'A coming-of-age tale  ...ing

TSUNAMI GIRL
is a GUPPY BOOK

First published in the UK in 2021 by
Guppy Books,
Bracken Hill,
Cotswold Road,
Oxford OX2 9JG

978 1 913101 466

3 5 7 9 10 8 6 4 2

Papers used by Guppy Books are from well-managed
forests and other responsible sources.

MIX
Paper from
responsible sources
FSC® C020471

GUPPY PUBLISHING LTD Reg. No. 11565833

A CIP catalogue record for this book is available from the British Library.

Typeset by Falcon Oast Graphic Art Ltd
Printed and bound in Great Britain by CPI Books Ltd

JULIAN SEDGWICK

TSUNAMI GIRL

CHIE KUTSUWADA

GUPPY
BOOKS

小高（福島県南相馬市）の方々に心から敬意を表します。この物語の小（お）相馬（Osōma）は小高ではなく、2011年3月11日とそれ以降の地震、津波、放射線の三つの災害に見舞われた様々な町や村が混ざり合った場所です。『津波少女』は、これらの町の人々と、彼らの思い出や語りに触発された上で書かれました。しかし、全ての登場人物、物語の設定、出来事は著者の想像によるものです。

Dedicated with deep respect to the people
of Odaka, Minamisōma, Japan.

The town of Osōma in this story is *not* Odaka, but a
blending of various towns and villages that suffered
the triple disaster of earthquake, tsunami and
radiation on 11th March 2011 – and afterwards.

Tsunami Girl is inspired by the people of these
towns, and their memories and stories.

But all characters, timings and events are
the work of the imagination.

This is the story of a girl called Yūki. 勇希

The syllable 'Yū' (with a long 'oo' sound) can be written using many different kanji characters. Yūki's name is written with 勇 – meaning 'courage'.

But Yū can also be written 幽 – as in the first character of 'yūrei': 幽霊

And that means 'ghost'.

PART ONE
The Wave

波

Once upon a time, deep down at the bottom,
of the ocean, there was an underwater boy.

His hair was blue like the sea at Matsushima
on a summer's day, his clothes like they
were cut from the sky ...

...and he moved through the water like a thought in the mind of a Great Buddha.

He controlled the waters of the world ...

... and sang lullabies to calm the monster catfish that send the earthquakes.

He was clever and curious. But he was lonely ...

1

Eternity

AN HOUR BEFORE THE WAVE comes, just ten short minutes before the earthquake shakes her world to pieces, Yūki starts to smile.

At first it's almost too small to see. But the smile is real, and therefore beautiful – and Grandpa spots it at once from across the table. He feels his own face mirroring hers, the deep lines on his forehead relaxing.

Ahhhhh, he thinks, maybe it's all going to be OK, maybe I'll be the one to bring you back to life Yūki-chan and rescue you from your troubles – and you can again be that girl who wanted to fly the biggest carp kites on the coast of Northern Japan, no matter how strong the wind came thrumming off the sea. Who demanded to light the fireworks yourself when we launched rockets from the hill on warm summer nights.

His bad dream of last night dissolves in his granddaughter's smile. She's trying to maintain some precious teen cool, he can see that – but she can't quite manage, and the smile's kind of out of control now, lifting her mouth, spreading, brightening her eyes like winter sunshine. Grandpa Jiro watches and waits patiently as she pushes a hand through her long, not-quite-black hair, her eyes fixed on the drawings in front of her.

The clock in the kitchen ticks a loud minute, and the heater purrs away under the table.

Finally Grandpa clears his throat. 'Well, Yū-chan? What do you say?'

Yūki tilts her head, considering. Outside the old family house she can hear the pines sighing in a cold March wind, a few crows calling blackly like always. But under the quilt at the sunken *kotatsu* table it's warm and snug, and it feels so good to be here again.

She looks up from the sketchbooks to find her grandfather peering back at her, his sparse white eyebrows arched.

'Yū-chan, you're *damn* well smiling! The first time I've seen you do that since you arrived.'

'I smiled at least twice yesterday, Grandpa . . .'

'Hmmm. When?'

'At the restaurant. At the station?'

'Well, just about, I guess.' He taps the table with a heavy index finger. 'Anyway, the point is that this old stuff of yours is *so* very good, Yūki!'

She pulls a face. 'But all kids do drawings like these.'

'No. You're wrong – there's real energy in them. And focus. I know what I'm talking about. Look how you *place* it all on the paper!'

'I kind of remember them being bigger.'

He laughs. 'Sometimes you drew *huge* seascapes and you'd yell, *Grandpa, more paper!* and I'd have to tape extra sheets on the sides. *Yū-chan no kaita umi ga afureteta yo*!'

'My seas . . . what?'

He repeats the Japanese slowly. 'I said: the - seas - you - drew - used - to - overflow! The more paper I taped on, the more you kept just adding wave after wave.'

'Sorry, my Japanese is so rusty . . . Mum keeps correcting my verbs all the time.'

'I never care what damn politeness level you use, as long as you're talking to me. And you always get quicker when you're here . . . Your Japanese is fine.'

He points at the sketchbooks stacked in the black biscuit tin, their Japanese cloth covers glowing burnt orange, indigo, moss green. 'We're supposed to be talking about how good your old drawings are. Most little kids don't do the amount you did, and they certainly don't do anything as good as these. Remember, you're talking to a Tezuka Award winner!' He puffs his chest out, pulling down the corners of his mouth like some fierce Japanese ogre.

'A big shot!'

'Right!' He laughs. 'Only you know how to talk to me, Yūki. I've missed that.'

'You should put that award out on a shelf or something.'

'Pah.' He wafts the thought away. 'I'd forgotten old Half Wave. He used to be all you talked about . . . kind of part of the family . . .'

Something catches in his throat, and he clears it loudly again. 'You worked like a real pro, Yūki! Look!'

9

She watches as Grandpa flips the concertina pages of the dark blue book in front of her. The thick paper has yellowed a tiny bit, but the coloured pencil is still vibrant. So certain – so childish – it feels like someone else drew the images. But the weird thing is, she remembers doing *every* single drawing as soon as they pop into view:

a *kappa* monster, sunk to the shoulders in a pond between tall green reeds, his saucer-like head balancing a massive cucumber, grinning at the viewer with teeth so sharp they could be biting the paper . . .

a rounded hill with a dark sky and fiery lanterns floating up from it past a grinning moon, and the words 'WELCOME HOME DED PEOPLE. PLEAS ENJOY YOUR STAY' jammed into a buoyant speech bubble.

a little shrine with a curling roof line – the paper screens of the doorway alive with eyeballs, one to each panel, thirty or more staring out at the viewer, shaky Japanese characters around it, spelling out '*MUKASHI MUKASHI*' – and the English squeezed in below: 'ONCE UPON A TIME, IN A PLACE FAR FAR WAY, THERE WAS A VERRY HAUNTED PLACE . . .'

And on every page there's at least one simple, but sure-handed drawing of a boy with bright blue wavy hair: running on the shrine roof, diving down between clouds of fish to a sinking ship, gliding through tangled fragments of Japanese, misspelt English and sound effects.

'HALF WAVE TO RESCUE . . .'

'IN ONE LEEP HE JUMPED OVER THE VOLCANO. *Fwoooooshh!*'

'THE KAPPA SMILED AND WENT TO SLEEP AND THE VILLAGE WAS SAYVED. THE END!!!' おわり

Grandpa sits back, and instinctively Yūki leans forward and turns the next page to reveal a mountainous wave, coloured in every shade of blue you could imagine – or at least every single blue in the huge pencil sets Jiro used to gift her for birthdays.

Riding barefoot on the wave's back, there he is again: the boy, in traditional summer clothing, his bright hair standing straight up, his face more smile than anything else. From his mouth a speech bubble: '*Han Nami desu*!! I am Half Wave!! I will do my honourable best.'

'When you smile like that,' Grandpa says quietly, 'you could chase *any* shadow from *any* corner of *any* place. No matter what.'

Yūki's eyes are still on Half Wave. 'How old was I – when I did these?'

'Six? Maybe seven. Remember you always wanted to use my special Rotring pen? *I want to be just like Grandpa*, you shouted!'

'I ruined the nib, didn't I? And you shouted at me, Grandpa!'

'I doubt that! I always encouraged you.' Grandpa starts to get up stiffly from the *kotatsu*. 'These skills skip a generation, I hope you're still drawing a bit?'

'Not really.'

'Not really?'

'It just comes out lame.'

'Everyone thinks that. You've just got to find your own style. Borrow things from other people and mess around until you find your way. Make it fun, and maybe,' he leans forward, 'and maybe

11

it can help you get going again, you know – get rid of some of your problems. Wake you up, like cold water in a sleeping ear? Maybe?'

'Grandpa,' Yūki groans, 'not you as well.'

Jiro winces, flapping his hand again to wave his words away. 'Sorry. Ignore me. I'm not about to nag like the rest of them, Yū-chan. I promise.'

'I just need a break from all that.'

'I know. I absolutely promise I'll give you that break.'

She nods, and looks away to the high window. You can just see the tree-covered shoulder of the bluff behind the house from where she is sitting – the steep-edged hill they always used to call 'Little Mountain' when she was small. The crows are busy in the branches, more of them gathering now, calling louder.

'I'm doing my best, Grandpa. Mum and Dad don't think I am, but I *am*.'

'I know you are, Yūki. You'll be OK. Of that I am sure.'

As if on cue the crows suddenly fall silent and then – as one – lift from the pines, scattering into the white sky beyond the frame of the window. She watches the last one go, then finds her eyes pulled back to the rolling wave, the boy riding its arched back, the peacock blues of his hair.

Somehow, some-*when*, she can still feel her fingers gripping the pencils super tight, smell the graphite as she scribbled away, trying to make her lines like the ones Grandpa effortlessly drew – if she nagged long enough.

Grandpa, draw me a real karakasa *haunted umbrella!*

12

How many eyes should there be in a paper screen to make a proper moku-moku-ren?

The more eyeballs the better for a haunted house, Jiro would murmur. *But I want your version.*

He sighs now. 'I've got a whole box more of those books, you know. I kept them all. And even one or two of those huge seascapes rolled up in the studio. I always felt a bit sorry for him though, to be honest.'

'Sorry for who?'

'Half Wave, of course. He needed a companion of some kind . . . you know, someone special, instead of always battling on his own. It's no fun singing on your own all the time, right? Want to see more?'

'Maybe later. I want to look at some of the original drawings for your stuff. You promised me you would this time.' She's boasted about Grandpa's grown-up manga to her almost-friend Joel back in Cambridge, and wants to take pictures home as proof. An excuse to talk to him again.

'As long as your mother doesn't have a fit. Even I'm shocked at some of what I drew back then. Sex and violence and death and all that jazz, particularly when I was still in Tokyo.' He scratches the back of his head. 'Drinking a bit too much, getting all worked up like things mattered!'

'I'm nearly sixteen, Grandpa,' Yūki says, 'I know about that kind of thing.' She reaches out to nudge the dark blue sketchbook away.

But as she touches it – and maybe it's only her memory playing

13

tricks when, later, she's back in these precious minutes with Jiro – it's as if an electric charge zips through her, and she jerks her hand away with a sharp intake of breath. Jetlag? Sometimes she gets this kind of zingy feeling on the first day after landing in Japan. Or something else?

'Are you OK?'

She nods. 'I'm just glad to be here, Grandpa.'

'We're a team, you and me. Which reminds me,' Jiro says, 'I have a belated birthday present for you.' And unlike the usual Japanese way of making light of a gift – *it's nothing at all really, sorry for burdening you with it* – he says, 'It's something kind of special. I want *you* to have it.'

'That's a very late present, like eight months late!'

'Or a very early one. Happy sixteenth!'

'Oh, yes, wait!' Her smile is back. 'I've got something for you too. It's in my room, hang on.'

Grandpa watches as she bounds away up the polished stairs, drafting an email to Yūki's mother in his head: 'Dear Kaori. Your wonderful daughter seems pretty fine to me . . . Some of us just take longer than others to find our way, right? Maybe lighten up on her a bit? Just my opinion, but . . .'

Once upon a time, *mukashi mukashi*, there was a boy, an underwater boy who could ride the waves on bare feet and loved to sing – and whose song controlled the waters of the world. He came from out of the sea, but loved the land and the people who lived on it, and had a huge heart and eyes that could see clearly.

14

Who calmed the catfish, and rescued sailors in distress and dealt with any trouble that came along: vengeful ghosts, naughty *kappa* monsters and *kitsune* fox spirits, volcanoes.

Tsunamis maybe.

And Half Wave's song floated under the stars as he surfed the waves, and everything was fine, totally fine. Young Yūki dreamed him up from wherever heroes come from, and he – in turn – made her. But in the end the little hero slipped away into the water, forgotten in the usual mess of growing up, just as a wave breaks and merges back into the ocean again.

Jiro looks at his granddaughter now as she comes back slightly out of breath, holding a wrapped box of fancy biscuits. 'From Kazuko and Mum. The ones you like.'

'It would be good if they brought them here in person.' He glances at the string of black letters and kanji written on the back of Yūki's hand as he takes the station gift. 'You know, I asked your Grandma this morning what would help you. I still talk to her every day – and she told me what to do.'

Yūki nods, trying not to let her disbelief show, but he spots it. As always.

'It's a crying shame to be such a sceptic at your age,' Jiro says, shaking his head. 'I blame your father. He doesn't come from here. We have ghosts and shrines on every corner. Every big tree and rock has its *kami-sama*, right? Warriors, waves, wind. You can *feel* them! Your grandmother got it, and she was from England, so it can't be just that.'

'She was from Wales, Grandpa.'

'She always used to get mad about that.' He bows slightly, switching, into three awkward words of English. *'Forgive me, Anna.* Anyway, you know what: I don't believe you. You still feel that stuff. You – don't – fool – me!'

Yūki fixes her gaze on the sun logo on the old black biscuit tin from which he's conjured the sketchbooks.

'Listen to me, Yū-chan. Please.' Jiro's voice has become serious now, and as she glances up she sees that shadow that just occasionally flickers across his face. There a moment, then gone.

'Are you OK, Grandpa?'

'Totally fine. We're talking about you, my girl. You come from here. At least a quarter of you does, physically, and far, far more in here!' He taps his heart. 'You told us all you saw our *zashiki warashi* once, our little phantom who helped look after the house . . .'

Yūki shakes her head. 'It was just a game, just imagination—'

'Damn it!' Jiro thumps the table with his fist. 'Never – never – say "just" before the word "imagination". Never. It gives us power, life. If people had never imagined being able to fly, we'd never have invented planes, right? And we'd never have had Astro Boy or Godzilla or Laputa. That's not a world I'd like to live in! Never forget the power of imagination. Right now I can imagine flying high up above our house and looking around . . .'

He gazes up.

'Imagine being a superhero and you can jump right across the sky! Imagine being in love and you can be in love. Only

16

imagination can capture eternity, right? You were always the *best* person to do Obon Festival with, Yūki, because you and I were the only ones who *really* imagined the dead coming home. The rest were just going through the motions, but we did it properly. To honour them. Full stop.'

'Yeah, it *was* good,' she murmurs.

She follows his gaze upwards, remembering the cicadas and frogs calling as they went up Little Mountain through the lengthening summer evening, lighting the lanterns at the top, and waiting in the dark to welcome the dead home, just for a while. Those nights seemed like they would last for ever.

'It was really good.'

March 11th, 2011. 2.36pm. Ten minutes to the quake.

To the south: the towns of Okuma and Futaba, schools and an old peoples' home. And the Fukushima Number One Nuclear Plant.

To the west there are mountains, and to the north, the town of Osoma.

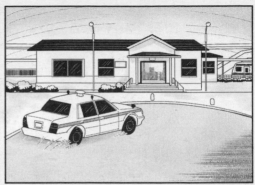

And to the East?

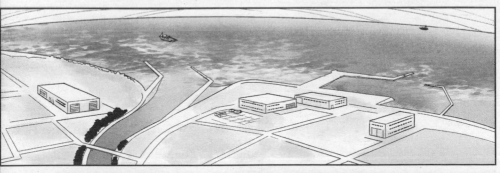

2.45pm

Grandpa stumps off to get whatever it is he's going to get, whistling the scrap of tune he always whistles, seven notes repeating, and then singing the next line of the song, his voice breaking as it clambers up into the higher notes.

'*I can't forget how the tears blurred my eyes, can't forget happiness under starry skies . . .*'

Yūki feels her smile stealing back. Apart from that one little misstep when he brought up her problems – and the moment when he snapped a bit yesterday evening – he's on great form, she thinks. He's not nagging like Mum and Dad, he's not like wild Aunt Kazuko, talking super-fast about *hopeless* boyfriends and tarot readings. He's just Grandpa Jiro: feet on the ground, a bit gruff at times, but always the same. Always here, just like the house has always been here.

She edges the dark blue sketchbook back towards her with her index finger, wondering vaguely if a book can actually shoot out static somehow.

And then she sees her finger has started to tremble like mad.

And every single thing around her is shaking with it: her hand, her arm, the books on the table, the black tin and its yellow sun, the table itself, the walls. A steady percussive rattling of crockery and cutlery and doors and windows in their frames – *gata gata gata gata* – that grows and grows until the house itself moves, and with a resounding shudder a bookcase next door tumbles to the floor, spilling its great weight of manga stories into the door-way in a landslide of paper and ink and card.

She looks at Grandpa in alarm as the noise gets louder and louder and louder

   . . . and the whole world is shaking,

   tumbling,

   breaking apart . . .

2

Samurai Check-In

IT WAS ONLY THE DAY before the day before yesterday that Mum and Dad had waved her off at the Heathrow security gate, Dad's eyes welling up (and him pretending they weren't) and Mum putting on the super bright expression she always did before running one of her half-marathons. Yūki had seen that so much in the last two years: her parents' hope – desperation – that she would be OK and start to have what they called a 'normal life' again, have 'real friends'. Sometimes she felt it was like looking in some kind of weird mirror, seeing her anxiety reflected back in Mum's half-Japanese features, Dad's English. You kind of lost track of who felt what first, and everything ended up in a muddle or an argument, trying to untangle hopelessly knotted wires, everyone frustrated.

'Take care, sweetheart. *Ki o tsukete*. Don't stress Grandpa out,' Mum said, shuffling back and forth between Japanese and English, straightening her rucksack strap.

Yūki shrugged off the fussing. 'Mum. It was your idea.'

'Well, no Yū-chan, I think you suggested it first. But, doesn't matter. You can be thick as thieves. Apparently there's some protest at the weekend he's planning on taking you on. Third nuclear plant or something. He's not happy if he hasn't got something to battle.'

Dad took a deep breath. 'He'd protest against his own mother . . . Maybe you could send a postcard to that friend of yours. Joel?'

'Dad, I don't really *know* him. And I don't have his address.'

Still, an image of Joel flowed back into her head: the last time she'd seen him, that day in the school library when she had hoped the ground would just eat her whole. Where the other kids had gawped at her, curled in a foetal position on the ground, he'd just looked like he cared, eyes reaching out from under his blond fringe – and gone to get help before they took her away to the office.

'Well, I bet we could get it. It's important you keep friends, right?'

Mum jabbed him in the ribs.

'Ow, only trying to help.'

Mum turned back to Yūki, holding her arm just a little longer than necessary. 'Have the *best* time. We're hoping this might, you know, sort things out a bit—'

'Now you're doing it!' Dad spluttered. 'Just go and enjoy yourself, Yūki. Remember we love you, but you need some non-Mum-and-Dad time, right?'

'*Ki o tsukete,*' Mum repeated.

'Mum, Osōma's got to be like the safest place in the whole world.'

'I know. There *was* a crime there once! Bye, sweetheart, remember what to do if – you know – if you feel an attack coming . . .'

'I know, I remember. Bye . . . *mata*.'

'Bye. Love you,' Dad said, turning away, a hand reaching for his balding patch like he always did when he was feeling emotional and didn't want to show it.

'I'll be fine. *Mata ne* . . .'

Yūki took a breath as the chaperone lady from the airline led her away across the mirror floor of Terminal 5. It looked like super-still water as she glanced down at her reflection, clouds beyond the huge airport windows billowing beneath her feet. The familiar grip of anxiety was coming up into her throat, but she tried to look as calm as she could.

'So, Yooki – long "ooo"? – am I saying that right?'

'Yeah, pretty good.'

'Have you got holidays from school? It's not Easter yet.'

'I'm home schooled.'

The woman's face, plastered in make-up, unable to hide the disapproval: 'Oh, really?'

Yūki reached for her usual response. 'It's so we can do half in Japanese and half in English.'

That was kind of true, but not totally. Angela, her therapist, kept saying it might be easier to be more open with people about what she's feeling, but what are you going to say? *Hi, I'm*

Yūki. I'm kind of a school refuser, I guess, and I don't have any real friends and I can't cope with secondary school and it's made me have these huge like panic attacks and now I can hardly leave my room on bad days, and anyway it's boring so please don't listen to me, but yes, I am a bit Japanese, but I'm mostly English. I guess. I grew up here, but I like being there more. But when I'm there people think I'm not really Japanese. And there's things I can't even begin to talk about really because it's just so stupid. Sorry. Sorry. Gomen ne.

'But what about friends?' the woman chattered on, giving her the usual *look*: the one that's trying to puzzle out who she is.

'It's OK,' Yūki said, glancing back at the gate. Mum was kind of hugging herself, and Dad was holding a hand up like a person hoping to catch a ball but not sure it's going to be thrown. Yūki made a furtive wave with her hand down near her hip.

The woman peered at her through her overly-long eyelashes. 'Parents! They'll be fine. Not your first time to Japan though?'

'It's like my second home.'

'But your first time on your own?'

Yūki nodded.

'Well, don't be nervous.'

Yūki felt a surge of irritation: *Haras don't get nervous! We're the nails that refuse to be hammered down, my grandpa stood up to right wing thugs in the sixties, he even goes swimming at Obon!... NOBODY goes swimming at Obon, right?*

Instead she stuttered, 'There were samurai in our family!'

'Gosh, I'll mind my step then.' The BA woman patted her arm.

25

'Come on, put your bag in that tray and your coat in that one. Any swords as well. Your mum said you worry a bit?'

'I like flying. I'm OK.'

But it wasn't true: she *was* anxious. Cooped up in the house for months and months, even the noise and bustle of the airport was a really big deal, and she hoped Mrs Make-Up couldn't see how her heart was beating so hard it was visible, pulsing *doki doki* against her dark blue hoodie. She glanced back, and caught one more glimpse of Mum crumpling in Dad's hug.

She felt a familiar twinge of guilt then, but swallowed it back with the rising tension, striding through the security arch, past the endless perfume and chocolate concessions – the usual consumer rubbish, as Grandpa would say – and on to the gate area magically marked TOKYO, trying to make it look like she did this every day, that the Hara blood was really coursing through her part-samurai veins.

As the plane made its turn for the Narita runway, Yūki pulled a fibre-tip pen from her bag and slowly re-inked the string of letters and Japanese characters on the back of her left thumb. Y for 'Yūki'; the kanji for 'Mum' and 'Dad'; J for 'Jiro' and the character for 'Hara' which is the surname she prefers; an infinity symbol for long life and health and the Japanese for 'smile'. Everyone kept asking her what had happened to the beaming smile she used to shoot at anyone and everything, but it's still there, in black ink at the end of her self-created good luck charm. The one chink in her rationalist armour.

Y J原母父∞笑

The woman next to her was watching as the wheels clunked down beneath and reverberated through the plane as it banked, bright light cutting across the cabin, across the magic formula on her hand.

'Are you OK, young lady?'

'*Hai, zenzen daijōbu*. I'm totally fine,' Yūki answered, then hurriedly corrected herself to make her answer more polite. '*Daijōbu desu.*'

The woman looked surprised. 'Oh, you're Japanese! Sorry.'

'I'm Japanese. Kind of.'

'Well. Try not to worry too much. It doesn't ever change anything in my experience.'

'Sorry. I'll do my best. *Ganbarimasu.*'

But it was so hard to do your best most days, and Yūki's heart was thumping away like crazy as the ground rushed up to meet them, the plane's tyres screeching black lines on the runway.

3

Ghost in the Cab

BRIGHT LIGHT FLOODED THE WINDOWS of the airport express as Aunt Kazuko glanced at her mobile for the umpteenth time and swept a hand through the lightning bolt bleached in her fringe. She had the brand-new iPhone on silent, but the thing was vibrating like a newly-hatched summer cicada. Yūki smiled, bathed in the warmth of the sun, and pointed at the phone.

'It's OK, Auntie, answer it. It might be the man of your dreams!'

'Still got your sense of humour then?!' Kazuko laughed. 'I'm glad. From what my sister said I thought it was ALL gloom and doom.'

'Mum says I always looked serious, even when I was born.'

'Well, you always made me laugh.' Looking down at her screen Kazuko pulled a face.

'Problem, Auntie?'

'It's definitely not Mister Right, just some idiot at the agency! He hasn't worked with a Hara woman before, poor guy!' She typed something back super-fast and thumbed 'send'.

'What did you type?'

'Never mind!'

She shoved the phone in her bag, and looked Yūki over from top to toe, taking in the long hair, caught somewhere between black and dark brown, oval face, round glasses, soft hoodie, black leggings.

'You're growing up, Yū-chan.'

'Mum doesn't think so.'

'Well, she sees you every day. But I see you like in one of those time-lapse films, every six months at most, right? I can see you've really grown . . . You're becoming a woman!' She cupped her hands in front of her own chest, her eyebrows halfway up her forehead. 'Mat-ur-ing, right!'

'Auntieeeee . . .' Kazuko had a habit of being *way* too inappropriate in public. And loud.

'So, want to go to that old manga place again? Or see some cool friends of mine, boys in this weird noise band? One of them wears a dress! We went on a date like that, but it didn't work out . . . Or we could go shopping, buy you something nice.'

'I just always look lame.'

'You look gorgeous. Always. Or how about dinner out?'

'Could we just eat at yours?'

Kazuko frowned. 'OK. But let's do *something fun!* Fancy trying some make-up? You could drive the boys crazy, you know!'

'I – I'm not really interested.'

Kazuko thumped Yūki's knee very lightly. 'I know school's rubbish, but you're not becoming one of those *hikikomori* are you? Locked up in their rooms, never coming out . . .'

'If that's what they need to do then why don't people leave them be?'

'Fair enough, but I guess I just don't think that's what you need to do. You need to, I dunno, *dive* in to life.'

'I just don't like loud places right now, lots of people and movement and stuff. You know. It brings on the attacks.'

'Well, Osōma's the place for you then. Quiet as the grave! That's why I got out.'

'I still like it.'

'Good for you.' Kazuko's phone was buzzing again in her bag. 'I'd better give this guy a piece of my mind from the vestibule. I'm going to call him something biologically complicated, and I don't want you to hear.'

'*Dōzo*,' Yūki said, making an exaggerated 'help yourself' gesture. 'Have fun.'

'Don't worry, I will . . . Ah yes, *moshi moshi*, Tanaka-san, could I just ask you to listen for a moment, if you would be so kind, you might need a pencil to make notes . . . and a working knowledge of anatomy. Sorry to take up your time, but . . .'

Yūki smiled as Kazuko threw her a conspiratorial wink, and then her aunt's voice faded as she retreated to the space between the carriages and the door hissed shut.

She settled back into the warm patch of sun, trying to shrug off Kazuko's advice. From the Skyliner window now: blue tiled houses and winter browned fields dashing past. A heron lifting slow wingbeats to the sky. A big modern Buddha statue there and then gone, the one with the funny expression on his face –

kind of more cheeky than wise. And yet like he knew some big secret you didn't yet know, but maybe was coming your way.

At Nippori, entering the concrete sprawl of Tokyo, there was still no sign of her aunt. Three schoolgirls got on, locked tight in chat and laughter, throwing the odd glance Yūki's way, quickening her pulse. Just like school, always on the edge of the joke, wanting to find out what it was and not wanting to all at the same time, because it might be about you.

She gazed down at her own phone, pretending to text somebody, wondering what it would be like to *be* one of them, part of an in-crowd, and not always on the edge looking in. Easier to imagine what it was like to be that Buddha.

In the entrance hall to Kazuko's 'mansion' block Yūki thought she felt a brief trembling pass up through the ground into her feet, her legs. Another hint of panic bubbled in her chest. Angela had gone over the breathing exercises – and in the constricted, swaying space of the lift she did them as best she could, only half listening as her aunt talked a blue streak, swerving topics that her sister had obviously warned her not to touch: friends, school, anxiety.

Still she bumped against one or two of them, Kazuko style.

'So, you know, there's no rush for boyfriends! But is there anyone you're interested in?'

'Not really.'

'You don't fool me.'

Yūki puffed the hair out of her eyes. Sometimes the only trick with Aunt Kazuko was to fight fire with fire: 'Yes, Auntie, I'm like doing *it* all the time.'

'Jeez. I'm just trying to help, Yū-chan. Well, if you want to chat about that kind of thing, time of the month et cetera, I'm always ready for a natter!'

'I'm fine,' Yūki said, firmly. 'Auntie? Wasn't that a little quake? Should we have used the lift?'

'Bah. This place has got a top notch seismic certificate, so don't worry for a moment! It was nothing.'

'I'm not worrying.'

Last month, Dad - wiping his glasses like he did when he was holding forth - had described the tectonics beneath Tokyo: three plates riding each other, with a broken chunk of one stuck between them, like food caught in a giant's throat. 'One day he's going to cough that up,' Dad had said, 'and I wouldn't want to be in Tokyo then. Not for a trillion yen. You know what the third chapter of the Tokyo Disaster Preparedness Manual is titled? *Accepting Death!* Honest, I'll give them that!'

'Thanks, Steve,' Mum had said. 'Very helpful.'

Waiting for the takeaway to arrive, Yūki gazed at the sea of sky-scrapers towards Shinjuku, the red aircraft warning beacons blinking messages to the clouds above, the neon beneath glowing, pulsing. Suddenly another wave of tightness gripped her chest from nowhere, the city swaying in her vision.

Breathe. Breathe. Breathe.

Breeeeeathe.

36

'You OK, Yū-chan? You look pale.'

'Yeah, yep, fine,' Yūki managed to say. 'How's Grandpa?'

'Same as ever!'

'I mean – last time he seemed kind of grumpy most of the time. You know, that look he sometimes gets.'

'Not with you,' Kazuko laughed. 'He just finds his daughters exasperating! The whole world some days . . . God knows why he ever stopped working – people buy old issues of Garo magazine with his work for a fortune now. Crazy money. He's just stewing there day after day, surrounded by the past, brooding. All that stuff. He needs a clear out, but . . .'

'Brooding?' Yūki didn't recognise the Japanese word, and Kazuko tapped it into her phone to show the English.

'Too much imagination. Runs in the family, right? I mean you were always–' Kazuko pulled up sharply.

'What?'

'Do you still like ghost stories?'

'Not really. I don't believe in ghosts.'

Kazuko exaggerated a comic squint. 'Reeeeeaaallly?'

'There's always explanations. I dunno.'

'Hmmm!' Kazuko splashed herself another glass of wine. 'You know that old cemetery near here? Aoyama?'

Yūki nodded, remembering the graves under the pines and gingko trees, the crows thickening the air.

'OK, so ever since they tunnelled the Chiyoda subway line underneath it, there's been stories about travellers late at night looking up from their seat to see people in like these ragged, old-fashioned clothes sitting opposite them. Clothes from the Edo period, right? And then they just vanish!' Kazuko took a swig, eyes bright. 'It's like the dead people don't know they're dead, and they end up getting on the underground by mistake. And then they have to find their way 'home' again, to the cemetery. And taxi drivers get flagged down late at night by people who ask to go to somewhere near the cemetery – and when they get there, and the driver turns round to take the fare, the back seat is empty!'

Yūki shifted uncomfortably. 'But–'

'But this is the best one,' Kazuko raced on, gesticulating with her free hand. 'The drummer in one of the bands we promote told me. I always trust drummers, and he heard it straight from the taxi driver. So it's gotta be true! One evening last March this driver was near Aoyama and he saw a woman sheltering from the rain, holding her coat over her head. No umbrella, and she was soaked through. So, he picked her up, and the girl – not much more than a teenager – gave him a run-down address a few kilo-metres away. The driver thought nothing of it, and when they got to the apartments the woman said, *Could we just wait here a few minutes? OK*, the taxi guy said, *but I'll have to keep the meter running*. The woman said it was fine, and just sat, staring up at a second-floor window. And silhouetted in the window was a man, looking down at the car, motionless. They just looked at each other, and looked at each other, and neither moved.'

Yūki shivered suddenly, and Kazuko nodded, the lightning bolt dancing.

'Creepy, right?'

'I'm just tired.'

'But listen! The driver says, *So, where do you want to go next?* And the woman says, *Take me home,* and gives like this posh address in Shibuya. *Fine,* the driver says and they make their way through the pouring rain to her house. As he pulls up, he turns round to tell the woman the fare, and guess what?'

'There's nobody there.'

'Right. But even better, there's just a patch of rain water on the seat. So, the driver gets out, seriously creeped, and goes to the door of the house. Even though it's *really* late, almost immediately an old woman answers, and without being told what's happened, she holds out the EXACT FARE for the ride, including the stop at the first house. The *exact* fare.'

A shudder bumped down the length of Yūki's spine. 'Yeah, but—'

'And when the driver looks astonished the old woman says, *My daughter was killed by a speeding car in the rain. She was crossing the street to meet her boyfriend and was killed instantly. Now, whenever it rains, she flags a cab in Aoyama, and goes to wait outside his house for a few minutes, and then she comes here. She comes* home. *We all have to go home, don't we?* Wow!' Kazuko paused, and took another gulp of wine. 'That's the detail, right? The *exact* money.'

Yūki could still feel the shiver flicking up and down her back. 'But it's just that people exaggerate and misremember and that kind of thing. I think.'

'Well, they're real *enough* if you ask me. Look at how you can get a cheap house if somebody's died in it. If some Tokyo fat cat is prepared to take a hit in his rental there has to be something to it, right? Come on! What happened to that girl we all knew? I mean the one—'

Yūki shook her head. Not again! 'I wish everyone would stop saying stuff like that! I was always funny, or always serious, or always believed in ghosts. Or Grandpa, always on about the stupid totem pole . . .'

Kazuko puffed out her cheeks. 'I'm sorry, I'm sorry. We all just want to see you back to your old self.'

'Everyone's *always* on about it.'

Kazuko smiled and dropped her voice. 'Well, you can't blame us for wanting that . . . Imagine what it's like for your mum. You must remember how long it took her to have a child, and she took *our* mum's death really hard, and then *at last* you came along . . .'

Yūki nodded, the old story settling on her shoulders. *You're so precious to us*, Mum always said. And once, unguarded, she added, *There were a lot who didn't make it before we had you.*

'How come you and Mum are so different?'

'What do you mean?'

'You're so – so . . .'

Kazuko laughed. 'Cra-zeeee?'

'I guess.'

'Until your grandma died, your mum was the wild one. Like one of the wild horses at the horse festival! I dunno, maybe she's

40

frustrated with herself. She got tamed.' She leaned forwards. 'Hey, don't tell her I said that!'

Yūki's eyes widened. 'Mum? A runaway horse?!'

'The local boys used to tease us both for being *hāfu*, right? *You're not proper Japanese, you're half-breeds*, that kind of rubbish. On and on they went and one day she just punched one of them right in the kisser! She'd been doing some karate so he really went down hard, bleeding! A real ninja girl in those days!'

'Mum *punched* a boy?!'

'Knocked him out!' Kazuko laughed. 'It never really bothered me so much – that *hāfu* stuff – I just snogged them instead. Come on, get some sleep. Every day is a chance to turn a new page, right? So let's turn another one. Waxing crescent moon, the horoscope said, in Gemini. That means it's a time for spontaneity and change!'

'Dad says astrology is a waste of time.'

'Well. Luckily there's room enough in this world for people to be different. Find their own way.'

Despite the jet lag Yūki lay awake for an hour or so, thinking about Mum and Kazuko growing up in rural Tōhoku, fighting, kissing . . . Mum now so changed from that younger version of herself, Kazuko still somehow the same by the sounds of it. How did it happen? How did you know which way you were going? And one day maybe you were just running across a road and thinking about the future and *bam!* that was it. Dead.

She turned off the light and rolled herself in the duvet and tried to will herself to sleep, but somehow when she closed her eyes she could *see* that poor girl standing soaked in the rain, the wet puddle on the taxi seat, the silhouette of the boy at the window. The sadness of it all falling through her thoughts like a rainy season downpour, saturating everything.

A train thrummed on the Yamanote line and she listened to it come and go, and then tried to concentrate and count carriages as the next train rattled across the points, and then did the same with six or maybe seven more rolling on through the restless city, until at last her breathing lengthened and calmed.

There – right on the very lip of sleep – she heard the distant sound of waves breaking.

4

Mr Kickboxer

THE 10TH OF MARCH DAWNED bright, and Yūki felt her spirits lift as she blinked away half-remembered dreams. Something about the sea or rain – a lot of water. And maybe something to do with a boy. Kissing? Not Joel . . . But it felt nice, she thought, the blood coming to her cheeks.

Kazuko guided them both through the Yamanote line rush hour to Ueno Station, and safely to the train armed with a bento box lunch and the gift for Grandpa – and a flurry of plans for her return to Tokyo.

She swept the lightning bolt away, hugging Yūki tight. 'Just enjoy being with the old rascal. Take a breath of ocean for my lungs! And get him to chuck one or two things away! And remember, you're a Hara. No matter what *anyone* else says. Warriors, right!'

'I don't feel like one.'

'Not yet. I guess a caterpillar can't imagine being a butterfly. Or maybe it does . . .'

Yūki squinted up at the station roof. 'So, I'm like a warrior butterfly or something?'

'Cheeky. Take care, Yū-chan. See you at the end of next week.'

The concrete and criss-crossing railway lines of Tokyo sped past, slowly giving way to channelled rivers, jigsaw fields, smudges of distant pale mountains. Eventually, the moment beyond Mito station that thrilled her younger self: the first glimpse of the vast Pacific, always bigger than you remembered, its silvery blue chopped up between the trees – the whole thing revealed like a magic trick.

And when it did come now, she gazed out at the white horses rippling to the horizon and felt a breath come and go, loosening something deep inside just a bit. She settled back into her seat. No expectations, no pressure, just space and time opening up as she rumbled north in a half empty carriage, all good. She opened the station-boxed sushi, squirted dark soy sauce from the plastic fish onto the first piece and turned to look at the bright sea again, shimmering in the sun *kira kira* all the way to the horizon, the tang of vinegar on her tongue.

At Iwaki she was cleaning her fingers with the bentō's wet wipe when two boys got on and plonked themselves down diagonally across the carriageway, facing her.

Maybe sixteen or a little older, one chunky, with a squared-off face and a regulation school crew cut, the other long and lanky, his curly hair a messy cloud over his oval face. Big orange

46

headphones clamping the black hair down, and a sports holdall that he thrust between the grubby trainers on his outstretched feet. Kind of nice looking, Yūki thought, sneaking a glance, but a bit full of himself. Like one of those boys at school with their voices set to loud, keen to tell you just how great they are. Not like Joel, keeping himself quietly to himself.

Every now and then she felt that prickly sensation you get when somebody's staring at you, and sure enough, when she plucked up courage to glance over, the curly haired boy was looking straight at her, a smile flickering on his lips. Then he turned and muttered something to his stocky friend, and they both laughed.

Warning lights fired in Yūki's head.

She tried to suppress the hot rush of blood to her face, forced herself to look out at the waves, but kept feeling the taller one's gaze on her. Hot and bothered now, the tightness in her chest started to build. She took out her Nintendo DS and tried to concentrate on where she was in *Dragon Quest*, but her fingers felt clumsy, and her eyes kept sliding off the screen, the tightness rising, rising to her shoulders now. Much higher than that would mean it reaching her throat, and then she would be lost, gasping for breath. Shaking, or – worst-case scenario – a meltdown on the carriage floor in front of everyone, just like that last day at school when Joel found her and went to get help.

Damn it, leave me alone.

She shoved the DS back in her bag, considering a dash to another carriage. She looked again, trying to do what Angela had told her – feet flat, slowing her outbreath until it was longer than the one in – and saw to her horror that the lanky one was getting up now, the other boy kind of egging him on, and was coming over to the empty seat beside her.

What now? It would all be, *Oh so you're not really Japanese then? Hāfu? Can you eat Japanese food? Your Japanese is sooo good.*

Without a word the boy dropped himself down into the seat next to her, and turned and grinned again, eyes peering into hers. He leaned closer, into her space – and then snapped his fingers.

'Ahhh! I knew it! Recognised you!' he said, in rough Japanese. 'You're that manga guy's granddaughter, right? From just outside Osōma?'

Maybe he was kind of familiar? With an effort she pulled herself together to make half a bow in her seat, stuttering out a formal greeting. 'Yes, pleased to meet you. I am Hara Yūki. Please be kind to me.'

The boy pulled a comic face. 'Waaah! Super polite! No need for that stuff. I'm Taka, remember? Stupid old Taka! Jimi's son. Taxi driver?'

He mimed a steering wheel.

I know what a taxi is, she thought. 'Yes, I remember you . . . I think.'

'Ha! You don't sound that excited!' he beamed. 'Last time I saw you must be . . . ? I dunno, seven years?'

'I guess. I remember you on the beach. At Kitaizumi.'

'Yeah! I was a real brat then, probably! Sorry. *Gomen ne.*'

'You were shooting everyone with a huge water gun.'

'Sounds like me!'

48

She remembered for sure now – he was madly curly haired even back then, racing around the beach. He'd even shouted, *Hāfu, hāfu*, as he blasted her, and Grandpa had shooed him away with a harsh word or two . . . And feeling super self-conscious in her swimming suit, way whiter than anyone else as Mum fussed with the sun cream.

'Well, anyway, sorry about that,' Taka went on. 'So. Visiting your grandad?'

'Yes. How about you?'

'Been at a tournament in Iwaki.'

'Doing what?'

He took a look around, and threw a couple of imaginary blows with his left hand, a flick of a trainer. 'Kickboxing.' He leaned closer and whispered, 'I'm in secret training, don't tell anybody.'

Figures, Yūki thought, nothing much going on under all that wild hair. But as she summoned the nerve to return his gaze she saw something else: his eyes were bright, kind of knowing.

He held his hand out to shake hers, Western style, and said, 'Very pleased to meet you,' in really badly-accented English, and she had no idea if he was pulling her leg.

But his hand felt big as it gripped hers, and warm.

'So, do you have two names – like an English one and a Japanese one? Two family names?'

She nodded. 'I don't use the English one here. Jones.'

'Yeah, that was it. *Jo-on-zu*. So you'd be like Yūki Hara Jo-on-zu? Sorry, my English is rubbish, I'll stick to Hara. Are you going to be around for long?'

49

'A week or so.'

'Want to hang out a bit?'

Now she was really puzzled. 'And – do what? Why?'

Taka shrugged. 'I dunno. Anything. I always thought you were kinda cute if you want to know the truth. Sorry.'

Yūki looked away hurriedly. 'I – I think Grandpa's got plans.'

His mate was still snickering, legs thrust out into the carriage-way, and she felt her breath tightening again.

'So how come you aren't in school then, Hara-san?'

She went for a Kazuko move. 'Got kicked out.'

'I doubt that.' He smiled. 'We were at the summer horse festival in Odaka, I dunno, seven or eight or so years ago, do you remember? The last day when they try and catch the wild ones. You were drawing and drawing. Your grandpa brought you, and he was showing you off to everyone. People say he used to keep a fox, bit crazy—'

'He's not crazy,' Yūki cut back. 'He's a . . .' Damn, what was the word for 'genius'?

'Hey, cool it,' Taka said, cocking his head to one side. 'My dad says he's a good guy. And if Dad says someone's OK, then I go with that. He's a good judge, you have to be in his line of work. So he was like a manga artist or something? What kind of things?'

'*Gekiga*.'

She had expected that to draw a blank and bring the conversation to an end, but Taka just nodded thoughtfully, sucking the air in through his teeth. 'Oh the alternative stuff! Riiiggght. Not

50

just animals and lame love stories, right? Tatsumi, Shirato Sanpei, people like that?'

'Yeah,' Yūki said, surprised. There seemed to be just a little more air in the carriage now and she took a gulp. 'Exactly. He knew Tatsumi-san, and he won a Tezuka Award.'

'Wow.'

'He did politics, protest type stuff. Grandpa always says you can do things in a picture that take pages and pages in a novel.'

'I guess. Like if we were in a manga you could just draw us side by side. You'd see how totally different we were. But both super good looking?'

'Are you making fun of me now?'

Taka threw his arms wide like a footballer protesting innocence. 'Just trying to be nice. Honest.'

Yūki looked at him. 'Really?'

'Cross my heart and hope to die, Hara-san. So. What's with all the writing on your hand? That's an infinity sign, right?' He reached out, and very lightly touched the string of letters and characters.

Yūki tugged her sleeve down over the marks. 'I'm just trying to remember something.'

'Me too.' He showed the back of his right hand, scrawled with the numbers 2.38. 'Train I've got to catch tomorrow. Secret mission.'

Yūki nodded. There was an uneasy silence.

'So,' Taka hesitated, scratching behind his ear. 'How about it?'

'How about – what?'

51

'Hanging out with me?'

'I'll – are you going to join your friend again?'

Taka glanced at the stocky boy opposite, and leaned his head towards hers, whispering, 'Him? Shuto? He's all right, but thick as sludge. Listen,' he added, 'I've grown up. A bit. You can get hold of me via Jimi's Taxis. If you want to, I mean.' He smiled again. Then – thankfully, at last – he sauntered back to his seat.

Gradually she felt her heart rate drop down the gears, the level of constriction in her chest going down, down, down.

And as the last few familiar stops came and went, the boys seemed to have lost all interest, as they grunted short, blunt sentences to each other, the sound of the rails drowning out the words, and eventually the shorter one buried his gaze in his Gameboy, and Taka pulled the earphones over his curly hair and slumped back in his seat, nodding his head steadily to something only he could hear.

Yūki tried to refocus on the DS game, but kept finding her gaze drifting back to him, when she was sure he wasn't looking. One time she got it wrong and found herself looking straight into his eyes. He raised his eyebrows, and again it was hard to tell whether he was having a laugh as she turned away, cheeks warm.

Nice he knew about *gekiga*, though.

But he felt like trouble. And as for 'hanging out' . . . ?

The ocean was there again: waves caught in shafts of early spring sunshine, falling through clouds of blue and grey.

5

Silver Trainers

AT OSŌMA TAKA MADE A show of holding his friend back to let Yūki get off first.

'After you, Miss Hara,' he called after her. 'Don't be a stranger.'

For a moment she felt the heat rising on her neck again, but then she saw Grandpa and the boys fell away. Energetically tapping the tarmac with his silver-topped walking stick he stomped towards her, the other hand raised in greeting, calling out from a distance.

'Yūki! A beautiful flower amongst the local weeds!'

Beneath his black wool cap Grandpa's face was lit with the energy she remembered so well. The sun slipped between the March clouds again, and she saw the shoes on his feet: brand new silver Nike trainers! She pointed at them and he mimed a comical running action.

A couple of strides away he suddenly stopped, and bowed formally. 'Please be kind to me as I will to you.'

Yūki bowed back, sensing Taka and the other boy whispering past.

When she glanced up Grandpa was still bent low. Then he raised his head a little, winking at her. 'OK. We've got to set the world to rights.'

'Your trainers look so cool!'

She let herself fall into his embrace, breathing in the familiar smell of aftershave, a hint of wood smoke.

'I don't think I've been cool since the sixties! I've got something I want to show you. A blast from the past.'

'What do you mean?'

'You'll see! I ordered you a limousine to get us home. Couldn't trust the starter in mine to get me here on time.'

Outside the station Taka was standing beside the 'limousine' – an ageing brown taxi, Jimi's of course. The other boy was walking away towards the cycle racks, calling, 'See you tomorrow, Taka, you jerk!' Taka waved vaguely, but seemed more intent on talking to his dad.

Jiro had insisted on wheeling Yūki's case and she had given up arguing.

'How are you, Grandpa?'

'Pretty good, pretty good. If you can ignore the idiots running the country, Mrs Takeda's dog digging up my plants. Who still calls a dog "Pochi" these days, for God's sake?!'

He frowned as they approached the taxi, his eyes on Taka. 'That young man give you any trouble? Got up to a bit of bother last year, I heard.'

'Like what?'

54

'Never mind, I'll tell you later,' he whispered behind his hand.

Taka gave the taxi roof a thump, flicked one more smile at Yūki and sauntered off down the main street with his bag over his shoulder. Jimi was already getting out, opening the boot for Yūki's case, every inch a thirty-year-older version of Taka, hair a little shorter, shot with white and grey, but just as curly.

'Hara-sensei! Miss Yūki! Shall I take you two home?'

'Yes please, Jimi-san.'

'Nice trainers!'

'I'm taking up marathon running!'

Jimi laughed, and turned to Yūki, 'Long time no see, young lady. Good grief, you're growing up,' he said. 'In my head you're always this high, and drawing and drawing. You still do that?'

'Not really,' Yūki said, but smiled a thank you.

Grandpa eased his way onto the seat beside her with a sigh, tapped her shoulder lightly and then peered into her eyes. 'Yūki, *daijōbu ka*?'

She nodded. '*Daijōbu*. I'm fine now.'

'OK. Good.' He smiled, held her gaze for a long moment, then turned to the driver. 'And how about your boy, Jimi?'

'Yes, fine. Why?'

'Yūki and him were chatting on the train apparently.'

'Oh, I'm glad,' Jimi said over his shoulder as he guided the car towards the port area, and the coast road beyond. 'He fell out badly with friends last year. Well, I say friends, but they were a dodgy lot. Bit lonely now with only his old man for company. Did he say how the tournament went? I forgot to ask!'

'Tournament?' Jiro muttered.

'Kickboxing,' Yūki said, pleased somehow to be able to tell Grandpa something about Taka.

Jimi laughed. 'Kickboxing? *Last* thing he'd be doing. No, he was at a chess competition. Did he say kickboxing?! Ha!'

The car slammed over a pothole, making a string of polished wooden prayer beads hanging from the rear-view mirror dance.

'Um, yes,' Yūki said, feeling a bit stupid.

'I wonder why he'd say something like that!' Jimi said, guiding them down through the tangle of little houses towards the sea.

Grandpa coughed. 'Trying to impress a beautiful young woman, of course!'

Yūki groaned. 'Grandpaaaaa!'

'No, he's really good though,' Jimi went on. 'High in the prefecture ranking. God only knows he didn't get it from me, those brains. Mine are like miso paste! All I do when I get off work is sit in the *pachinko* parlour and watch those little silver balls ping around and around for hours!'

'Gambling is a mug's game,' Grandpa grunts. 'I should know, I once lost a lot on the bike racing.'

'Probably. But I find it kind of soothing, Hara-san, watching the balls fly around. Meditative. *Pachinko Zen*! You just have to *accept* whatever happens, right?'

Jimi turned around again, beaming: a real northern face, rounded and weather beaten. 'How about that shake yesterday?' he went on as he steered through the cluster of buildings in the port. 'They say it was 7.3 on the Richter. I was in Minamisōma, and it felt like an upper 5 on the Shindo scale.'

'Relieved the pressure,' Grandpa said. 'But it toppled one of my stone lanterns in the garden.'

The taxi driver nodded eagerly. 'Port office said there was a fifteen-centimetre tsunami!' He lifted his hands in mock horror. 'Ha! We'll all be swept away, right!'

'Probably best not to joke about stuff like that.'

Jimi glanced in the mirror, the bags under his eyes weighing his smile down. 'No. Sorry, Hara-sensei. You ever write a story about a tsunami?'

Grandpa screwed his face up. 'Don't - think - so. Did a typhoon. The firebombing of Tokyo. Student riots. The battle of Narita. Ainu rebellions . . .' He glanced at Yūki. 'I saw an oarfish washed up, dead on the beach day before. They say they only come up before big quakes. Poor thing. I'll show you if it's still there, Yū-chan. If you want?'

She nodded vaguely, but Grandpa's list had nudged a memory: the day when she grabbed a stack of *Garo* magazine – feeling a rush of excitement and knowing she was breaking a house rule – and took them to her den on Little Mountain behind the house. Crouched in the long summer grass up there, focussed on turning page after page of tattooed gangsters, and lechy *kappa* and naked women and weird mutant monsters. Not understanding much, but knowing that whatever this was, it was good. That the man who had drawn all this knew what he was doing.

'Do you want to see it? The oarfish?'

'Sorry I was thinking about one of your stories.'

'At least somebody still is then!'

'That one about the kamikaze pilot who decided he didn't want to kill anyone on the morning of his mission and flew his plane up and up into the clouds.'

'Ah yes. Quoting Shakespeare and haiku as he went. He renounced Japan, threw the flag away, and then met a kind of angel in the clouds. A very sexy angel!' he laughed.

She nodded, looking away out of the window. The story had made her super, super sad, then embarrassed and intrigued all at once as the young pilot and the angel kind of melted into each other. And then she'd been discovered. Mum had lost it with her, then Grandpa and Dad got in a big row somehow, before Aunt Kazuko and her then boyfriend had taken her to one side and tried to tell her all about 'the birds and the bees' Kazuko style.

Jimi laughed, changing gears. 'Sexy angels, that's nice!'

'Bit cheap maybe,' Grandpa sighed, following Yūki's gaze towards the sea. 'I was proud of that big, last panel of the story though. Spent ages trying various things. Do you remember it, Yū-chan?'

'Mmm. It was just blank, right?'

'White. Empty. The void! You have no idea how much I had to argue for that!'

The taxi chugged up from the port area, past a couple of fishermen strolling towards the harbour in wet weather gear, and

58

then along the narrow coast road that hugged the cliffs, past the little roadside Inari shrine on its outcrop, vermilion *torii* gates against the ocean and clouds piled beyond. A breeze tugged at the faded red bibs hanging around the scowling fox statues guarding the entrance.

'Snow on the way,' Jiro grunted, watching them pass. 'You got enough warm stuff with you?'

'I'm fine.'

The road jinked inland, through the pine and wild camelia, then back out to skim along the edge of the cliffs, flying high above the ocean. Beyond that Jimi's taxi dropped down from the cliff road, taking the long curve around the rocky bluff that hid the Hara family house from the rest of the world.

And beyond that, no more land, just flat fields running to the sea wall, the ocean and the sky beyond. A house not quite belonging totally to either the water or the land.

On the hillside the pines and firs and *hinoki* sighed and shifted in the wind as Jimi gave a short toot on his horn, and his old Mazda pulled away towards the sea.

'*Okaeri*,' Grandpa said, unlatching the gate with its familiar *snick*. 'Welcome home.'

And, one hand resting on the big ornamental rock beside the path, Yūki whispered, '*Tadaima*.'

I'm back.

6

Swimming Prawn, Silent Foxes

SHE WAS HOME.

And she felt it, the tension dropping off her shoulders as Grandpa set about making her some instant noodles and she drifted from one room to another in the sprawling house, fingers trailing on familiar surfaces and objects. To the left of the *genkan* entrance hall through the old, emptier tatami-matted Japanese part of the house, with dusty folding screens and scrolls in the gloom, the family *butsudan* shrine with the framed photo of Yūki's grandmother beside it. Above her and her soft smile, the row of formal black and white photos of the generations before, stern gazes staring out unblinking. Yūki's eyes drifted again towards Grandma Anna's face – a face she'd never seen in real life. That hint of a smile in the corner of her eye caught for ever and ever, the one European face amongst all those Japanese Haras.

When Yūki was small and she and Grandpa went up on the bluff at Obon, climbing up behind the house through the warm and humid August evening and the cicadas whirring *miii miiii miiiinnnn* all around them, it was always Grandma's spirit she had hoped to see returning out of the darkness from *anoyo* – the 'other place'.

'Is she here yet, Grandpa?' she would whisper.

And Jiro would squeeze her hand, and make a grunt that could have been yes, or could have been no, or could just have been him clearing his throat – and the lanterns would flicker around them as a sudden warm breeze stroked the hill and put a delicious shiver through her body.

'Is she here?'

'Just wait. Just let's wait and be calm.'

Nowadays standing in the dark like that would freak her out.

Yūki gazed a long moment more at Grandma's picture, then rang the bell quietly on its red cushion and held her hands self-consciously in brief prayer position while the tone resonated and died into the silence. Then on, across the glassed-in walkway to the modern Western-style annexe to the right of the *genkan* and into a world of *stuff*: the bookcases groaning with Grandpa's artbook collection, papers and magazines overflowing from old box files, and rows and rows of the *gekiga* he wrote and drew in the seventies and eighties. Photo albums above that, an Eiffel Tower model, souvenirs from travels to Europe and America, a model Kabuki theatre, an old mouse cage, a typewriter. High on a shelf at the end, Great Grandmother's teardrop-shaped *biwa* lute with its crescent moons and tuning pegs and strings silent and still and cobwebbed.

61

She dragged a finger through the dust on the bookshelves, before pulling out a book at random, gazing at Grandpa's name, flicking the pages: a woman in a kimono on a motorbike tearing along under a black sky and the title: ESCAPE FROM SHINJUKU; a mushroom cloud boiling over a coastline that could have been Osōma and a caption: NUCLEAR NIGHT.

'Want sushi this evening, Yū-chan?' Grandpa called, making her jump.

'Yeah, that would be good.'

'What are you doing in there?'

'Nothing.'

'Don't just look for the rude bits!' he laughed, coming into the room. 'Hey, listen, tomorrow I want to talk about something important.'

Yūki pulled a face. 'About what?'

'Your future.'

Maybe it was all a set-up after all – Grandpa enlisted to push her to get a grip, get friends, get a life. But now he smiled reassuringly.

'Trust me.'

He joined her at the window, gazing out at the bits and pieces that he had collected over the years: the two shop dummies, one male, one female, their pale bodies naked and slowly greening with lichen; the little Buddha; an old Japanese postbox painted white. Even the garden was jam-packed.

'Remember when I told you that you could write to the foxes if you posted the letter in my special fox postbox?'

She smiled.

'And you got replies, right?'

'From *you*, Grandpa!'

'You believed it. For a bit.'

She had kept the letters for ages, the strange shaky handwriting and drawings just like a fox would do.

Dear Yūki,

It is very cosy in our den. We like to see you playing on the hill and we keep an eye on you with our fox magic. Look after us and we will look after you.

From, the Foxes

Above the postbox a bronze bell hung from a low branch of one of the pines, waiting for a strong wind to ring it.

Grandpa followed her gaze. 'One of the best things I ever bought, that bear bell! Got it the year I met your grandmother. On a hike in Nagano, one summer's day, ooh fifty plus years ago.'

'But you never get bears down here, Grandpa.'

'Shows you how effective it is!'

'You always do that joke.'

'Well it makes me laugh!'

Her eyes fell on the faded windmill toy, wedged in the border of the little rock garden. 'Why do you still keep that? I'm not a kid any more.'

Jiro sniffed. 'Not everything's about you, Yū-chan!'

'Maybe you should chuck some things away, Grandpa. You've got too much stuff!'

'Oh, I see. They've sent you to nag me as usual—'

'No, I just meant maybe you could get rid of a few things like that old windmill . . .'

'Damn it!' Grandpa's voice was sharp, abrupt. 'The trouble with young people is sometimes they think they're an expert on everything. Including what it's like being old! And by 'young' I mean anyone under sixty.'

'I'm sorry.'

'No, no. I don't mean you. I mean my daughters. Come on, noodles.'

In the afternoon they walked the wide, flat beach on the far side of the sea wall, the wind blowing as they hunted for the dead oarfish.

But there was not a sign of it, and after half an hour Jiro scratched his head.

'How could something that big have just disappeared? Maybe it wasn't dead . . . You know Katsumata-san – the manga guy I used to know – he wrote a bunch of stories about the nuclear plant.' Grandpa waved his stick in the direction of the towers of Fukushima Daiichi. 'He stayed with me when he was doing it. Wrote a great one about a huge octopus getting stuck in the reactor's cooling channel. Maybe our oarfish went off to sabotage that place for good.' He smiled. 'Imagine that!'

Later they sat in the sushi restaurant in town, the warm smell of cooked rice making her drowsy as she watched a huge prawn swimming lazy pink circles in her miso soup. She yawned.

Jiro laughed. 'I'm boring you!'

'Just jet lag,' Yūki said.

'You haven't smiled much.'

'I have! I did on the platform.'

'Hmm, just about. It must have been tough. School, and your parents nag-nag-nagging.'

She nudged the prawn with a chopstick.

'I don't really want to talk about it.'

The sushi master came over and set down a big platter of glistening rice and fish between them.

'I remember you when you were this big, Miss Yūki!' the man said, holding out his hand, palm down, his little finger no more than a stub.

He winked at Jiro. 'How have you been, Hara-sensei?'

'Well . . .' Grandpa tilted his head, considering. 'A friend of mine became a Zen priest when he got fed up running his club. He always said any problem you've got now is going to look pretty attractive when you're lying in your coffin!'

The master laughed. 'Enjoy your food.'

Jiro watched him go back to the pale wood counter. 'He used to be a *yakuza* gangster. Kind of person who made my life tricky once upon a time. Great sushi though.'

Yūki followed Jiro's gaze to the man, already busy again shaping rice. He muttered something to a pretty girl beside him, who hurried out through the door to a backroom, and, as it swung open, there was a clear view of a slim figure bent over the sink, washing pots in a cloud of steam – Taka, surely? Yes, definitely him, even though most of his curly hair was held in place under a tightly-tied white headcloth. As if feeling her gaze, he looked up and into the restaurant just as the door swung shut again. Had he seen her?

'Are you listening to me?'

'Huh?'

Jiro was peering at his granddaughter. 'She's still there, you know.'

'What? Who?'

'Young Yūki.'

'I'm sixteen in October.'

'I mean the one with the Hara spirit! The one who was mad for drawing. That girl that climbed the totem pole . . .'

Yūki rolled her eyes. 'You *made* me do it. And everyone *exaggerates* it!'

'The only day they ever left me in charge of you!'

Grandpa took a swig of his beer, savouring the memory. 'I merely suggested it would be fun to climb, and next thing you were over the rope and climbing and climbing. Eagle's wing and bear's paw and whatever, boy, could you climb like a monkey in those days. And the guard was shouting at you to get down – and at me too – and I just blanked him and said I don't speak English, and you shouted back at him too, from the very top.'

'It wasn't the very top. And I don't remember.'

But she did. She remembered exactly what it felt like being perched up there on a carved eagle's wing, high above the Cambridge museum floor, the other kids gawping in amazement.

It felt like being alive.

'You, me, Kazuko, we go our own way in life,' Jiro said, slurping his beer. 'Even your mum in her own way.'

'Did she really punch a boy?'

'Who told you that?' Grandpa snorts. 'But yes, it was Jimi's brother! That's why he still gives me discounts!'

'Was Grandma like that?'

'Anna?' Jiro tilted his head. 'No. But she was – just about the strongest person you'll ever meet. And so elegant with it. Came here *on her own* in the sixties to study with Hamada-sensei. You had to be tough to do that, you know – a woman, and a foreigner. What I liked was how she took this dirty old clay – basically mud, right? – and shaped it, and glazed it and made something as perfect and light as a flower. Like a lotus, you know, their feet are in the mud, but on the surface they are just light.' He turned away as if gazing into some huge distance, and shook his head. 'And well, just before your mum and Kazuko were born we moved back here to the family house. And some people were sniffy at first, but she had a smile like yours, and she even learnt a bit of dialect, and she carried on making her pots, and if anyone gave her the old *gaijin* foreigner nonsense, she just charmed them harder.'

'Grandpa?'

'Uh-huh?'

'Did you stop because she died?'

Jiro let out his breath, and looked back at her. 'Partly. I – I had nothing more to say. No more fish in the sea for me to catch . . .'

'Don't you want to draw again?'

'Oh, it's a young person's game these days anyway. Seven pages a week at least is OK when you're twenty. But . . .' Jiro swallowed the last of his beer, and banged his glass down.

'But what?'

He signalled for the bill. 'But, well, I *have* been fiddling with something.'

Yūki's eyes opened wide. 'Really? What?'

'I'll show you tomorrow. I had some work done on the studio – there was a leak and we had to replace some floorboards, so it's all shipshape now. The guy is just finishing up. Found a whole bunch of stuff!'

'Like what?'

'Things that got me thinking, that need to be talked about in the daytime,' Jiro said. 'Not at night.'

Outside, the street was quiet, and after the warm fug of the restaurant, the night chill sent a shiver through Yūki. A few paces down the road Jiro suddenly stopped, one hand slapping his forehead.

'Damn, left my cap. Won't be a moment.'

The sparse street lighting picked out pools of light: cherry trees with their blossoms still tightly rolled against the last of the winter, a car stopping outside the little Peacock *ryokan* hotel, steam from its hotbath billowing shifting shapes into the night over the two red vending machines.

A bang made Yūki jump, and she looked round to see a figure

coming out of the side door to the sushi shop, hair springing free as he hurriedly untied the headcloth.

'Ah good, caught you!' Taka beamed. 'Did you have a good meal?'

'Yes, thanks, it was good. *Gochisōsama deshita.*'

'You're so polite!'

'Mum's always on about it.'

He stood there, hands in his pockets, the smile lopsided on his face. 'Long time no see!'

She nodded at the lame joke.

'We're about to go, so . . .'

'So did you think about it?'

'What?'

'Hanging out with dumb old Taka?'

She bit her lip. 'Your dad said you got into some trouble or something?'

Taka looked away, but she saw the colour rise in his face.

'You're going red.'

He looked back. 'Yeah, it happens. When I talk to girls sometimes.'

'You didn't on the train.'

'Because I didn't have time to think about it, I guess. I've been getting ready to come and say something to you for half an hour!'

The sushi shop door rattled on its runner, and Jiro's silhouette filled the doorway.

Taka fumbled a small card from his pocket. 'My mobile. In

69

case you want it! See ya.' And without waiting for a reply he thrust it into her hand, turned and disappeared back inside the kitchens.

'Interrupt something?'

'No, no.'

Yūki glanced at the card. On one side was the address and phone number of the sushi place, on the other a scrawled string of digits. And, at the end of them, a large question mark.

'Was he chatting you up?'

'We were just talking.'

'He's a good lad. I think.'

As usual it took two or three goes to fire Grandpa's old Nissan into life.

'You should get a new car, Grandpa,' Yūki said, sliding the card deep into her jeans pocket.

'I hardly ever need one these days . . . besides it's getting a new starter next week.'

The car lurched forward, round the corner by the station, clipping the kerb.

'Should you be driving? Don't drink and drive, right?'

'It was just one beer. And we'll never meet anything on a night like this.'

Jiro's headlights picked out the sleeping town, the cluster of houses on the higher ground just above the port area. He accelerated up the wide sweep of tarmac, past the community centre, the engine and his reflexes settling, and then on to the smaller coastal road, starting to hum to himself, that same half a tune.

'Why do you always do that bit over and over, Grandpa?'

'Do I?'

'Yes.'

He paused. 'Is it annoying?'

'Not really. What is it?'

'Just something from *way* before your time . . .'

At the top of the slope the little Inari shrine and its two small *torii* perched silhouetted against the brighter space of the ocean beyond. As they passed it Jiro suddenly swerved to the kerb, cranking on the handbrake, his eyes bright as they strained into the darkness.

Yūki looked at him. 'Grandpa?'

'Just give me a minute.'

He switched the engine off, but then just sat there, gazing at the darkened shrine.

'What is it?' Yūki said, feeling cold now. The shrine had always felt a bit spooky – those angular muzzles of the shapeshifting foxes and their chiselled eyes seemed to follow you – and now, in the winter darkness, the power of the place felt very real.

Grandpa went to open his door, then appeared suddenly to change his mind.

'Are you OK?'

'Of course,' Grandpa said. 'You know, the Inari god is normally about rice. But ours is different: fishermen and storms and that kind of thing. I always prayed here, after I got back from Tokyo –

when we were starting out again. Storytellers are like fishermen, that's what I used to tell my assistants.'

'I don't understand.'

'Sometimes you get a good catch. And sometimes nothing. And sometimes you sail too far out.'

Grandpa sat in silence a long moment, then sucked the air in through his teeth.

'Are we going home now, Grandpa?'

'In a minute. But we'll come back tomorrow and bring the foxes some fried tofu. I want to make a special prayer.'

Under the eaves the ritual paper twists were fretting in the night breeze.

Back in her usual room on the upper floor of the annexe Yūki changed for bed, her mind still full of that moment beneath the shrine and Grandpa's suddenly darkened face. Chinking the blinds she took a long look out into the night: the lit windows of the houses dotted out on the flatland, one or two of the fish processing units burning midnight oil, and beyond, on the invisible sea, the lights of the local trawlers setting out into space.

She heard Grandpa whistling as he moved around downstairs . . . thought of the piles of clutter everywhere, the silent typewriter, and Grandma and her delicate ceramices, the cobwebs on the *biwa* lute – and suddenly felt the loneliness of all the time he must have spent on his own these last twenty or so years.

I'll be brighter for him tomorrow, she thought.

*

72

The kitchen clock ticks steadily through the morning of Friday 11th March. And Grandpa lets Yūki sleep in, humming to himself as he moves into the morning, making coffee, trying to shake the weird dream that he woke from in the early hours. Well, forget it. Just a dream. He thinks instead of the conversation last night, how occasionally Yūki's smile had threatened to break loose, push away the clouds and confusion, but had then faltered each time.

Poor kid, he thinks, nagged pillar to post I bet, she needs a good break. Well, let's try some manga healing . . .

Carefully, he prepares the stack of sketchbooks, piling dark blue on orange on moss green, making sure the very best one is on the top. He flicks the pages and Half Wave beams back off his curling blue wave.

Everything will be OK.

The coffee bubbles blackly in the filter machine and the crows come down into the trees above the house and everything's OK.

Around lunchtime he hears Yūki padding down the polished wooden stairs, and there she is, yawning, stretching.

'Morning, sleepy head! All OK?'

'All OK, Grandpa.'

'Good. Then drop your mum a quick email on my machine and let's have some fun. I've got a surprise for you . . .'

'Can we have pancakes for breakfast?'

'It's already lunchtime! But you can have breakfast and lunch together if you want! We'll make our own rules.'

So Jiro makes her breakfast and lunch and then shows her the first of the Half Wave sketchbooks . . .

. . . and Yūki smiles, and Jiro thinks, Ah! there you go! Good old Half Wave to the rescue!

But then he sees her smile has been wiped away, and her mouth is opening, her face turning to something more like horror as a cacophony of rattling and chattering erupts around them. And he realises something very bad indeed is happening.

7

11th MARCH, 2.46 p.m.

YŪKI WATCHES HER FINGER TREMBLING, the letters and kanji along the back of the hand shaking with it, faster, blurring. Some kind of weird panic attack? No, it's her whole arm, her shoulder, her feet, the sketchbook in front of her, even Half Wave looking back at her from the back of his curling wave, the *kotatsu* table itself, everything - *everything* - starting to shake like mad. From the living room there's a thud and a strange twanging sound, and then the bookshelves give way and drop their load with a roar. The shuddering gets worse, the chattering of crockery from the kitchen louder and louder, and Jiro falls to his knees. A second later the display cupboard - the one that holds Grandma's best pottery work - leans out from the dining room wall, hangs for a moment at an impossible angle, and then smashes down and explodes like a bomb, bright slivers of glass shooting across the floor.

'Grandpa!'

'Quake!' Jiro shouts. 'Get under the table, Yūki. Now!'

But she knows the drill.

It's a huge, vicious side to side shaker, the frequency getting faster, faster – way stronger than anything she's ever experienced before . . .

The dining room light is swinging wildly on its flex, drawers and cupboards opening and closing around her as if grabbed by unseen hands. Something big breaks on the tiles in the kitchen, and the light flickers as she scrambles under the table, banging her knee. It's weirdly difficult to move with the shaking this hard, and her limbs won't seem to go where she wants them to go.

'Grandpa!'

'I'm – coming.'

She crouches in the darkened space under the *kotatsu*, hugging her legs to her chest, counting the seconds as the world rattles and bangs around her. Must be almost over now surely . . . but as Grandpa clambers down to join her, the quake just gets worse and worse, gathering power, kind of thrusting up from beneath as if some monster is trying to break free. And the sound with it is horrible: a roar that seems to be emanating from everywhere at once, punctured by the noise of things breaking and falling, cutlery splintering to the kitchen tiles, a shattering of glass from upstairs, the whole timber frame of the annexe creaking and groaning.

'Grandpa! We should get out!'

'Stay put!' Jiro growls. 'This house can take it.'

The shuddering is even worse now. She tries to look at her watch to see how long it has already lasted but the face is a shadowed blur. At least two minutes now surely. A kind of claustrophobia is stirring, and something in her wants to move, to get out.

'Hold tight,' Grandpa shouts. 'It's not done yet.'

She feels the dry warmth of his hand take hers, and she squeezes it back, fighting the fear rushing through her body. There's a kind of lull, things quieten for a few seconds, and then another spasm grips the house, and there's a crash from the hallway, something big falling as the movement changes again, jerking everything from side to side. Her legs and stomach feel like jelly, and she's starting to worry she's about to throw up when another massive bang jolts right through her, and suddenly it's pitch dark under the table.

'We'll be trapped!' she shouts, trying to struggle out from under the table.

But Grandpa holds her tight. 'Keep still. Until it's finished.'

A minute more of the shaking, another, every second stretching out – and then there's one huge lurch from side to side, and all the movement and fury grinds to a halt, and – apart from the warbling of the alarm in Jiro's Nissan, and some kind of distant, quick thumping – there is total and utter silence.

It takes Yūki a long moment to realise that the thumping sound is her own heartbeat, battering away at her ribcage. The room smells funny – dust or smoke or something – and it's hard to get a proper breath.

Grandpa groans. 'Damn. You OK, Yū-chan?'

'Is it over? That was a really big one, right?'

'Very.'

'What now?'

'We're going to grab the emergency bag and go up on the bluff.'

'Why?'

'Just in case.'

'In case what?'

Grandpa drops his voice very low and utters a single word. 'Tsunami.'

'Oh? Really?'

'Could be.'

Her heart seems to miss a beat or two and she worries a panic is coming, her stomach still churning instant ramen round and around. Need air, need to get out, she thinks, starting to scramble from under the *kotatsu*.

'Careful. Don't cut your feet.'

Grandma's precious cups and bowls lie smashed all over the floor, porcelain shards everywhere, and a set of lacquer miso bowls are broken into bright red and black half-moons amongst them.

She runs into the hall, picking her way carefully on socked feet. The huge cupboard that holds all the shoes and coats has fallen across the *genkan* and gouged a chunk of plaster from the wall, but she finds a pair of outside sandals and clacks across the tiles to the front door. The thing won't budge even though it's unlocked, jammed in its frame somehow.

78

The need to get out is almost overwhelming, and she pushes the door hard with her shoulder, once, twice, her breath still held. On the third desperate shove it flies open, and she clomps out onto the *engawa* walkway above the garden and takes a huge gulp of air, eyes shut. Then another, and another. She opens her eyes again. The second massive stone lantern has fallen and smashed against one of the big rocks, its pedestal split neatly in two. Otherwise, apart from branches and hundreds of pine cones strewn under the trees, there's not much obvious damage. The alarm in Grandpa's car stops mid-note, and in the electric silence that follows there's just the quick tapping of her heartbeat in her ears, and the whirr of the windmill toy tucked in the edge of the rock garden. The falling lantern has missed it by a whisker.

Behind her Grandpa flicks the light switch in the hall back and forwards, the car key gripped in his other hand.

'Power's gone. Damn. Must've been lower 6 at least on the Shindo scale.'

'But it's over, right?'

'Mmm. There'll be aftershocks for sure. But nothing's going to fall on us for now.' Jiro sighs. 'The living room's a real mess, Mother's *biwa* is broken. She'd be really annoyed about that. She always hoped somebody else in the family would play it.'

'Grandpa! What about the tsunami?'

'We'll be OK.' Jiro glances at his mobile phone. 'No signal. We'll get the radio on.'

'Do you think one will come?'

'Depends how deep the quake was, epicentre, that kind of thing.'

Already Yūki's mind is full of images of Tokyo lying in smouldering ruins. 'Do you think Aunt Kazuko's OK?'

Grandpa pulls his face to one side, considering. 'I think we must have been much closer,' he says. 'Given what that felt like. Unless this is the end of the world. And I doubt that. It must have taken the phone masts out though. Put some proper shoes on. And keep them on. What a pain! At least we'll have to have that clear out! Your mum and aunt will be pleased!'

Yūki grabs her trainers from the *genkan* and starts lacing them as Grandpa takes a pair of heavy work boots from the fallen cupboard. 'I should have told you to stay put in Tokyo.'

'What do you mean?'

'Doesn't matter.'

She can make out distant alarms now from houses out towards the sea – but other than that, the silence is extending, deepening, like some huge space is opening up in the world.

Yūki looks at her grandfather. There's no panic on his face, just a hint of that same shadow that drifted across his face last night.

'So, what do we do?'

'Grab a coat and phone quickly. Passport. I'll get the earth-quake bag.'

'Will Little Mountain be high enough?'

Grandpa nods, trying to look casual. 'If a tsunami was that high it would be bigger than anything ever.'

But again she notices he utters the syllables *tsu-na-mi* very quietly, and she runs her right index fingertip along the faded magic letters on her left hand. Forgot to re-ink them this morning in the luxury of her lie-in.

'But let's move it, just in case,' Grandpa says, snapping into action. 'Your mother will kill me if anything happens to you! And then your dad. And Kazuko would probably have a go as well.'

Yūki runs up the stairs. It feels weird to be wearing shoes indoors, and her legs are still wobbly, her body swaying as she runs like she's just got off a storm-lashed ship or something.

Glancing out of the corridor window she sees a yellow haze hanging over the bluff behind the house, as if a fire is smouldering there amongst the pines. Her trainers crunch glass under foot, and she looks down to see the framed photo of Grandpa as a young man. He's grinning at the camera with a bunch of other manga artists, Anna next to him, their faces all flattened by a flash bulb, haloed in smoke and light.

In her room everything is a mess, drawers open, the blind roll has fallen diagonally across the window, slashing the view to the ocean. A butterfly has been shaken to life from somewhere, and is battering white wings against the glass. Quickly she goes over to open the window, ushering it out with shaking hands, the wingbeats fluttering against her palms. The butterfly dances away towards the sea and she follows it, half-expecting to see a disaster movie wall of water bearing down on them.

But the ocean looks really calm, and you can even see a couple of fishing boats out there, so still they could be painted on the grey water.

Maybe it's going to be OK.

It's even kind of exciting really, she thinks, like something's happening, something real. Something to talk about when I get home, tell Joel about it.

A sudden thumping from under her feet startles her – Grandpa banging on the ceiling now with his stick, his voice muffled but loud. 'Yūki! Come on, will you?'

She grabs her jumper, fumbling it over her head, and decides to change her thin leggings for the black jeans from last night. Her fingers are still shaky and it makes everything take ages, her heart rate picking up speed again. What else should she do? A Japanese word pops into her head, something that was drummed into her in disaster drill in those two short terms at the elementary school here: OKASHIMO. O for *osanai*, don't push. KA for *kakenai*, don't shout. SH for *shaberanai*, don't chat. MO for *modoranai*, don't go back. You don't go back ever until the disaster is over . . .

Might be outside for a long time. For good measure she whips her hoodie from the chair, and shoves that in her rucksack, checking the passport is still lodged in the inner pocket with her spending money.

'YŪKI!'

Jiro's shout has real urgency to it now, and she glances out of the window again. Still nothing but coiled clouds and the un-moving boats, and she hurries back along the corridor, thumping down the polished wood of the stairs. Picking her way through the chaos of the dining room she sees the open blue sketchbook and Half Wave looking up at her, determinedly riding his wave.

For a heartbeat she thinks about grabbing the book, but no – in an emergency you just take the vital stuff, right? – and so she rushes on to find Grandpa on the *genkan* step, a radio beside him crackling away.

'We've got to go. There's a tsunami warning for the *whole* of the Tōhoku coast.'

It's hard not to keep looking towards the ocean. Out across the flat land it seems like a typical Friday lunchtime, but about a hundred metres away a car is speeding along the coast road, much faster than normal. Somewhere away to the right she can hear a woman's voice shouting something, and distantly – towards Osōma Port – an amplified voice is coming from a loudspeaker, the syllables blurred by the wind.

At the edge of the stone garden the windmill toy is spinning like crazy, *whirrrrrrrrrrrrring* as the breeze stiffens, and the woman's voice is closer now.

'Hey, Hara-san? Are you there?'

'Ah. Takeda-san. Are you OK?'

It's Jiro's stern-faced neighbour, cycling head down like a *keirin* racer towards the Hara house, her beret a red flash in the gloom.

'*Daijōbu*. How about you, Hara-san?'

'We're fine,' Grandpa calls back. 'There might be a tsunami though. Come up on the bluff with us.'

'Oh, do you think so?' she says, stopping, putting one foot down on the tarmac, breathing hard. Her face is creased up with worry.

'There's a warning for a big one,' Jiro shouts.

'I'm supposed to pick up my nephew from middle school, and I'm trying to find Pochi,' she calls back. 'Have you seen him? He ran off in the quake.'

'Animals are smart. He'll have found somewhere safe. Get to high ground, Takeda-san.'

'No, I'd better go to the school. You take care of that grand-daughter of yours, Mister Hara!'

'Don't worry,' Jiro clamps a hand on Yūki's shoulder and waves his stick in the direction of the path around the side of the house. 'Some animals are smarter than some people if you ask me!' he adds under his breath. 'Come on. Let's climb.'

They head round the side of the house, past the toppled lanterns, the shop dummies lying on the ground trying to curl into their own foetal positions.

'Hurry a bit!' Jiro grunts.

Yūki glances over her shoulder, stumbling. 'Why? Is it coming?'

'No. But if it is, it'll be soon. Probably be . . . something tiny, like Jimi said!' he puffs. 'Damn it, should've put my new trainers on.'

The back garden is overgrown, but a path winds its way past the long, low studio, a pile of old boards and some fresh offcut timber propped against a workbench outside. Then on past Grandma's old pottery at the back with its wheel and kiln, silent and dark.

'Thought you might need some . . . excitement,' Jiro pants. 'But . . . maybe not as much as this!'

Winter has left the long grass dry and faded, and it whispers against her legs as she follows him all the way to the foot of the bluff. Quickly they climb the rough wooden steps up the first half dozen or so metres to the spot where Grandpa has planted bird feeders on iron stakes. All of those lie on the ground now, seed scattered.

'Won't this do?'

'Better go to the top, Yūki. Then we can see what's what. Just let me get a breath.'

From here a faint track zigzags up through the tangle of bushes and scrubby pine and fir, the familiar route she always used to take, but steeper somehow than she remembers. Her feet slip, but Grandpa steadies her with his reassuring grip. Every ten or so paces he has to pause and plant his stick though, cocking his head and listening for a moment, before urging her higher with a wave of his hand, and she pushes on up through the overgrown bushes scratching at her face, panting a bit now herself as she overtakes him and climbs higher. When she pauses to get her own breath, she looks back to see Jiro rooted to the spot below.

'What is it, Grandpa?'

'Listen!'

The wind is sighing through the dead winter leaves, and you can hear the blurred words from the distant loudspeaker, a car on the road. Nothing else.

'What is it?' she repeats.

'There's no birdsong. None at all.'

It's true: not even a crow calling. There's always at least one crow calling darkly in Japan – here, Tokyo, everywhere. Or sparrows chirping like feathered clockwork through the under-growth. Or migrating swans honking overhead. But there's not a single scrap of birdsong now.

In the pause she realises how dry her mouth is, how clammy her skin feels under her T-shirt. 'I feel weird, Grandpa.'

'It's probably the shock. We'll get warm at the top. I've got an emergency blanket in the bag.' He clambers up to join her. 'Are you doing OK?'

'Yep.'

'I mean – you know – as regards these panic things?'

She manages to find half a smile from somewhere. 'Panic-wise I'm surprisingly OK, thank you for asking.'

Grandpa smiles back. 'Come on then. You used to practically live up here! Show me the way!'

The path jinks onto an angled slab of rock, very rough steps cut into it, and grabbing saplings to steady herself, she clambers the last few metres, up and up, her feet remembering the move-ments, and suddenly she's at the top, safely on the moss and needle-strewn earth and jumbled rocks beneath the stunted pines – the whole thing about the size of a tennis court, dipped in the middle where they always built the bonfire to send the spirits home on warm summer nights.

But now the top of the bluff is cold – and that strange yellow haze is filling the air and her body is shivery.

Grandpa joins her, breathing hard. 'God, years since I've been up here. Any sign?'

She peers out through the trees towards the ocean, but those two boats are still as good as nailed to the waves.

'Nothing. What do we do now?'

'Find out what's happening,' Grandpa says, pulling a small radio from the emergency bag and crouching down to fiddle with it. His blunt fingers conjure a swish of white static, and then a man's voice, speaking very fast, formal Japanese from which all she can catch is the word 'tsunami' and the names of places further north. Ishinomaki, Sendai, Miyako.

'Is it coming?'

'Nope. Just the warning.'

Yūki shivers again, looking around. The summit slopes away steeply on three sides. On the fourth, to her back and inland, a sheer cliff drops to the little back road.

'Grandpa, I think some of it's fallen down.'

'Hmm, probably a landslip.'

'What's the yellow stuff?'

'Pollen I should think.'

The ground gives a faint shudder again, and Yūki braces for an aftershock. Grandpa glances up but nothing comes and he goes back to fumbling with the radio, trying to get the signal clearer.

'If you're cold, get the emergency blanket out.'

'I put my hoodie in my bag.'

'Smart thinking.'

Below them a solitary car passes on the road and, far away, there's the wavering rise and fall of a police or ambulance siren, the amplified voice still echoing beyond that.

She tries to focus on the radio.

'They're saying there's a chance of a big tsunami, right?'

'Uh-huh,' Jiro turns the volume down a bit, 'maybe as much as six metres. There's a lot of quake damage being reported too, must have been a huge one. The epicentre seems to have been offshore – not far away. If it felt that big to us, you'd expect the tsunami to have come by now. They travel really fast. I remember one that came all the way from Chile – crossed the Pacific faster than a plane and it caught a lot of people out. Good grief, I was only just a bit older than you! Twenty. We were fine but a lot of people weren't so lucky . . .' He looks away again. 'I dunno . . .'

A car horn is hooting somewhere to their left, and Yūki turns to look towards the road that leads to the cliffs and Osōma Port and the town beyond. Two cars – one black, one beige – have stopped and are facing each other, and then the one heading away starts to do a three-point turn, and both come back towards the Hara house. Somewhere beyond the cliffs a plume of black smoke is rising.

'There's a fire.'

'Not surprised.'

'Grandpa?'

'Yes?'

'Last night at the shrine you said you needed to make a prayer. It wasn't about this was it?'

Grandpa looks up sharply. 'What do you mean?'

'Like you knew it was coming or something?'

'I thought you were meant to be the sceptic these days.'

88

'I'm right, aren't I?'

'Good grief, you always could read me.' He puffs out his cheeks. 'No. It was about something else. But I did have a silly dream *last* night.' The tone in his voice is heavy. Not very 'Jiro' at all.

'About what? Tell me.'

'I was walking on the beach – near where I found the oarfish the other day. And I could hear somebody singing, and suddenly I saw a boy walking towards me. And when he got closer his feet were making huge footprints in the sand and each one was filling with water, leaving a trail of big, blue puddles. Kind of beautiful really, but he looked miserable and soaked through. And I said, *Hey kid, what are you doing out here?* And he said, *I just want to go home because there's a tiny tsunami coming and it's going to kill me*, and I said, *If it's tiny then what's the problem?* . . . but he just looked really sad.'

Grandpa's voice trails off.

'And then?'

'Nothing else really, I woke up and had a drink! Must have been Jimi going on about the fifteen-centimetre wave yesterday, right?'

Yūki looks at him, then out to sea, then back again, the shivers pulsing through her.

'Maybe it was a – you know, a dream about the future . . . ?' She can't remember the Japanese word for 'premonition'.

Grandpa shakes his head. 'Forget it. I should be chatting bright and breezy to keep our spirits up, right? Lousy grandfather really.'

'You're not lousy.'

He grunts. 'Thanks. Still glad you came?'

'Yes. Hundred per cent.'

'You said I was a bit grumpy when you came last year. Sorry, heh?'

'It was a bit like you were frustrated with me.'

'No! Maybe I was just fed up with everything else. But not you. You're special, Yūki. I always thought that. Grandma would agree with me . . . she told me that once.'

'Like - in a dream?'

'Kind of.'

They fall silent, listening to the sirens, the hissy swirl of static around the announcer's voice, the swaying of the branches in the stiffening wind overhead. Another five minutes pass, their gazes both glued to the sea - and then another five.

'Do you think it's coming, Grandpa?'

'Probably not now.'

But when she turns to him, Jiro looks - sad, kind of defeated somehow and she tries to think of something to lift his mood. 'Thanks for finding the Half Wave stuff. I'd forgotten it all really until I saw the books.'

'Well, thought it might be good to remember. I wonder where he's been all this time!'

'Did you say you had done a drawing?'

'Hmm?' Jiro mumbles, as if he's only half listening. 'Nothing really. Just thought I'd have a go at something. I'll show you later. Had to give all my pens a clean out, especially that lovely Rotring of mine. It felt good though! Pens and pencils want to draw, you know, they don't want to sit around all dried up. I apologised to them, formally.' He joins his palms in a *gassho* and bows. 'There is absolutely no excuse for what I have done.'

'I wish I'd seen you doing it all, you know, when you were famous. The Tezuka Award and everything.'

'Oh, well . . . things change . . .' His face brightens. 'I was thinking *I* might draw your Half Wave a companion.' Grandpa peers at her. 'I keep worrying how lonely he might have been. It's no fun being on your own.'

'You could do a proper version, Grandpa.'

'It's your story, Yūki. I'd just be your assistant! Just promise me one thing.'

'What?'

'Try and learn to trust your instincts. Even if they seem silly – follow through!'

'OK.'

The wind gusts coldly across the hilltop.

Suddenly Jiro plants his stick on the ground with a thud. 'Listen, I need to do something. I'm going to nip back down to the house, but I want you to stay here. Sit tight, listen to the radio and see what you can make out.'

Yūki grips his arm. 'No! I'll go, I'll be faster. Just tell me what—'

'Out of the question. You're staying put here until they've *officially* given the all clear.'

'What about *okashimo*? 'Mo' means *modoranai*, right? Don't go back.'

Jiro pulls his arm free gently. 'Until it's over. The quake is over and it was so close if there was going to be a tsunami it would have come by now. The authorities just like to play on the safe side.'

'But what's so important?'

'Need to do something, fetch something.'

'But what?'

'My new trainers, of course!'

'Don't be stupid—'

'It's a joke! You're on guard.' He hands her a whistle from the emergency bag. 'If you see or hear anything coming, just blow this as hard as you can. There'll be plenty of time for me to nip back up.'

'But—'

'I'll be back. Promise.'

He takes one more look out to the ocean and then is away down the steep slope, boots slipping, a hand grabbling for hold on the trunk of a tree, the stick braced in the other, moving surprisingly fast. Within seconds he's gone from sight and she listens as he crashes on down through the undergrowth, hears him whistle a scrap of that familiar tune, and then the sounds fade slowly and are gone and the hillside falls into silence. For a moment she stands teetering on the verge of following. But stops herself.

There's no arguing with Jiro once he's made up his mind.

And she's been given a job as lookout, so she turns the radio up and fixes her gaze back to the sea. The reception is better again: quake reports, a bridge down, a school damaged, the tsunami warning repeated every minute. Still sounds serious, but no news of anything beyond the quake. She scans the sea again, ears pricked for Grandpa's return as the seconds lengthen into long minutes.

Come on, Grandpa, come on.

Her hands are cold and she shoves them into the tight jeans' pockets, and feels something there, and pulls it out to see the sushi shop business card, the scrawl of Taka's phone number on the back. Hopefully the earthquake didn't hurt him or his dad – wasn't there something about a train he had to get this afternoon? She thinks about calling him and takes the phone from her bag, and then remembers the masts are down and shoves the card and her mobile back in her pocket and scans the flat landscape in front of her again. A few cars are beetling along the little roads between the houses and the sea wall, and you can just make out the pale concrete buildings of Osōma Port Elementary, half hidden behind a line of scraggy pines. A lorry is moving towards it along one of the narrow, straight roads that criss-cross the old marshland, but now it slows and comes to a halt a hundred or so metres past the school. It looks horribly exposed out there if anything does come . . .

Her eyes move on to the sea wall beyond, the ocean waves stretching out to the horizon beyond.

Come on, Grandpa.

Even if he is fairly sure the danger for a tsunami has passed, it's just like Grandpa to ignore a warning. She remembers Kazuko scolding him for swimming in the sea at Obon.

'I was doing samurai stroke!' he boasted as he towelled down with a grin, his chest out.

Yūki locks her eyes back on the waves.

Amidst the cold sea, the wind, the distant sirens, her heart beating, beating, beating.

That dark blue lorry is moving again, coughing up exhaust from its smoke stack and heading towards Osōma, a few other small white vans dashing along the low-lying roads. A sudden burst of white noise dissolves the radio voice, and Yūki crouches down to fiddle with the tuning, trying to find the station again – and in that moment she misses something important. Slowly – but gathering pace with every second – the entire ocean is retreating towards the horizon, as if a vast blue-grey rug is being pulled away to the clouds piled beyond.

Unable to get a signal Yūki peers down at the house, edging a little down the steep rocky slab. She cups her mouth and shouts, 'GRANDPA! The radio's gone! Come up!'

Her voice sounds uselessly small, and she knows it won't reach the house.

Why isn't he back yet? She strains to listen to the space below her. Is that the sound of the Nissan's engine turning over under the car port? A long dry coughing that dies to nothing . . .

'Grandpa! Should I come down?'

The ground gives a violent heave, and then begins to shake hard again beneath her feet – and she sits down heavily, clutching the roots of a tree to hold onto the ground as a big aftershock shakes the bluff, rattling her bones, her teeth in their sockets.

Harder, harder . . . Is it as strong as the last one? Maybe the whole thing will slip . . .

The bluff bucks violently again beneath her, and she hears herself making a weird kind of 'ahhh ahhhhhhhh aaaaaaahhh' sound, something more like an animal whimpering than her own voice.

98

She clings tighter to the ground, pushing herself into the pine needles and earth – and then after another few seconds, the aftershock rocks to an abrupt stop. The air smells of soil, and there's fine dust hanging in the air, the sharp tang of pine thick in her nose. Better go down and find him, Yūki thinks, and looks away just to check the sea again.

It takes her a moment to make sense of what she is seeing, to realise why everything looks so weird out there.

The Pacific has disappeared.

Or rather it's not where it should be, but much further away than normal, steadily retreating even further from the shoreline as she stares in horror, exposing a huge stretch of rock and seaweed and sludgy black *hedoro* mud.

Oh my God. It's coming.

She struggles back to her feet: 'Grandpa! GRANDPA!!!'

No reply from below, not a sound – even the car alarm has died – but then the radio comes back, loud and very clear:

'TSUNAMI REPORTED AT SENDAI PORT! Ten-metre tsunami! Please evacuate all East Tōhoku coastal areas immediately. Evacuate to higher ground. TSUNAMI COMING!!!'

8

The Thousand-Year Wave

SHE TRIES TO SHOUT FOR Grandpa again, but all the air has gone from her lungs. Tries to will her legs to move, but it's as if they are stuck to the ground. And try as she might it's impossible to pull her eyes from the ocean.

The exposed sea bed looks so strange, so otherworldly, so impossible. Beyond that, one of the boats is still visible, motionless on the water some three or four kilometres out now. But then – horribly – it seems to lift up, and up, and hang high in what seconds ago was air, floating impossibly, then suddenly disappearing as if it has winked out of existence.

It's coming.

Not a disaster movie tidal wave, just a vast swell on the sea like a dark mountain ridge – it must be dozens of metres tall – and it's coming, the tsunami is coming.

Yūki raises the whistle to her mouth, takes a huge breath and blows as hard as she can. Nothing. Just a fluttering, wheezy sound. She shakes it hard and then tries again, fingers trembling as she holds it to her dry lips, her rapid heartbeat chopping away in her ears.

Not a peep, the stupid thing must be bust.

One more soundless blow, and a second later she is sliding, running, slipping down the steep path, bellowing, 'GRANDPA! GRANDPA!' over and over again at the top of her lungs. She stumbles in the soft earth, and a branch slashes her face, leaving a hot line on her cheek, knocking her glasses askew. Grabbing a tree trunk to stop the freefall, she clings to it for a few seconds, pushing the glasses back into place, and glances back out to see where the wave has reached.

There's a great puff of white that at first she takes to be smoke, erupting all along the line where the furthest houses and pines mark the coast. But it's not smoke, it's a long, foaming mess of water and spray hitting the land proper, detonating over the sea wall, the dunes, the trees, smashing anything in its path, obliterating everything. A moment later the noise follows: low and ominous, like a wall of thunder filling the air as the water crushes the shore and starts to eat across the flat land towards her, into and over houses, foam churning above its thick black body as it slams into the elementary school, swamping it to the height of the roof in seconds. Caught in the wave she glimpses a small white car, then something else, square and boxy. A shed? No, something bigger: a small house – a house! – splintering to bits even as she recognises what it is, and all of it, all the black water and white thundering wave crest, seems to pick up speed, the sound getting louder and louder and louder.

She manages to shout for Grandpa again as hard as she can, and peers down at the house, leaning further out, straining to see through the trees. Not a sign of him – or any movement – but to her left, out of the corner of her eye, there's something moving, near the road. Squinting through the branches she sees a silent, stealthy out-runner of the wave – water flooding the tarmac, advancing fast, growing and deepening across the tarmac. A car is heading towards it from the far side, its hazard lights blinking. It brakes hard, then reverses away fast, the engine shrieking in protest.

She shakes her head, and before she knows what she is doing she is hurtling down the hillside again in a mad whirl of arms and legs.

'Grandpa! *Ojīchan*!' she screams against the growing roar. 'It's coming!'

Beyond the fallen bird feeders the rest of the path is gone, the last shake has caused a mini landslide that angles down onto the grass.

She hesitates. Hidden now by the house, the wave sounds horribly close, like a huge express train bearing down on them. Only a handful of seconds to make a decision. She is still a few metres above the garden, level with the eaves of the roof.

'Grandpa! GRANDPA!!!'

Where is he?!

She edges three more tentative steps down the landslip, but it gives way suddenly beneath her feet and she falls, bracing with her right arm just as she hears a huge *whoomph* as the wave smashes into the front of the house. She rolls to a half-sitting position in the loose soil, just in time to see the front edge of the tsunami round the corner and come racing across the garden towards her, its leading edge clawing the ground with white fingers.

Time slows to a crawl.

Under the carport Grandpa's white Nissan has lifted on the wave's back, its hazard lights flashing as the alarm sounds again, turning towards her and floating through the bushes beside the carport – nobody at the wheel but the windscreen wipers flapping as it accelerates like an out of control boat, rearing up and then ramming hard into one of Grandpa's beloved trees with a sickening crunch. The car yaws in the current and goes half under. A fraction later she sees a figure rolling in the clutch of the black water, swimming towards her.

'Grandpa!!'

She edges lower, getting ready to reach out her hand – but then realises it's just one of the stupid mannequins from the front garden. Flailing and rolling it disappears under the surface, swallowed by the blackness as the surging water breaks onto the slope just below her. The sound, the vibration, the smell of sea and earth being mushed together is overpowering . . .

She turns, feet scrabbling, and grabs for a branch, hauling herself up with every bit of strength. But already the tsunami is at her feet, and it claws at her ankles, calves, at her knees – and then it has her and pulls her down. Something thumps into the back of her left thigh, spinning her around, arms flailing, as she pirouettes into the water, a shocking coldness crashing over her, taking her under, blinded, gripped by a fierce current, turned helplessly. She tries not to swallow or breathe, but finds herself making a kind of watery scream that merges in her ears with the muffled roar of things being crushed and drowned.

The ocean forces itself into her mouth and nose, and she swallows some as she instinctively makes a strong kick – and either the kick itself, or the thrust of the current, lifts her up through a tangle of submerged branches, scragging her clothes and skin, her elbow striking something hard, sending a tingling numbness the length of her arm.

Her forearm and hand go limp, and she rolls in the water, the bluey-blackness enveloping her, churning her over, objects dimly seen, then gone . . .

. . . no, no, no . . . it can't be . . .

. . . maybe that dummy again? A flash of white . . .

. . . her strength is ebbing, draining away, as she keeps trying to fight and kick with her good leg and arm, struggling to find the surface. But it's like the water has been thickened into a kind of black porridge . . .

. . . roaring and churning, like it's right in the middle of her skull.

Something bangs the back of her head and sparks flare in her vision, bright stars fizzing like fireworks, and she's starting to swallow more water, desperately holding the last of her breath, but can't any more, and she takes a big gulp, and another, seeing nothing, and she knows she is drowning, feels ready to let go and stop struggling and even though her mind is losing its grip, suddenly a strange feeling of peace comes with it, almost a sense of calm and relaxing.

There's nothing left to worry about because she knows how it's all going to end now. Here, in the wave, in the raging waters flooding the Hara house.

It's all fine, Yūki.

Maybe – just maybe then – she sees something: a patch of light in the corner of her vision, like a big fish or something has just brushed past, the sensation of something close.

She swallows more of the wave, and her vision goes dark.

On the edge between consciousness and nothingness, she feels something against her – not hitting, but a force kind of pushing her through the water. It feels alive somehow, and she panics again, but there's no strength left, and she just gives in to whatever is coming.

The current or the wave itself – or whatever it is – shoves her on through the darkness. Strangely, in that moment of calm and resignation, Half Wave flashes in her head, a fleeting image of the boy on his wave, head held high, smiling at the spray.

Weird.

Am I dying?

Probably.

She feels cold.

She feels heavy.

There's no breath to be had. And the image of Half Wave fades into blue darkness.

It's my fault, she thinks vaguely. But I did my best.

And now it's over.

In a fury of noise and cold her head breaks the skin of the water.

Spluttering, thrashing at the surface, blinking sea and salt out of her eyes, she sees a slab of debris floating right next to her. It's about the size of a garage door – and there's something crouched on it.

No time to think – she takes one big stroke with her good arm and grabs hold, trying to pull herself to safety, kicking hard with the sodden trainers on her feet. But it's impossible, the thing's bobbing up and down and slippery, and her strength is almost gone. Nothing to do but cling on as long as she can and hope somehow that they drift into the shallows eventually. She blinks at the thing on the 'raft' – and sees a small dog. A sodden little dog, steadying itself as it struggles to its feet, legs splayed, shaking . . .

Stuff under the water keeps banging into her legs and lower back, and her grip is already weakening. Now her head is above water it's somehow almost worse than the moment when she thought all hope was gone. This tiny chance of survival is almost like she's being teased. She can taste the salt and mud in her mouth, the back of her nose. Again she tries to propel herself up out of the water's grip, her fingers desperately clawing the shiny wet surface.

No good. She slips and nearly goes right under again, her fingertips just keeping contact, the cold shocking her again. But then there's a sudden upthrust of the water, and it lifts her, and she's virtually catapulted out of the tsunami and onto the piece of flotsam where she lands in a mess of arms and legs, half-dead, choking up seawater and sludge.

For a moment she lies there clinging to the slippery surface as best she can as the wreckage pitches up and down. She takes a deep breath, then steadies herself on all fours, and retches again and again from the pit of her stomach, coughing up muck that stings the back of her throat. As it eases – through the blur of water clinging to her eyes – she sees the bedraggled animal edging away to the far side of their makeshift raft. It yaps sharply. Maybe by some miracle it's Mrs Takeda's Pochi? About the right size, and the same reddish brown colouring. She holds out a hand, overwhelmingly glad to see something else living.

'Pochi? It's OK, *daijobu!*' she coughs, and the animal suddenly whimpers and comes closer, paws skittering on the shiny debris as something bangs into them, tilting the raft, threatening to spill the creature into the water. She reaches out and grabs it by the scruff of the neck, pulling it to her aching chest.

More water chokes up from her insides, and for a minute or so all she can do is cough and heave until the spasms pass. She manages to get up into a half-sitting position, braced better against the rocking of the chunk of whatever it is they're riding, doing her best to hold onto the animal.

She blinks again, holding one edge of the raft tight. Without her glasses everything beyond arm's length is a blur, and she looks down at the shivering dog in her other arm, taking in the sharp ears, the pointy muzzle, the thickly-matted fur of its tail.

It's not a dog at all . . .

A small, bedraggled fox is staring back at her in terror, its eyes two pale orange orbs, dark ovals in the centre of each, perfectly reflecting her silhouette in both. The poor thing's shaking like crazy.

'It's OK,' she whispers. *'Daijōbu daijōbu daijōbu* . . . keep calm. Don't bite me, please. Don't bite . . .'

She keeps a tight hold on the scruff of the fox's neck, watching it to make sure it doesn't nip at her as she takes another few long breaths. Then raises her head to stare in amazement again at the watery world around her. Without glasses she can recognise nothing at first, then realises the island poking up through the ocean behind them is the bluff – Little Mountain – just the top third peeking out through the green and black waters, the family house totally under save for the roof ridge of the old house, everything else swamped.

The current is turning them again, sending the smudge of the cliffs to the north through her vision, the debris-strewn water raging high against them too. And then she gasps as the rotation continues and takes her gaze out to open sea: there's a house floating there, about two hundred metres away – an entire house lifted off its foundations but still intact – with smoke and red flames streaming from it as it burns against the lowering clouds and dull blue Pacific beyond.

And further off another house – with a tiny figure clinging to the roof, maybe? Yes, there's somebody on it, but no more than a distant silhouette.

The fox is really struggling in her arms, and she lets go long enough for it to shake from muzzle to tail, and then she hugs its wet fur to her again, both of them shivering hard.

111

'I'll look after you,' she whispers. 'I promise, Fox-san.'

Her arm still feels a bit numb, and she knows it would be senseless to swim for it. Signal for help maybe? But what with? And who's going to see? The whistle was useless and that's lost anyway, and the phone is gone from her pocket – and when she tries a shout it's instantly lost in the vastness of the ocean, and all she manages to do is to panic the little fox again.

'Shhh. It's OK, Mr Fox. *Dai-jouuuu-buuu.*'

She looks out at the water turning huge circles around her, and her heart drops. Slowly, but inexorably, they're being carried away from the bluff, from the cliffs, following that floating house out towards the wide open sea.

The towers of the nuclear plant, some three or four kilometres south, spin through her vision, then the submerged family house again and the bluff – but they're already getting noticeably smaller.

Her gaze drops to her mud-stained hand on the deck, the letters of her safety charm blurred by filth and water.

Another series of coughs erupts from deep within.

'Fox-san,' she whispers, when the fit has subsided. 'We're in a lot of trouble. I hope you're a *kitsune* spirit or something and a good one at that . . .'

The fox stares wide-eyed back at her, like it's not sure whether to leap off the raft or cling close.

'Don't leave me,' Yūki says into its wet fur, starting to cry. 'Stay with me.'

9

Shipwrecked

SHE LIES FLAT, HUGGING THE shivering fox tight, trying to calm the shakes rattling her to the core. Numbly her mind reaches out for Grandpa, trying to calculate the odds that he's made it somehow.

Maybe he got to the cliff road? He always was a strong swimmer, he's still fit. Chopping wood most days in the winter for the stove, walking miles some days.

But looking out again at the power around her, it's impossible to keep hope alive. Nothing could match that.

Maybe he was the person clinging to the rooftop? But that house has sailed so much further away already it's impossible to shout or wave, and she can't make out the figure on it anyway.

She remembers the dry cough of the Nissan's starter motor, and tries to focus. He must have got in the car at some point. Maybe the hazard lights would have gone with the movement from the wave, but that wouldn't have set the wipers going, would it? Maybe he was in it when it rammed into the tree? Or maybe he tried to get away in the car and then made a run for it at the last moment? Maybe back in the house to take cover in the attic?

The fox is whimpering now, and she strokes its head, trying to reassure herself as much as the animal as they float, bob and ride on the swell of the water, further and further away from the coast. There's wreckage all around them – it looks like everything from the land has been washed away: fishing nets, and crates and bits of furniture, and chunks of broken building like the thing they're on. Planks of wood and plastic drums, a garden chair part submerged – most of it is so fragmented you can't make out what you're looking at.

Bodies too? Or do they sink straight away?

She shoves the thought aside and looks down at their raft. Under her are black kanji characters and she moves a bit, carefully, scared of upending the whole thing, to see what they say.

KITAIZUMI LIFE–

Must be from a lookout post on the 'summer beach'.

It makes her thinks of Taka again. What about him and his dad? Maybe their house is high enough above the port, but given how high the water has come, most of that bit of town must have been destroyed. And what time was that train? The line would have taken the full force of the wave just south of here . . .

From that direction now there's the pulse of a helicopter, and she looks around, trying to see where it is, imagining her and even the fox being winched to safety. But when she does make out the chopper, it's low and somewhere off to the right of the nuclear plant, moving fast inland – no chance of them seeing a tiny speck down here amidst the chaos of burning houses and wrecked towns.

If only the debris would stop spinning - the movement is making her feel really sick and it's hard to think straight. At least her numb arm is coming back to life, thousands of pins and needles starting to shoot through it now. She shakes it hard, then closes her eyes, trying to keep both her and the fox warm. I'll rest a bit, she thinks. And then I'll try and think of something. Some kind of plan.

But for a long five minutes her mind goes kind of blank and empty. Not a single thought, just the water and rubbish swirling in her gaze, shivering as her wet clothes cling to her. And then when thoughts do come again, all she can do is berate herself for letting Grandpa go down to the house.

Why on earth didn't he stay put with me? What was so important? It's so stupid - his joke about the silver sneakers as if it was all a game or something. What was the last thing he said?

I'll be back. Promise.

Oh God, she thinks, if he *has* drowned then I'm going to have to tell Mum. But then again I'm probably going to drown anyway, so maybe I won't have to do that.

She and Dad are probably still asleep, must still be early morning there, probably fast asleep, cosy, warm . . .

Need to think of something else. Something totally different, but positive.

Strange how that image of Half Wave flashed through her head at the moment she was giving up - so clear and bright. If

115

I'd drowned then that would have been the last thing I saw, she thinks, and tries for a few cold minutes to imagine her imaginary hero running across the water towards her. Half Wave would save us if he was real, right? He wouldn't stop until he had saved every person and every animal he could.

'*Mukashi, mukashi*,' she whispers into the fox's wet ear, 'there was a g-g-girl who got caught in a wave. And she found a small fox, and they were rescued by a little superhero with b-b-blue hair who helped them to safety . . .'

But exhaustion washes over her again, and a fresh wave of shivering stops her story dead as the raft turns and heads for the open ocean and – who knows – America? Chile? That bottomless trench in the middle of it all. What's it called? Maybe I should swim for the land now?

But when she looks back towards the coast it is far away and the black currents look like they would swallow her in one easy gulp.

Silence descends beyond her quiet sobs and the fox's snuffling and there's nothing else but the sound of water and dark clouds in the immense sky overhead. From towards Futaba comes the pulse of a siren – and she closes her eyes and her mind goes blank as they drift on the cold spring sea.

.

It's hard to know how much time has passed – it could be ten minutes or thirty minutes or an hour or more – but Yūki realises the sounds around her have changed. The noises of the open sea – the slap of water against the raft, the sigh of the wind – have given way to a growing murmur, like something's churning close by, a propeller or something. She lifts her head wearily, bracing for the sight of a tanker coming at them.

But instead of ocean she sees the unmistakeable shape of Little Mountain, now not more than a hundred or so metres away. Somehow the wave has turned, and is surging back at the land again, carrying them with it, the flotsam thickening the water around them, almost back to where she was swallowed by the wave in the first place. Adrenaline kicks back through her, and she sits up.

'Hey, Fox-san,' she rubs the animal's thin back briskly, 'look – the land!'

It's still way too far to swim, but there's a chance. Maybe only half a chance, but the current is bringing the raft rapidly towards the bluff.

Can't leave the fox though, she thinks, scouring the water for something to grab and use as an oar. Can foxes swim? I can't make it with him under my arm . . .

The debris around them is no use – broken flimsy shards of plastic, a barrel of some kind – but then she sees a bit of plank floating close to them, and makes a lunge for it. For one horrible second it feels like the raft is going to tip and her pulse leaps, but – no – it's OK, and she has the board in her hand, and the fox is still pressed against her. The piece of wood is about a metre long, broken diagonally, and she grips the narrow end in one hand, the middle of it with the other, and leans forward, scooping the water, working as fast as she can to help the raft through the swell.

'Stay close to me, Fox,' she shouts. 'We'll do it!'

Twenty, thirty dips of her improvised paddle and she looks up to gauge her progress. None at all, damn it, damn it. Hopeless. If anything we're drifting away again?

She leans further out, the jagged wood splintering into her palm. Twenty more frantic splashes, throwing all of her remaining energy into the movement, and – yes! – now they're nudging a bit towards the roof of the house.

Ganbare Yūki! she mutters under her breath. *Do your best.*

The current shifts again, and suddenly thrusts them towards the bluff, just four or five metres away now.

'Get ready, Fox-san!'

She takes two more messy digs with the paddle and then hurls it aside, grabbing for a sapling thrashing out in the water – just as they strike the hillside or something rams into them, and the raft flips . . .

. . . and for the second time she experiences the horrible shock of cold rushing over her head filling her ears and eyes, feels the buffeting of debris against her. But this time she is ready for it, and with three determined kicks and a clawing action she manages to turn herself, find the surface and reach again for the sapling. She closes her eyes as something soft brushes across mouth and

119

nose, and she grabs that instinctively as the water rolls her, and then she is out of it somehow, out of the tsunami, her knees and one hand finding the ground.

Solid ground!

With the last of her strength she crawls a bit higher up, and collapses again, laughing and crying at the same time, and finds to her amazement that gripped in her hand is the scruff of the fox's neck. It's wriggling furiously, and makes a nip for her now, but she keeps hold and then puts him down carefully beside her.

'Easy. Easyyyy. We're OK. We did it!'

The animal looks back at her – those big orange eyes ringed with black gazing right into her – and then gives a sharp yap, wrenching itself free to shake the length of its body, showering her in droplets of water.

'We made it, Fox-san!'

She sits up and looks back at the water. Their piece of debris is already bobbing away, spinning around the edges of a succession of roaring whirlpools, the wave grinding and growling against itself, metal and wood snapping, being mushed to nothing. The white board gets pulled into a kind of vortex and spins faster and then is sucked under.

And doesn't come up again as far as she can see.

Inexorably the wave is pulling away from the land again, and when she looks back down to the house, the blue tiles of the roof are emerging row by row, as if a huge blue whale is breaching the surface, the sound of the water overwhelming.

Without warning the fox lurches at her, and she recoils thinking it's about to nip her. But instead she feels its rough tongue whip across her hand. It shakes again and suddenly darts away, into the undergrowth, towards the summit of Little Mountain. And is gone.

For a full five minutes she sits there, exhausted, as the wind frets around her and the ocean retreats, taking her gaze away with it. She knows she has to move, but there's no energy anywhere in her body, and she just watches as the water subsides, shivering, hoping somehow she will see Grandpa clamber out onto the roof, or perched in one of the bigger trees, but fearing she will see his body any minute . . .

Got to get warm, she thinks. I can't just sit here on my own and freeze to death waiting for someone to find me. If only the fox hadn't run off. And I can't give up on Grandpa.

She waits a moment or two more, then hauls herself to her feet and trudges up the rest of the bluff, through a high-tide line of rubbish, and up the slab of rock to the top of her old hideout to where – surreally – the battery radio is yammering away, the emergency bag and her rucksack untouched beside it.

The fox is there, sniffing at her bag, and she crouches down trying not to scare him. He looks round at her, then skips off to the far side of the clearing and into the undergrowth.

'D-d-don't leave me, Mr Fox!'

Her teeth are chattering like crazy, and with numb fingers she pulls the dark blue hoodie from the bag, wriggling it over her head.

121

Through blurry eyes she sees the whole roof of the Hara house clear of water below her. Grandpa is the type of man who would smash his way up through the roof to safety if he found himself trapped inside. But the tiles are intact and empty, and below them every corridor and room must be submerged. The house would have been a deathtrap.

She sinks back on her haunches, water and black muck squelching in her trainers, and looks up and down the transfigured coast.

Beyond the cliffs to the north there are palls of smoke smudging up into the clouds, and south too, smoke and flames beyond Futaba. And out at sea another floating house, this one listing badly like an ocean liner that's struck a rock and is going down.

Another house beyond that . . . the tsunami retreating, gathering speed, carrying away the splintered houses, tons and tons of unidentifiable wreckage, trees and bushes and barrels.

Huge shakes are going through her every thirty seconds or so now.

Taking a breath, as deep as she can, she raises her right hand to her mouth and bellows.

'HELP! ANYONE?'

And waits and waits for a reply that she knows isn't coming.

She tries to shake and rub some life back into her fingers, then reaches for the earthquake bag, shivering even harder, and pulls out the packet with the emergency blanket. It crackles as she unfolds it, the aluminium material reflecting her face back in a hundred pieces. One reflection holds her, and she stares back at it, almost not recognising the person looking back at her: the classic face of a Japanese *yūrei* ghost – white face, the hair looking black now and hanging straight.

For a long moment Yūki and the ghost version of herself stare at each other, and then she wraps herself in the blanket and walks to the edge of the cliff.

There are more fires now, dozens of them, up and down the coast. The flaming house has rounded the cliffs and disappeared, past where a chunk of the land has collapsed into the retreating ocean.

It *is* the end of the world, she thinks.

Maybe far away Tokyo is flattened. Maybe the tsunami was so big that the whole of Japan has been hit.

All she can see are the grey clouds, the fires, the wreckage-strewn ocean.

All she can smell is the stink of the filthy *hedoro* of the sea bed.

Maybe a hint of the fox's fur.

All she can hear is water, water, water, as if it's still churning inside her ears.

The cold is reaching deep into her now, and she sits again watching the last of the tsunami running for the sea, leaving big, muddy ponds where once there had been gardens, small fields, roads. In the distance the school is gushing water from its upper windows.

A snowflake falls.

Another, and then a few more, fluttering past her face,

dissolving on the ground where they land, and suddenly she finds herself panicking, shouting wildly, and wandering around her hilltop like a crazed, shipwrecked sailor – and then sits down abruptly and pulls the blanket around her again.

It feels like the cold is inside her bones.

That image of herself staring back was a shock. Wretched.

I mean, she thinks, would you know for sure if you were a ghost? A cold, wet phantom who drowned some time ago. There was something strange about that fox too . . .

Kazuko's taxi ghost story floats back into her head, and she shivers so hard it feels like her teeth will come loose.

Come on! Nothing to fear now.

10

Body in the Mud

As if summoned, the fox has materialised again, its eyes fixed on a spot just behind and to one side of her. And it feels – weirdly – like she's being watched, like there's somebody else on the bluff just out of sight. Something cold brushes her cheek, and she looks round expecting to see somebody, but there's no one. The fox edges closer.

'Hello?' she calls. 'Is anybody there?'

No answer, but it really feels like somebody was close by, just a moment ago. The wind sighs across the bluff, through the pine branches overhead.

It's so cold. She needs to get warmer . . . and then look for Grandpa properly. He could be alive but injured. Or trapped somewhere. And she's so hungry she realises now, and rummages in the earthquake bag until she finds a pack of *kanpan* biscuits and rips it open. She's taking another before she's swallowed the first biscuit, spilling a third to the ground.

The *kanpan* are dry and hard but the taste of food in her mouth lifts her spirits just a little. Maybe Grandpa *has* survived by some miracle, she thinks – look how I ended up on that bit of debris. Anything is possible, right? Anything! And I can't be dead, because I'm eating. Ghosts don't eat.

The fox is coming closer, sniffing the air. It must be the biscuits it's after, and she crouches down, holding out half the second one. 'Come on then. Have a bite.'

Gingerly, the fox takes a step, another – and then shoots forward and makes a bite so fast Yūki only just manages to avoid having her fingers bitten. She fumbles another biscuit out of the pack and throws it onto the ground and that's gone in a moment too. The fox licks its lips and looks back at her.

'Sorry, Fox-san. One more and then I need the rest.'

The animal's ears prick up, and then it turns and sprints across the clearing, and turns to watch her from the safety of the undergrowth.

Yūki gets to her feet. That little surge of optimism is still with her and she climbs up on the biggest rock on the summit, scanning the garden.

But there's nobody: no Grandpa – no *body* – just the studio ripped open like a cardboard box, and plastic crates and splintered wood and wreckage everywhere. If only everything wasn't such a blur. The house itself is still choking water from every broken window and door, but it looks incredibly intact.

He could still be in the house, trapped in an air pocket, or unconscious somewhere? Quickly she takes a few swigs of water from the bottle in the emergency bag, then jams the roughly folded aluminium blanket into her own rucksack. There are more *kanpan*, and a second bottle of water. A torch with a red handle. She stows them all quickly on top and swings the bag onto her back.

'I'm going, Mr Fox,' she calls. 'I hope you're OK. Be well!' Kind of crazy to be talking to a fox, but it feels good to say things out loud. Not totally on her own. 'See you soon!'

Then quickly she edges back down the rock slab and the saturated hillside below.

Beyond the high-tide line of tangled plastic and fishing gear, she finds the path has dissolved, and it's hard not to slip and slide on the mud and loose stones. A larger chunk of the hillside has come away and as she shuffles down it, grabbing branches for balance, in her haste even more gives way beneath her, and she slides a few metres, arms thrown out to balance, almost like she's surfing down the hill. She grabs a tree trunk and looks again at the mess in front of her. One of the pale mannequins is lodged in the top of a tall tree not far away, gazing up into the sky. God, the water came that high then . . .

'Grandpa? Hellooooo? Can you hear me?!'

Nothing: just alarms and sirens, but all from so far away it feels as if they are coming from some other world, and she squelches as fast as she can through the water and wet grass of the back garden, past the ruined studio, its insides exposed to the air and scoured clean. Everything – all the plan chests with his original art, every brush, every pen, every manuscript and sketchbook – all gone.

She splashes on, up onto the big stone that makes a step onto the *engawa* at the rear of the house.

The back doors have ripped away, and dark water is still streaming out over the wooden walkway. Yūki peers in to the gloom, heartbeat quickening, takes a deep breath and then steps over the threshold.

'Grandpa? Can you hear me?'

The corridor is cluttered with stuff, all of it covered with black gloop so you can't see what it is. She calls again and listens, and then wades further in, the water thick against her legs, feeling her way slowly in case she bangs her shin into wreckage.

Or a body.

The reek of sea and silty mud fills her nostrils as she squeezes past a fallen cupboard, on into the kitchen. Here the water is still a good thirty or more centimetres deep, swirling around her feet as if trying to find its way out. As she stares at it the surface starts to ripple, and then the whole house with it, rocking backwards and forwards.

Another aftershock . . .

What if it isn't? What if it's the wave coming back?

Frantically she goes splashing back down the corridor, out onto the veranda – but the aftershock has already passed by the time she's in the open, and silence has descended again. She breathes the smells of crushed foliage and cracked pine branches, maybe the rotten egg smell of gas too? Maybe the whole thing could just blow if there's a gas leak?

From somewhere above comes that foxy bark again, and she looks up.

For a brief second she thinks she sees someone standing on the hillside, then bending over.

'Hello?'

Frustrated with her useless vision, she rubs her eyes hard and then looks again. No. It's just a bush bending to the sea wind. The light is already fading, and her shivers are returning now, sodden clothes clinging to her, but she knows she needs to check every corner of the house, and quickly.

There's no sign of Grandpa in the utility room or the kitchen, the water's low enough you'd see a body lying on the floor. The clock has come off the wall and lies half drowned in the sink, stopped just past quarter to three.

In the dining room she feels bits of Grandma's pots crunch under her feet as she sploshes to the sunken *kotatsu*, takes a breath and then gropes around in the flooded space under it in case his body has been washed there.

Nothing. Just cold black mud that shines darkly on her arm as she pulls it back out.

The living room is a mess, books and manga pulped on the floor, French windows smashed, blinds hanging loose, furniture swept at crazy angles against the far wall. And to the other side of the hallway the older Japanese rooms are no better, thick brown-black sludge oozing across the tatami, an antique screen floating its golden dragons on top of it, the family Butsudan shrine gone, all the old framed photos of Grandma and the other relatives swept away or buried.

She heads upstairs, hurrying now, up past an obvious water

131

line just below the highest step. Somehow the windows have held against the force of the water, just a few places where it's come through, and the corridor is wet but no worse.

'Grandpa? Are you up here?'

She picks up her pace, calling out again, banging open each door, past the big photo of Jiro and Anna in its broken frame, in and out of her own saturated bedroom, and as each possible air pocket turns out to be empty the last of her hope fades. And when she reaches the loft hatch round the corner at the end of the corridor, it is firmly closed, the ladder retracted.

He's not here then. He's not in the attic and he's not in the house.

Outside again, she runs her hand through her wet, mud-caked hair. The gas smell is stronger – and the light is almost gone and the shivers are chasing through her every few seconds. No point going back up on the bluff and no point just hanging around hoping for rescue. The snow is falling to the wet ground and it's so cold. She scours the garden again for any trace of Jiro, then heads round to the front of the house, clambering over a sofa wedged on the walkway, a packing crate.

Have to try and make it to town.

From the front steps she surveys the carnage in front of her. Trees and houses gone, cars turned on their sides and not a hint of another living soul. Beyond, fires are lighting up the clouds to the left and right. As the sky darkens they burn intensely at the base of towering columns of smoke. Away to the south there's an occasional faint flash of light from the direction of the nuclear plant, and a distant alarm warbling on the wind. Nothing else.

One last time she calls, 'Grandpa!' at the top of her voice, and then, teeth rattling, she looks at the daunting ground between her and the cliff road, choked deep with mud and great piles of wreckage.

The snow starts to hold on the mud and the cold bites deeper.

Darkness is filling the space between here and the cliff road, light fading in the sky even faster it seems. Something about it feels really oppressive. Scary.

She fishes for the torch, and shines it briefly on her muddied palm to check the batteries are strong.

OK.

She takes one more quick look towards the ocean, and then clambers down the steps and across the wrecked garden. The foot-gate is gone, and the stone path itself lost beneath the debris. The stone Godzilla lies face down in the mud, but everything else has been scrubbed away: ornamental pine trees, the rock and gravel garden, the fox postbox. At the rock she pauses in the gateway, looking back at the house one more time.

'Ittekimasu,' she whispers quietly. I'm going now, but I'll be back.

From the darkened eaves, a single note from the bear bell rings in the silence.

The snow keeps falling as she slogs through the gloop towards the cliff road.

A few hundred difficult metres down the wreckage-strewn road, a dark grey car lies on its side. It takes a long moment to realise it's Grandpa's white Nissan, the windscreen smashed, its white body painted all over with tsunami mud. She rushes forwards, flicks the torch beam on and trains it through the passenger window, half expecting to see a bloodied face staring back at her. Or Grandpa just slumped at the wheel. But there's no trace of Jiro inside, not in the front, not in the back seat either, the footwell. Nothing but mud and an orange fishing buoy that's somehow ended up inside.

Bracing herself she swings the torch in wide, shaky sweeps, scanning the ground for any sign of life, her shivers shaking the beam so much it's like the objects caught in it are moving.

A big fridge, door jarred blackly open.

An armchair balanced in the stump of a broken tree.

An upright object that at first, with a start, she mistakes for a person but then realises is just a standard lamp rammed upright into a pile of unidentifiable muck. She calms her heartbeat as best she can and then checks every mud-shrouded object in sight to make sure it's not Grandpa's body, and then nearly drops the torch she's shaking so hard.

Got to go, a voice inside her says. Or you'll freeze to death out here. Move.

Just beyond that the going gets harder as the road drops slightly, the mud deeper, thickened with debris. Every single step now threatens to suck the trainers off her feet, sapping what little strength she has left. The darkness is getting thicker too, pressing

134

closer, the wind carrying strange sighing sounds she can't quite place. Something pale seems to move on the edge of her vision out towards the sea, and she flicks the torch on again and probes the oncoming night with the beam. Snowflakes spiral down through the light, but she can see nothing else moving, and she turns the torch back to her path ahead, negotiating bits of splintered wood and jagged metal as she clambers on over a mound of wreckage. It moves beneath her, unsettling and unsteady.

Is that a voice out there somewhere – ahead and to the right? Someone shouting? Or more like a weird kind of cry?

She stops and calls out, 'HELLO?' and waits and listens.

But there's nothing again.

Maybe she's the only person left alive on the whole Tōhoku coast.

Can't be. And it won't help to go to bits now. Got to keep going, keep spirits up somehow. Nobody around to pick me up. *Ganbare, Yūki.*

Her mind feels fuzzy, thoughts drifting in and out of focus, the snowflakes cold on her cheek, and she's hurrying her steps as best she can, suddenly from nowhere imagining long fingers of *funayūrei* ghosts reaching out for her, trying to pull her away to their drowned world. There's a sound behind her, and she turns sharply, flaring the torch into the nothingness, tripping and nearly going headlong down into the mud again.

For God's sake, get a freaking grip!

She steadies herself and starts to move again, her feet clumsy no matter how much she tries to take care with each step.

135

Come on, come on. You can do it, keep going. Keep walking.

Out of the nothingness she finds herself humming a tune – and it's a minute or so before she realises what it is: the melody Grandpa always whistled or muttered to himself, day in, day out, year in, year out, the first few phrases looping in her mind.

She can't really remember the words, so she hums most of it and mumbles the few phrases that come to her lips, and the melody climbs and lifts her spirits just enough, as she tugs her left trainer loose from the knee-deep mud, and staggers on another dozen paces.

A line comes back to her: *I'm all alone with far to go* . . .

Great! The words are sad, but the rhythm helps a bit, and she sings it through her chattering teeth, the cliff road within sight now, on through the mud, sodden step after sodden step, closer and closer to the road.

Can't forget how the tears blurred my eyes, can't forget happiness under starry skies. Walking with my gaze held high . . .

Nearly there, if I can get to the road I can make it . . .

Two things happen at once: her left trainer is sucked off her foot as she tries to free it from a particularly sticky, deep footstep – and she sees the body.

A figure – an adult – is lying on its side, arms at a weird angle up around the head, framing short, matted black hair. Not Grandpa. Yūki's stomach turns as she moves closer, playing the torch across the back of the figure's dull yellow puffa jacket. The face is planted in the muck, no sign of breath or movement.

Can't just walk past.

She gathers her courage and reaches out to grab the shoulder and shake it hard. There's no response, so she pulls, and with a horrible kind of sigh the body rolls, revealing a man's puffy face. The skin where it shows through the black mud is white, eyes open, staring past her lifelessly into the falling snow.

She gazes at the frozen face for a long, long moment, her breath working hard in her chest.

Not somebody she recognises, not any of Jiro's neighbours or anyone she knows from town. A youngish man, no more than thirty, his features blank, his gaze fixed on a point that seems both close up and very far away at the same time. She moves the torch across his face, making absolutely sure he's not breathing – wanting to look away. It feels a bit like looking at the sun a moment too long, the image searing onto her retina.

She's about to search for something to cover him with when she hears that unearthly cry again, louder now and floating out of the darkness: a weird, high-pitched kind of moaning, the note wavering, falling, rising. She can feel the skin on her scalp tightening as she looks around wildly.

The cry is coming from behind her now? Maybe out towards the sea.

She flashes the torch beam into the trees along the cliff road. Nothing but dancing pine branches, snowflakes, the empty road climbing beyond. She takes one more glance down at the dead man, and starts to stumble towards the higher land as fast as she can. Anything to get out of this deathly space.

'He-hello? Helloooo? Is someone there?'

The wailing stops abruptly, and a woman's voice comes down to her from the darkened trees, 'Up here! Hello, is someone there?'

Doesn't sound like a ghost now. And if one person's alive, maybe other people are – maybe even, miraculously, Grandpa is up there too? Yūki hurries forwards, shouting with all the air she can summon from her tired lungs.

'HELLO! DOWN HERE! HELP!'

At the foot of the slope Yūki stops, flashing her torch into the darkness ahead, and lights up a pale figure emerging from the night. The beam catches a flash of red and then lights a round familiar face: Mrs Takeda. Their neighbour is shielding her eyes in the bright torchlight, peering at Yūki.

'Oh my God! It's you, Yūki-chan.'

'I – I was in the water,' Yūki stutters, and sinks to the ground. 'Have – have you seen Grandpa?'

'Isn't he with you?'

'No. I was up on the bluff and he went back down to the house and . . .'

Mrs Takeda comes closer, her face red, eyes wild.

'I can't find Grandpa,' Yūki whispers again. 'And there's a body down there.'

'Yūki-chan,' Mrs Takeda says, her voice wavering. 'There are bodies everywhere. I was above the port when it hit. Everything's gone. I don't know about the middle school. Or what's happened to Jun. My nephew. Or Pochi.'

Yūki struggles back to her feet. 'I couldn't find Grandpa.'

138

But it's as if Mrs Takeda can't hear her. 'I don't know if Jun made it, Yūki. It looked awful from above. I don't know what to do . . .'

She's sobbing now, one hand clasping her beret to her head, and Yūki goes up to her, uncertainly.

'I thought maybe I saw a light or two at the nuclear plant so there must be electricity in some places.'

'Sorry, I should be comforting you.' Takeda-san shakes her head. 'They'll be on the back-up generators there. Got to keep it all cool you see.'

'Will – will it be safe?'

'Lots of safety systems. Don't worry about that. I worked admin there for years.'

But she gazes a long, long moment into the darkness where the nuclear plant should be, before slowly turning back to Yūki. 'You said you were in the water? For real?'

'I – fell into the ts-ts-tsunami,' Yūki says, teeth chattering violently again.

Mrs Takeda looks at her in amazement. '*In* the water?!'

'Uh, yes, I g-g-got out somehow. Onto something floating. There was a fox and I rescued it but I couldn't find Grandpa. And there's a dead man down there—'

'A fox? You're not making much sense. . .'

The steady thump of a helicopter's rotor blades is growing louder and louder, suddenly overhead, and then it's gone in a flash of tail light, heading north.

'My God, you're shaking like anything, Yūki. We've got to get you warm. You could get hypothermia.'

'There's an emergency b-b-blanket – in my rucksack.'

'Then for heaven's sake get it around you. And then we'll head for Osōma. Some of the coast road's gone – washed away. I saw it go, two cars with it. My house is gone, Yūki. And I've no idea about Jun.'

She looks out to sea, up into the sky, then back out to the blank void where her house had stood.

'I c-c-can't leave Grandpa out here,' Yūki says. 'He could be injured and needing help. I promised Mum.'

'Goodness, yes, your parents. Where *is* your mother, Yūki-chan?'

'At home. England.'

'Other family?'

'My Aunt K-k-kazuko is in Tokyo. Do you think T-t-tokyo's OK?'

Mrs Takeda tilts her head. 'The wave hit Sendai first, a woman up on the cliff road heard. So, it must have come from the north, north east. My guess is they'll be OK further south, but it was the biggest quake I've ever felt . . .'

'I can't leave Grandpa.'

'Yūki,' Takeda-san says quietly, 'he could be tens of kilometres away by now. Anywhere. We have to go.'

'But it's my fault. The whistle didn't work.'

'We'll talk later. I've got to get you somewhere warm.'

Yūki looks around one more time, back to the bluff, about to protest. But she knows Takeda-san is right, and numb with cold, she nods.

'OK-K-K.'

Together they start to trudge up towards the coast road, the cold wind crackling away at the silver blanket.

There's water in her eyes, but no energy to cry, and she focuses on putting one foot in front of another, then another, then another. The socked foot and the squelching trainer make a weird kind of rhythm and all she wants to do is to lie down, get rid of the wet clothes, get the smell of salt and mud out of her nose, to rest, and sleep and sleep. To be warm.

To be safe and warm and none of this to be real.

A little echo of the song comes back into her mind, the rhythm of her feet triggering it in a slow refrain.

Thinking about days from long, long ago, I'm all alone with far to go . . .

A three-quarter moon peers down through the shifting snow clouds.

Sometimes Mrs Takeda falters and loses her grip for a moment and starts to sob with worry about Jun, and it is Yūki that urges her on.

And sometimes it is the other way around.

Mostly they are both silent though, stunned into silence. Yūki's mind fogs as the cold and hunger grip harder, waves of fatigue coming at her over and over again until she wonders if she's awake and walking, or asleep and dreaming the whole thing. Not cold, not hot, not anything.

In the moments when she is more awake she can still remember those last few minutes before the quake as Grandpa pushed the book towards her, heroic Half Wave looking up at her, everything normal – better than normal: that bright blue of Half Wave's hair lifting her heart – like the sea at Matsushima, that colour, Grandpa had said once.

The wind rises, and weather closes in on them until her thoughts are just the cold and the wet, and they stumble into what feels like nothingness.

Another helicopter goes thumping overhead, and Mrs Takeda grabs the torch and flashes it on and off, signalling desperately, but it's already gone and they are alone. From above they are as good as invisible, lost in the dark woods.

All along the vast coastline north of them, towns and villages and houses lie ruined. Whole cities have been flattened and swept away, bridges washed to nothing, cars carried out to sea. Communities plunged into broken cold and darkness and snow-fall and falling temperatures. Fires still burning where oil and gas and petrol has ignited. And bodies lying close to home and far from home, out at sea, on beaches, washed up inland, buried.

Close to twenty thousand souls are lost now and looking for home, roaming the empty spaces left by the wave.

Out on the flat margins where the sea and land blur into one maybe you can see them: pale forms shifting in the night, taking shape out of the snow and mist and sea spray, trying to retrace their steps, working out what has happened and where they need to go. Do they know they are dead?

Maybe not quite yet. Or maybe they can't admit it fully to themselves.

For her part Yūki keeps walking, now almost seeing nothing ahead of her – like the world is fading, fading, fading away from her. Just one step in front of another, on and on and on. Got to get to wherever it is we're going . . .

She closes her eyes.

On the very edge of nothingness comes a sound: maybe the blood pulsing in her ears – or hundreds of unseen sparrows thrumming in the bushes around them.

A whirring sound, that comes and goes, and sometimes feels like it's inside her head, and sometimes like it's far, far, far away . . .

What is it?

Maybe it sounds like the whisper of the wind in the spinning blades of a toy windmill.

PART TWO

Between Worlds

世界の間

1

The Great Parting

Two months later, in the stillness of her therapist's consulting room on a quiet street in Cambridge, Yūki still only has broken pieces of what came next.

Her eyes drift across the familiar nature images on Angela's walls – a huge, foaming oak tree, a wildflower meadow under clouds pierced by rays of light – the same as always, but somehow changed now. In the tree's curling foliage she sees the tsunami's fury, above the meadow she sees the dark clouds as coming, not going, rolling in to blot out the sky. May sunshine fills the consulting room, and yet she feels cold – always does these days. There's a new picture surely? A flower and its underwater root seen in cross section, white petals tinged with pink, dark bulbous root sunk into mud.

Heavy, dark, cold mud.

Her eyes stick there.

Angela leans forward.

'Can you say a bit more about what you felt at that moment, Yūki?'

'That picture's new, right?'

Her therapist glances back over her shoulder. 'Yes. It's a lotus, do you like it?'

'Ummm.'

'I can take it down if it's bothering you. Is it bothering you?'

'No. It's fine.'

'Sure? Well, I was saying, when you were in the water you suddenly felt *peaceful*? And I said, *Can you explain that*?'

Yūki's eyes are still on the root. 'Um, no. I can't. It doesn't make sense.'

'Why do you think that is?'

'Because – because when I try it's like the words don't sound like it felt. It was – cold and noisy and horrible. But like it didn't matter at the same time. Sorry.'

'We can talk about anything. Doesn't have to be that. I guess you were immersed in Japanese when it all happened. Thinking in Japanese?'

'I – maybe?'

'Well, tell me in Japanese then.'

Yūki closes her eyes, thinking. '*Nemimi ni mizu*.'

'What does that mean?'

'Water in a sleeping ear. Cold water.'

'I don't understand.'

'Just something Grandpa said. He said I needed to wake up, just before the wave . . .'

She trails off. She can say 'wave' in English, but 'tsunami' feels too difficult. That word - that *thing* - lurks still like a slumbering beast inside her. And when buses rumble, or thunder shakes her bedroom window, it grabs her again and tumbles her like a ragdoll in a washing machine, and she is lost.

Worst trigger of all: a trip to the north Norfolk coast last weekend - somewhere whose wide spaces always used to make her feel a bit better about the world - but which left her a shaking mess on the back seat of the car. The warm late spring day was idyllic, but one sight of the gentle waves put her straight back in the monster's grip, and she ran to the car park, fighting to breathe, shivering in one of the worst attacks she's ever had.

She likes Angela well enough, and has agreed to more regular sessions, but has resisted her cautious nudging to talk about the day of the quake in detail, and only told Mum and Dad the bare bones. When they welcomed her home - huge hugs, of course, tears, talking, talking, talking - they pushed too hard for detail, and Yūki retreated to her room, desperate for silence, and lay curled on the bed, hearing the roar of the wave, watching it swirl in the plaster patterns on the ceiling.

Mum, Dad - everybody - nod patiently, and say, 'There's no rush,' but, boy can she feel their desperation for the full version. Mum, in particular, is struggling to come to terms with her own loss, and tiptoes round stuff for ages before a kind of damn breaks and the questions come at a great rush: *What did he say, Yū-chan? Tell me again exactly what he said before he went down to the house. And what time was that? I don't understand how you got back up there? And you looked in the house, right? Everywhere? No, I understand, I know we've been over this, but are you sure he didn't say what he was doing . . . ?*

'Mum, I'm doing my best.'

'I know, Yū-chan. Sorry.'

'I just can't. Sorry.'

It's not just that she can't find the right words to answer everyone's questions. The thing is, it feels wrong to say anything out loud about it at all, like she's giving away a kind of secret that she shares with everyone else who saw or died in the disaster. What she wants to say is this: if you weren't there, you can't possibly understand.

So she holds everything, pressure building, and nods when people talk about Post Traumatic Stress and give her handouts to read, but not even that seems to do justice to what she feels inside.

To help let it out she takes an old notebook and crosses out the dumb pages of an abandoned diary, trying to order the broken pieces of memory from the moment the quake struck to the moment she shuffled through the arrivals at Heathrow and fell into the family car.

One fragment: being high on the cliff road, the moon breaking the clouds, and the ocean back in full view, vast and forbidding all the way to where it became night. Wilder and more alien than she had ever seen it before – and she and Takeda-san had just stared at it, awed into silence.

And another, that *might* have been real: there was a sound, a sound that was super familiar, but which she can't now place, like the noise you get in your ears just before you faint.

And sometimes it seemed there was a light in the trees, moving ahead of them. Maybe another survivor with a torch picking their way towards Osōma.

A definite memory of coming out of the woods, and seeing the little cliff road, smooth tarmac and guard rail running to . . . nothing. A huge chunk – maybe thirty metres or so – bitten out of it by the wave, the ocean grinding the remains far below.

Other tiny pieces:

Eating hard, cold chocolate and shaking uncontrollably.

Brushing snow off Takeda-san, and waking her up, when their neighbour had slumped down for a rest and kind of passed out. She tried polite language, then really direct stuff, blunt verbs like you'd use with a little child. *Come on! Enough! Get up and get moving!*

And she's pretty sure she caught a glimpse of a fox, fleeting orange in the torch beam. Presumably not the same one she pulled out of the tsunami, but it looked like it, maybe it had followed her . . .

Dutifully she adds that in the notebook, and then adds a big '?' after it.

ぱきっ!
CRACK!

Grandpa! He's OK!

Yūki-chan! There's nobody there!

I'm OK. I need to give you something.

I – I can't hear you!

Yūkiiii. Come back.

Grandpa?

♪Love and happiness lie beyond the stormy waves, love and happiness written on your face ... ♪

She knows she was drifting from waking to sleep and back more than once as she and Takeda-san trudged through the long night. That bit about Grandpa must be a dream of course.

But it lingers, and so does that fleeting sensation that lifted her heart for a moment now and then: a feeling that somehow things would be OK, and her feet found the ground that bit more firmly.

The fragments start to join and become clearer when she remembers first light coming on the morning of the 12th of March: in the pale dawn they saw the two fox sculptures guarding the steps to the roadside Inari shrine, one leaning perilously now, and the further red *torii* gate and the little temple building itself shunted off-centre by the quake. On the steps beneath an elderly man and woman lay huddled together, asleep under a blanket. Yūki heard Takeda-san gasp then and, turning, she saw the devastated port area below: a confusing, thick mess of oozing mud and upturned cars and boats, splintered houses, flames smouldering at the edge of it all and smoke swirling up into the murky air.

A fishing boat was jammed into the top floor of the port office building, its back half sticking out over the sea of wreckage. Through her no-glasses blur Yūki could just make out figures picking their way through the mud and debris, and hear the distant, urgent shouting of names, somebody crying, *It hurts it hurts it hurts* . . .

She thought of Taka, but had no idea where Jimi's house was, and then the exhaustion came washing over her again.

Further down the road beyond the shrine, emergency lights were burning in the community centre, and people huddled around the entrance wrapped in duvets and blankets. To one side of the path lay a few stretchers with sheets pulled right over them, and she hurried past those, wanting to look, to not look at the same time. Search parties passed her, the men's faces grim as they set out to scour the wreckage in the half light.

She remembers Mrs Takeda saying a brisk goodbye and hurrying off to look for her nephew, and then nothing much else, just a vague memory of sagging to the floor, being carried into the building – and that persistent feeling that the cold had filled her whole body and that the filthy black *hedoro* was still glooping at the back of her throat. Coughing and shivering, she was laid out beside a portable heater, but it still felt like ice was forming inside her and the people around her seemed a long way away, almost shadows.

Nothing more after that.

But it's not a restful nothing. More like one of those nights where you can't remember a single dream, but know that you have been fleeing something horrific from dusk till dawn, tossing and turning and knotting your legs in the sheets until you can't move even a toe.

It feels like there was something more – somebody she saw, or who sat with her for a while – but it is all lost in the numbing cold.

The next thing she remembers for sure is waking up in a hospital bed. Not a clue where she was until an exhausted-looking nurse came to tell her she was in Fukushima City, and that Osōma and all the neighbouring towns had been evacuated after a bad accident at the Daiichi nuclear plant.

'Accident?'

'There's been a radiation leak. Something's gone wrong. Explosions. But you're safe here.'

'But what about the people still out there?'

'Apart from the brave guys working at the plant, everyone's been evacuated, there's a big exclusion zone and it just got made bigger. Nobody really knows what's going on. Maybe we'll even have to move from here . . .' The nurse wiped a hand across her face.

Yūki tried to sit up, but her body wouldn't do it and she gave up and slumped back on the pillows. Still some of that horrible chill lingered inside. 'No, I mean the people who got swept away. My grandfather is out there, I think.'

The woman laid a hand on Yūki's. 'There's nothing we can do for them but pray.'

'I want to go back, and look for him—'

'The Self Defence Force are doing what they can. You got bad hypothermia, you're not going anywhere. The hospital office is trying to contact your parents. You were really lucky you made it, you know. You were . . . very close to the edge.'

'The edge?'

'Of leaving us. You know. The Great Parting. The one you don't come back from. Be glad you're here . . .'

Another tremor shook the ward, glasses and equipment

157

chattering, and the nurses and doctors all paused and looked at each other, then quietly carried on their work as the trembling subsided, and Yūki slumped away into half sleep.

After that there's another muddle of fear and restless dreaming and aching, trying not to think about what happened, but her mind looping the last minutes on the bluff, the feeling of the wave taking her, the emptiness of the ocean. Like her own personal twenty-four-hour news feed stuck with a limited number of images to cycle.

She repeats the phrase in her head: *The Great Parting*.

Lying on her own in the hospital bed it felt like she had taken half a step out there on the bluff, maybe a full step, over a border and into some other place.

Days later, feeling just a little stronger, with the reactors spilling out caesium and who-knew-what, there was a hurried evacuation from Fukushima City. She was helped onto a coach chartered by the UK embassy early one morning, blinking in the cold, winter light, where an English man took her under his wing. He peered at her through his round glasses and introduced himself in really good formal Japanese and then asked her what language she wanted to talk in.

'I don't mind,' she said. 'But I don't really want to talk much.'

'Well, talk if you want.' He switched to English as the coach pulled away, a soft Liverpool accent noticeable now. 'Tell me to shut up if you want! Are you scared?'

'What of?'

He shrugged. 'The accident and the radiation.'

'Not really.'

'Well, I am. I've been teaching at the university for years and years but I never experienced anything like this. I'm glad to have your company. It was raining yesterday. Nobody would leave the bus station until it stopped. Radioactive rain, it's like we're in a disaster movie . . .'

'I think I'd like to talk in Japanese.'

'No problem at all, Yūki-san.'

Something about him reminded her of Grandpa. He treated her like an adult, and in the end she talked more than she'd meant to, not about the wave, but about Grandpa and his work, and school and the effort to fit in, and the man nodded and made just the right noises you make in Japanese to encourage the other person to go on, the drawn out rising 'eeeehhhhhh?' – finally bringing her to the meltdown in the library.

The man looked at her as the coach rolled through a grey afternoon into the outskirts of Tokyo.

'It's a hard thing, finding where you fit. But you'll get there.'

'It doesn't feel like it.'

'I'll tell you what, Yūki-san, you seem very strong to me. They told me you were on the coast when the wave hit, and here you are, looking after an old fool like me. Your smile has cheered me up.'

'Was I smiling?'

'Just about. Every time you mentioned your grandpa.'

'Yeah,' Yūki groaned, 'but I couldn't save him.'

The man rubbed his chin. 'It was nobody's fault, just the tectonics. Nobody can stop that force once it's built up.'

'He showed me something. Just before the quake. He wanted to cheer me up and I was kind of – I dunno, a bit of a sulky brat really.'

The man patted the back of her hand. 'Let's not be too hard on ourselves. Right? In my experience most people are too hard on themselves – apart from the ones who ought to be and never think of doing it at all. Like the ones who built a nuclear plant near a fault line! Idiots!'

Back in Cambridge she has tried to gather some facts in her notebook to add to her memories – and make things more solid, more real.

Fact: the earthquake was the fourth strongest ever recorded on earth at 9.1 on the Richter scale.

Fact: it moved the earth fifteen to twenty centimetres on its axis, making the earth rotate very slightly faster, the day minutely shorter.

Fact: the tsunami that followed raged at incredible heights, bursting over sea walls, flooding emergency refuge centres to the fourth or fifth floor in places, destroying more than 100,000 houses and taking 18,000 lives with it.

Of those, 3,000 are still missing, and Grandpa is one of them, lost to the nothingness of mud and ocean. Over the following weeks Mum and Kazuko and Dad slowly tip towards talking about him in the past tense rather than the present. Once a week or so the sisters have long, intense conversations on Skype. The old family house is now locked within an evacuation zone, rumours and counter rumours flying about the level of the radiation, the state of the four reactors at the plant. Three of them have melted down and a fight is on to save things from getting worse. There's talk of radioactive water leaking into the sea, of areas of Osōma, Ōkuma, Namie, Odaka that will be closed off for years.

Yūki overheard one Skype, when Mum obviously thought she was still at Angela's. Kazuko was talking fast as always, but her voice heavier now. 'There's a rumour they might have to evacuate Tokyo, sis. Where the hell will everybody go?'

'So there's no chance of us getting up there,' Mum said, 'looking for Dad. I can't stop thinking about it.'

'I spoke to that neighbour, Mrs Takeda - she's living in a refuge centre now. Her nephew never showed up, you know. The aftershocks are still coming thick and fast, and there are parents further north digging in the mud for their kids when the SDF give up. Can you imagine it?'

'I mean the worst of it is not having a body. To do a proper funeral. It's like we're letting him down right at the end of his life.'

'But he wouldn't care about that,' Kazuko said. 'Passing the bones in the ashes and all that stuff. Would he? I remember him winking at me when we were passing his brother's remains with the chopsticks, y'know?'

'But it just feels wrong. It might help, Yūki too. Closure.' There was a silence and Mum dropped her voice. 'Did Takeda-san say

161

much, I mean about what it was like for her? She'll hardly tell us anything. She hardly talks to us at all. Angela says it's the shock.'

Round the corner Yūki strained to listen, holding her breath.

Kazuko sighed so loud you could hear it down the Skype link. 'Takeda says Yū-chan started to say some odd things. She was talking about ghosts, and some boy she wanted to find who could help. She says she was talking to Dad. For ages! And singing that old song he was always humming . . . I guess the poor girl was hallucinating with the hypothermia. How's she doing?'

'She's not really here. It's like half of her is still there. With Father.' Both sisters fell silent, them Mum whispered, 'It's like having a ghost in the house.'

Yūki let out her breath, and turned to the mirror in the hall to gaze at her own reflection – her shoulders and hair lit from behind and dust motes floating around her head, her face pretty much the same as always, but somehow paler? Thinner?

The Skype call ended and Mum came bowling out into the hall to find Yūki still rooted in front of the mirror. She hesitated, and then hugged Yūki hard.

'At least we got *you* back. We've just got to hold onto that fact and be glad of it.'

Yūki nodded, held in Mum's embrace, eyes still fixed on her own semi-silhouetted reflection.

The truth is *that* fact – *all* the facts – don't feel real.

It's all of the other stuff that comes seeping like water around, through, over the 'facts', that seeks Yūki out and grips her attention: rumours of strange creatures pulled up in fishing nets;

fire engines called to houses that turn out to have been swept completely away in the tsunami; ghosts glimpsed trudging along twilit streets; even – terrifyingly – stories of angry restless spirits and exorcisms. People who have strayed over that borderline, gone through the Great Parting and into the 'other place', *anoyo*.

And about that she can't say a word to anyone.

2

Not Alive . . .

ANGELA LEANS FORWARD AGAIN, HOOP earrings reflecting May sunlight through her black hair. 'So, tell me more about why you feel so bad about that?'

'About what?'

'You said, *I should have talked more.* Guilt is very normal after events like this. But it feels like something specific?'

'I should have been . . .' Yūki mutters, looking away, 'less sulky.'

'Maybe let's explore that. About what?'

Yūki thinks of Jiro's utter delight as he tapped the image of Half Wave atop his rip curl of ocean.

'It doesn't matter. Something silly from childhood.'

'So you were thinking about when you were little? And you didn't want to talk about it *then*?'

'I guess.'

'And you felt what?'

'I dunno. It all felt too childish so I think I didn't react right.' The tears are stinging the back of her eyes behind new glasses. This is just so hard, each word feels like she has to force it out. 'It's like I'm trying to grow up, you know, and it was already hard enough. And now . . .'

'You did your best, but right now you feel it wasn't enough.'

Yūki fights for a breath. 'I just stood there on the hill like an idiot. The stupid whistle wouldn't make a sound . . .'

'It's OK, take it slowly. From what I hear, you were a hero, Yūki. Saved yourself, helped a neighbour that night.'

Yūki shakes her head, and a silence descends. Her eyes rove across the pictures on the walls – the root in the mud, the weight of the tree, the clouds in the meadow. Wind chimes stirring in the breeze and on the window sill below some round river stones, a carved bird, and a little figurine of a . . . fox.

'You look like you want to say something, Yūki.'

'I – I did save a little fox. He was in the water.'

'A fox?!' Angela smiles. 'Really?'

Yūki feels her mood lift, just the tiniest bit. 'He was stuck on the raft thing. Or she. It felt like a "he". I got him back onto the land.' She nods. 'And I gave him some biscuits. It felt good, I guess. Grandpa liked foxes. He kept one once, before I was born. People thought he was strange, but he wasn't . . .'

'Great! There's no rush, Yūki, but that's about the most you've said in one go. We could try some art if you like, around that fox. Build around that positive memory. Do some stuff with clay. Or draw, your mum said you used to draw all the time.'

'I can't draw now.'

And as for clay, the thought of it just conjures up that man's

165

body wodged into the tsunami mud. His emptied-out eyes when she rolled him over full of nothing.

Her eyes wander back to the fox, remembering her last glimpse of the bedraggled animal watching her cautiously from the undergrowth.

And in truth, drawing is hovering on the edge of her mind.

Now and then she finds herself wishing she'd picked up that dark blue sketchbook from the top of the pile beside the black biscuit tin. Maybe tucked the whole box with its bright yellow sun under her arm as they ran. Something about the grin on Half Wave's face, that flash of it in the depth of the wave. It mattered to Grandpa after all, so maybe – *probably* – she should have trusted that.

All she managed to bring from out of the disaster is her passport, and the clothes she was dressed in that day. Dried but unwashed in a bin bag, they had been bundled into a small cheap suitcase bought in haste in Tokyo, then into the machine at home the morning after her return.

'I found this in your jeans,' Mum said, holding up a small white card. 'Is it important? It's the sushi shop right? But there's something on the back.'

Yūki shrugged, then suddenly realised what it was and took the card quickly from Mum.

'Just as a kind of souvenir, it was from the night before.'

'OK, sweetheart,' Mum said quietly, turning away to look out of the kitchen window. 'Dad loved to spar with that old *yakuza* guy: politics, whatever . . .' Her voice snagged.

166

Yūki glanced at the blurred number scrawled on the back, still just about legible, thinking about Taka grinning his lopsided grin, shoving it into her hand, the way he tried to impress her with the made-up kickboxing. That had seemed annoying at the time – now it just seems sweet, she thought, as she tucked the card into the front of one of Grandpa's *gekiga* books in her room.

A day or so after her old phone had been replaced she tapped out a text – corrected it two or three times, deleted it, retyped it, her finger hovering over 'send' for about half a minute before she fired it off.

Hi. It's Yūki. Are you OK? I hope you and your dad were OK. Did you get evacuated? Where are you now? (It's Hara Yūki) ☺

All the long next day she watched the phone, but no reply buzzed back so – carefully calculating the time difference – the next morning she shut her bedroom door, and called the number. The Japanese ring tone echoed distantly, almost a minute or more, her pulse tapping away at her wrist, and then clicked as if answered.

'Hello? *Moshi moshi*?' she whispered.

Nothing at the other end. Just static, or a sound like a strong wind gusting over the phone's mic. A voice lost in all that, just on the edge of being audible?

'Hello? Can you hear me?'

There was a click – and then the line went dead. She thumbed redial, heart going *doki doki*. But when the call was answered this time she heard a woman speaking rapidly with the typical voice of a Japanese automated message.

167

'*Unfortunately this number cannot be reached and we apologise but you cannot leave a message. Thank you.*'

Was he there? And declined her call for some reason? Or was his phone just lying somewhere deep in the tsunami mud and broken-up rubbish?

Or still lodged in his pocket? Dead?

Suddenly it mattered a lot to know what had happened to Taka. He would be good to talk to, *he* would know what it was like . . .

But every time she tried the line it always came up with the automated voice, and she worried about it eating up her credit and in the end she emailed Kazuko instead, and asked her to ask Mrs Takeda to find out what happened to Taka and his dad.

After almost a month of waiting, checking her email every day, she got a reply that Takeda-san's very sorry, but she doesn't know. She's heard nothing either way about Jimi-san, but thinks the son 'disappeared'. Kazuko copied and pasted the rest of the reply, and Yūki read it, mood sinking deeper with each line:

The new kasetsu *refuge centres are horrible: rows of metal make-shift houses a bit like lorry containers, baking in the sun. It's not like really being alive, we're all just sitting here, lonely, grieving, and the food's lousy and you're not even allowed pets or music. I miss Pochi. A young student with funny hair came and did some 'active listening volunteering' and some of my new neighbours enjoyed that, getting things off their chest. But it's not for me, that kind of thing, my business is my business, right? He told me*

168

he'd keep an eye out for Pochi on his travels though, which was kind . . . But at night you hear people crying, and we're all just waiting really, waiting.

She didn't specify for what.

One phrase of Takeda's email resonates like a bell inside.

Not like being alive.

That's the worst of what she's feeling. The PTSD panics are beyond horrible when they're happening, but with Angela's help she's learning bit by bit how to ride over them, like she's riding a wild horse samurai-style until it loses energy. But the long flat hours in her room, or silent at meals with Mum and Dad trying to engage her, are pretty much unbearable – even though she knows they love her and she loves them and all the rest of it.

Somehow Osōma feels closer than the other side of the dining table.

At their next session Angela offers her a box of pencils and paper.

'No pressure. But it's worth a go, Yūki. I've known it help people move their stuckness that way . . .'

'I'm sorry. It would just make me feel worse, trust me.'

'You still draw though?'

'No. Not really. Not since . . . And everything I did before was rubbish anyway. Just copying stuff.'

Angela raises her eyebrows, pauses. 'Your grandpa was a comic artist right? What did he draw?'

'It was grown up stuff. For adults.'

169

'Interesting. Love stories or do you mean - "adult"?' Angela makes the quotation marks in the air.

'Serious,' Yūki says quickly. 'About things like the Ainu people being repressed by the shogun, and them using shaman rituals to cope. Shapeshifting. And politics, and *hibakusha*–'

'Hibaku-sha?'

'The people who survived the Hiroshima bombing, but got discriminated against. Because of the radiation and birth defects and things.'

'I guess sometimes it's harder to survive something like that than not survive, right?'

The wind is blowing June warmth through the half opened window, setting the small set of wind chimes ringing. Yūki glances at the lotus, the water lapping at its stem.

'I was *in* the wave,' she murmurs. 'There was this boy - and I think he's drowned too. How on earth could *I* have survived? And so many people didn't?'

'Well, here you are. You can feel your breath coming and going, feel your feet on the ground–' Angela begins.

'But maybe ghosts think they're real. I mean, my aunt told me this story, about ghosts from a cemetery and they end up on the subway line because they don't realise they're dead. Maybe they can feel their breath too?'

Maybe a *funayūrei* could get on that evacuation bus, board a plane back to England, get through passport control.

Angela looks up to one side, judging something.

'So, what do you think happens after we die, Yūki? I'm curious

170

– I mean I remember you telling me once, before this experience – very, very firmly – that when you're dead, you're dead. I'm
interested to know if that has changed maybe?'

'I – what do you think?'

Angela smiles. 'I'm supposed to say it's not relevant . . .'

'I'd like to know.'

'Hmmm. OK. I think that probably you're right. But I'm also
almost certain I felt my sister's ghost once. About a year after she
died. She tapped me three times on the shoulder just like
she always used to, when nobody else was around. Maybe we
can allow ourselves to have both?'

The wind brushes the chimes again.

'When I was little,' Yūki says, 'we went up on the hill behind the
house at Obon, and we lit all these lanterns. And then we waited
up there for the spirits to come.'

'Wasn't it scary?'

'Not really,' Yūki says. 'Mostly it was just . . . really great.
Grandpa would hold my hand, and then we'd bow to the spirits
who came home. And Grandpa made a big bonfire to send them
back safely again at the end.'

'Where do they come from?'

'A place called *anoyo*.'

Frogs calling in the dark, smoke from the smouldering
mosquito coils scenting the warm air, multicoloured fireworks
taking to the air with a *fwooosh* . . .

'Your smile,' Angela says quietly. 'Apart from when you talked
about the fox, that's the first time I've seen a hint of it in – ages.

171

Maybe you should do some rituals for him, for your grandpa? Make something up. A way to think about him.'

Next day Yūki persuades Mum to let her make an improvised shrine in a corner of the living room: a tiny Buddha she once bought in Kamakura, a *kitsune* fox figurine, a bowl of rice and a glass of water which she refreshes every day in front of a framed photo of Jiro from about ten years ago. It's a strong portrait, the energy still in his eyes, hair already white but fuller, eyes as fierce as an *oni* demon as he stares into the lens – must have been taken against his will like most photos.

But there's that hint of a smile too, his eyes reaching out for hers whenever she kneels on the cushion in front of it and rings the bell on its little pad.

'Grandpa,' she whispers. 'What should I do?'

♪love and happiness lie beyond the stormy waves ...

love and happiness written in your face ...♪

And he is strong again, comforting the grieving survivors and lifting them with his strong heart.

I still worry about my dog. Pochi-chan.

Maybe he's starving in the radiation zone ...

I'll look for him for you. I'm visiting a lot of places.

THE EVACUATION ZONE
2km FROM THE NUCLEAR PLANT

You wait here.
It's too dangerous ahead.
I've got to help them.

FUKUSHIMA DAIICHI
POWER PLANT

UNDERNEATH
THE REACTOR

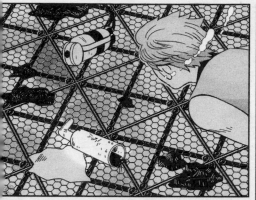

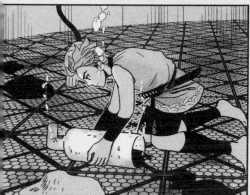

LATER

3

But Not Dead . . .

IF YŪKI DOES DREAM AT all now, she can't remember anything of what happens in them – just a vague sense of panic, of running – or trying to fight her way free, presumably, of the wave. But one Saturday morning in early summer she wakes with a start – and for the first time since Japan knows what she has been dreaming. Not much, just a fragment: Grandpa standing calmly on the *engawa* at the front of the house, looking out towards the sea, a sketchbook open in his hand . . . and that noise again, that thrumming sound, and with it a tremendous sense of Grandpa's presence that is still with her as she sits up blinking in the light.

Thirty minutes later, trying to pin the dream to her notebook, she hears the doorbell ring. She keeps scribbling, but a few moments later there's a knocking at her bedroom door.

'Yep? What is it?'

Dad puts his head through, sheepish. 'Um, listen, no problem if you don't feel like it. But I've got somebody here to see you. Are you decent?'

'Who?'

'Your friend Joel. From school.'

'Joel?! What's he doing here?'

'Ask him yourself.'

Flustered, she pulls on her jeans, throws a jumper over her head.

'Are you dressed?'

'Uh huh.'

'Go on, Joel. She's glad to see you even if she can't say it.'

Before she can say anything Joel is in the doorway, one hand raised in an awkward greeting. 'Sorry, if you don't feel like it, I can go. Honest I can.'

'No. It's OK.'

Dad retreats, miming a sock puppet, encouraging her to talk.

Joel takes a step into the room. 'Um.'

'Um yourself.' Another awkward second or two as Joel looks around her room.

'Don't laugh. I was rehearsing what to say, and then all I could think of was "um" . . .'

'What – what are you doing here?'

'I've been worried. Even before – what happened in Japan. I wanted to text you, but I wasn't sure how you'd react, so–'

'OK.' Yūki pushes her hand though her hair.

'I can go, honestly, if you don't feel like talking . . .'

'I mean, thank you. Really, I mean it.'

'I'm glad you were OK. In the tsunami I mean. Sorry, honestly I can go if . . .' Joel appears unsure what to do next, and the seconds draw out horribly. He turns to her bookshelves. 'Hey, got anything by your granddad here?'

It's a great move.

'I was just dreaming about him,' Yūki blurts out.

'I heard he didn't make it. I'm really sorry.'

'How did you hear?'

'Um, the truth is your dad phoned my mum. He asked me to come round.'

Yūki's shoulders sag slightly. 'Oh, so you didn't want to come?'

'No! I wanted to. Really wanted to – people were talking about you at school and saying you had, um–'

'Um? Gone mad?'

'No. Just that you weren't very well. You don't look very mad.' Joel smiles. 'I wish you'd come back.'

Yūki nods, and gets up and goes to the shelves. Kazuko has sent a package of vintage *Garo* magazine, along with a note saying, 'You're way old enough now. See how great our Manga Star was!'

'These are Grandpa's,' she says, handing them to Joel.

He perches on the very edge of her bed, then pulls a copy carefully from its plastic wrapper and starts to flick the pages with careful fingers. The images spring to life: the kamikaze pilot flying high into boiling, swirling clouds . . . a young man violently strumming a beat-up guitar covered in stickers.

Joel nods. 'I can't read a word. But wow they're – powerful.' He turns another page – and there's Grandpa's 'sexy angel' that finishes the pilot story. Stark black and white before the blank panel that finishes the story.

180

Yūki flushes. 'There's a lot of stuff like that. Is that OK?'

'How do you say "no problem" in Japanese?'

'You'd just say *daijōbu*.'

'OK then. *Daijōbu*.'

'I can read them for you if you like. Translate.'

'That'd be great,' Joel says.

'I wanted to be a manga artist, when I was little . . . I used to draw this one hero all the time,' Yūki says. 'But my drawing sucks these days.'

'How do you know?'

'Because it does.'

'What was this hero?'

'Doesn't matter.' She glances at her bed under which all the old sketchbooks from the last few years lie gathering dust. 'I mean, I still do a bit – or I was before the – before what happened.'

Joel looks up at her, for once making direct eye contact. 'I'd really like to know.'

'No, it's not anything.'

'Genuinely. Hundred per cent.'

She takes a breath. 'Well, he was like this underwater boy who controlled the sea. He was called Half Wave, he came from the ocean, but he loved the land, you see. And he was small, but very, very strong. That's why I called him Half Wave, and he saved people in distress and fought monsters . . .'

Joel goes to say something, then stops himself.

'Were you going to tell me to draw him again?'

'No! Just you should keep drawing.'

'That's what Grandpa said. My therapist too.'

'Sounds like everyone thinks it's a good idea then!'

Yūki shrugs. 'Can we talk about something else?'

'OK. How about reading some of this to me?'

'Like I say, some of them are a bit rude.'

Joel laughs. 'We've already covered that.'

'Oh yes, right.'

She sits down beside him.

And an hour and a half passes very quickly as they read the kamikaze story, Joel really listening, pointing out stuff in the background of the drawings.

It feels . . . OK. Maybe even a bit better than that, she realises as she slides the *Garo* back into their plastic sleeves, and so he visits three or four more times, and then Yūki even goes to his house. It's annoying how Mum and Dad are just a bit too eager for her to keep up the friendship, but she feels better when they're bringing Grandpa's stories back to life, glancing at each other when the story takes a bizarre turn, turning some pages a bit faster when characters get naked together. One day after he's gone she looks in the mirror and sees herself half smiling back.

'He's a bit hard to read,' she tells Angela at the next session.

Her therapist smiles broadly. 'Best books are, right?'

'What?'

'Hard to read. Sometimes, but rewarding if you stick with them!'

'I do like him. Just as a friend. It's nice.'

'Well, it's a good thing either way . . . you rebuild a life bit by bit you know. Let him help you.'

And when September comes it's Joel – not Mum or Dad – who is the one who persuades her to try school again.

'I'll be with you,' he says. 'You won't be on your own . . .'

She braces herself, teaches Joel to say *ganbarō*, let's do our best, as a kind of secret self-encouragement.

For a moment she is the centre of attention and kids who used to give her no time of day at all cluster round the first morning on the AstroTurf courtyard. But the onslaught of faces and voices is immediately overwhelming, and the effort she's made to get there is dwarfed by the effort she has to make to field questions coming at her thick and fast.

'Wow! What was it like? The earthquake?'

'Oh my God, Yoooki. Are you like radioactive now?'

'Did you see any bodies? It must have been way weird. Are you really OK?'

One of the louder boys leans in, the tight curly hair noodled on his head vaguely reminding her of Taka's mop. 'It must have been sooooo cool. I'm not getting too close! Haha! I don't want to get my bits fried!'

'Cool?!' she splutters. 'It wasn't cool, it was – so many people died . . .'

'All right, keep your hair on, Yucky.'

'It's *Yūki*, dumbass.'

'Close enough.'

Idiot.

She looks round, sees Joel at the edge of the scrum. The ground feels soft under her feet and the faces swim in her vision, her breath tightening.

Ganbarō, he mouths.

She nods.

When she gets a moment at break she finds Joel in the library.

'How are you doing?' he asks.

'I can't breathe.'

'You can. They've started a manga club. Why don't you come? Tell people about your grandpa. Bring some of his stuff in.'

She nods. 'Maybe.'

But a week and a half later she is stuck back home again, the panic attacks more intense than ever. In the worst of them she doesn't make it out of the wave, and wide awake she spirals down into the inky depths, like she's dying over and over again.

Angela and her GP start talking about medication to go along with their sessions and she spends a chunk of her sixteenth birthday tiptoeing around the cliff edge of a massive vertigo-inducing attack.

By December she feels like she will never be normal again. Her dreams are coming thick and fast now, saturated in noise and colour, twisted nightmares with different versions of the wave and her running through the flooded Hara house, stalked by pale *yūrei* ghosts and restless spirits.

One night she finds herself flying somehow over a wide beach, a canopy of blue sky overhead and gentle waves lapping the golden sand. There's a figure lying below her and she floats down to see it's the body from the mud, the young man face down in a yellow puffa jacket. She's next to him, her adrenaline pumping, crouching beside him and then rolling him over.

He seems to weigh nothing at all, and flips over onto his back, a cloud of black hair spilling onto the sand, exposing Taka's face to the bright sunshine. Black mud comes oozing up out of his mouth, but his eyes are still bright with life somehow, and they seek hers out – and she wakes in a rush like a diver surfacing way too fast.

When she meets Dad in the kitchen at breakfast he gazes into her face, and frowns.

'Bad sleep?'

'Yep. Nightmare.'

'They'll pass, I'm sure. Just got to give it time. Just the neurons trying to work it all out. They're not real.'

She thinks of Taka's face, alive and not alive at the same time. 'Dad?'

'Yes, sweetheart?'

'Are people going back? To Osōma?'

Dad pulls a face. 'A guy in the labs showed me the latest radiation maps and Hara Central is going to take ages to come out of the zone. Years.'

'What about nearby? I saw people visiting their houses on the news, in protective suits and masks.'

'That's further away from the nuclear plant. And it's old people and they only go for an hour or so. Why?'

185

'I just feel like I want to go. Pay my respects to Grandpa, and all the rest of the people who died. Maybe we should go and do some kind of memorial for Grandpa. There.'

Dad puts a hand on her shoulder. 'Yūki, it's out of the question, especially for someone your age. You might want kids someday. Maybe your mum and Kaz can go in a year or two. You need to concentrate on . . . getting your feet firmly back on the ground. OK?'

'We should keep looking for him.'

'People are doing that. Professionals. We can remember him here.'

Shaken by the dream she tries Taka's number again, gets nothing but the automated message, pesters Kazuko to try and find out what happened to him, but hears nothing. Steadily the cold seeps deeper and deeper back into her bones, and more and more it seems like that step she took in Osōma between this world and *anoyo* can't be fully taken back.

4

Half Wave's Return

EARLY ONE MORNING YŪKI IS at her desk, staring at a huge piece of blank paper in front of her, sucking the end of a pencil, tasting graphite. First light is seeping around the curtains, a bright light that seems almost too bright for January and the rest of the house is gripped by silence as deep as the moments after the wave. She knows she *needs* to be drawing something, but she can't make even a single mark. And there's a sound which at first she thinks is a butterfly or a bee caught in the blinds - no, it's something louder, like wind flapping the vent cover outside her window.

Suddenly the doorbell rings shrill in the hallway, making Yūki jump.

Who rings at this hour? Can't be Joel? She waits for Mum or Dad to head downstairs but nobody goes, and then the doorbell rings again. And then again, a long, long peal. Maybe there's been an accident or something . . . her heartbeat picks up pace as she thumps down the stairs in her bare feet. An insistent knocking now to go with it.

'OK, OK!' she calls. 'I'm coming.'

She steps off the stair carpet and as her foot hits the hall tiles it slaps into a puddle. Oh God, there's water all over the floor. A pipe must have frozen and burst. Maybe it's a plumber ringing . . .

She throws the bolt and opens the door wide.

And sees Grandpa standing there, bathed in radiant, morning sunshine. The silver trainers catch the dazzling light. And whirling in his hand is the old windmill toy from the front garden. Yūki's mouth drops open as she tries to find some air in her lungs, tries to say something.

'Yūki,' Grandpa whispers.

'What,' she gasps, 'what are you doing here? Are you dead?'

'It's difficult to come here,' Grandpa says. 'Thanks for putting out a drink for me. How about some fried tofu next? We like that.'

'What are you doing here?'

'I want you to come back home.'

'Why?'

'Got something for you,' Grandpa mumbles, like he's trying to clear something from his throat.

Yūki reaches out to hug him, but Jiro just kind of dissolves in her arms, and she wakes, sitting bolt upright, gasping, the tears wet on her cheek.

She lies back, heart racing, trying to hold the details, but already bits are fading, just that shock of seeing Grandpa stamped on her mind. Swinging her legs from under the warm covers she gets up, and pads downstairs. The tiles are cold under her bare feet, but bone dry. And when she unlocks and opens the door a sleety rain is falling in grey dawn.

She goes to the makeshift shrine in the living room and rings the little bell on its cushion, then lights a stick of incense and watches the coils of smoke drift up across Grandpa's face.

Quietly Mum comes in and kneels down beside Yūki in *seiza* position.

'I heard you were up. Did you open the door?'

'I had a really intense dream. About Grandpa.'

'Oh?' Mum says, voice rising to an edge.

'He came to the house. He wanted me to go to Osōma.'

She feels her mum stiffen suddenly beside her, her breath held. 'Just a dream, sweetheart. It's still only six-thirty, get back to bed.'

As if something has been unlocked, after that first dream Grandpa appears night after night, but always in or near the old family house.

In one he's sitting on the porch, beckoning her in from the road. She just about reaches him, and then he puts his finger to his lips and everything fades. In another he's helping her to climb that stupid totem pole again. But this time it's not in the museum, but somewhere outside and they are climbing in the swirling blue and white clouds.

'What happens when we reach the top, Grandpa?'

'We just keep going,' he says, calmly. And suddenly they are standing at the lookout post on Little Mountain and the light

191

is fading and the *higurashi* cicadas are shrilling full summer all around them. Deafening.

In another she sees him drawing, energetically filling an enormous sheet of paper with ink dipped from the pot beside him. The little orange fox is there, padding around on the waves, making inky footprints, and the paper seems to get bigger as Jiro draws, until it's filling the whole of the old living room in the family house, and when she gets closer he just keeps scribbling away and she sees a vast, choppy ocean inked to the horizon and fish and boats leaping about on them.

And suddenly - right in the middle - is Half Wave. Not childish like her drawings, but a kind of skilful, grown-up version of him now, with all the strength of Grandpa's *gekiga* in his inked lines. A boy, wise beyond his years, strong, his head lifted like always. The fox pads towards him, swishing its tail . . .

When she wakes she thinks about it all through breakfast, trying to remember details as she swirls her spoon in the bowl. The sense of power and lift and movement. Real movement.

'You going to eat that,' Mum says, 'or just turn it to mush? You look preoccupied.'

'I forgot to do an assignment.'

'Better get on with it then.'

She runs upstairs to her desk and pushes the tutor books away, pulls one of the old sketchbooks from under the bed and rips out four sheets of cartridge paper. For a long while she stares at the top sheet, pencil gripped in her fingers, then waggling loose as she slumps back in her seat, not one mark made.

But when she closes her eyes she can still almost *see* the dream burnt like an after-image on her eyelids, and she grips the pencil again, leans into the paper and starts to etch a line, an oval head, the one-two-three spikes of hair she used to give Half Wave, the smile, his body with arms thrown, one forwards, one back, as he balances.

All the time she is fighting the voice in her head that is telling her it's useless, but she keeps working until Half Wave is roughly there.

She pauses, eyeing the figure. Not good. The arms are all wrong, and there's something a bit odd about one eye, it's not looking the same way as the other one. Hmm. She adds a few waves, trying to make them look like what she's seen in her dream.

After ten or so minutes she scrumples the paper in frustration and lobs it into her bin, then goes to look out of the window at another dull morning. Another day stretching ahead, and after that another, and . . .

But all the while it's like she can feel Half Wave in the waste bin, crouching there – all his energy and optimism – as if he's calling out to her for help.

'It's just a drawing,' she says out loud. 'Stupid.'

Before she knows it she's back in the bin, pulling the paper out and smoothing the sheet flat on her desk, Half Wave smiling up reassuringly at her.

'Sorry, *gomen ne*,' she whispers, and pushes her tongue into the wall of her cheek, considering. There's lots wrong, but maybe it's not *total* rubbish.

She sits down again with a fresh sheet, working from what she's done, trying to take details from the fading dream, getting up to flick through the pages of *Garo* magazine for ideas, copying arms and legs from one of Jiro's old stories about an Ainu boy warrior. The figure *looks* better this time. But he doesn't really *feel* like Half Wave, not like the first lopsided drawing.

After an hour she has four attempts at Half Wave, none of them right, and then, on a whim, she scribbles a quick cartoon version of the little fox riding the raft – that isn't totally terrible. She adds more waves around him, a few more – and then puts all the drawings between the pages of a *Neo* magazine, and shoves it in a drawer.

Every now and then she finds herself taking them out again, smiling at the fox at least, and gradually she adds another few attempts to her secret file . . . even a kind of ninja girl to give him a friend like Grandpa said. She thinks of the grown-up stuff in Jiro's comics – and self-consciously adds some bumps for breasts under the girl's kimono, and then a bunch of waves to cover the legs because the angle of them is wrong. The figure comes out like a weird busty mermaid, and she puts it all away again, and goes to gaze at the street, silver birches swaying in the winter darkness.

One morning she's looking at the fox when her phone buzzes on the bedside table.

Joel? She hasn't seen much of him lately and worries it's her fault.

But when she glances down she sees a Japan code displayed,

and a number she doesn't recognise. Cautiously she presses answer and lifts it to her ear.

'Hai? Moshi moshi?'

There's a kind of staticky noise echoing down the line, but she can hear somebody talking in the midst of it – a woman's voice maybe? – and she puts a finger to the other ear, scrunching up her face in concentration.

'Moshi moshi? This is Hara Yūki? Can I help you?'

The white noise gets louder and she holds her phone away from her ear. And then – just for a moment – the line goes clear and she hears not just a woman's voice, but a whole bunch of voices, kind of overlapped, all talking across each other – a soup of Tōhoku accent and formal Japanese and dialect.

Who's there? Hello? Hello. This is . . . can you hear me? My name is– Is that you? Hello? Moshi moshi mossshhhiiii moshiii. Wow, this is weird! Hello? There's laughter mixed in there, and then she hears somebody say, *'Any foxes on the line?'* and more laughter and then there's a click, and the line goes dead.

For a full minute she stares at the phone in her hand, then brings up the call log with a shaky finger, and suddenly gets up and goes to the *Garo* magazines and pulls out the sushi shop card. Sure enough, when she turns it over to show Taka's handwriting, the numbers match. Could he be calling after all this time? Or winding her up with some stupid joke? Surely not. Maybe it's just some technical fault? All those voices trying to connect with each other, some laughing, some sounding more urgent, some close, some very, very distant.

She thumbs the return call button, but after four rings the automated voice comes again: *We're very sorry, but this number cannot be reached and you cannot leave a message. Goodbye.*

Technical fault or ghost call – or whatever it is – it feels that for a moment she has somehow reconnected to Osōma, to Taka, to those hours before and after the wave – and two minutes later she's in the kitchen, confronting Mum, determined.

'Are you all right, sweetheart, you look pale? I've got to get to work.'

'Could you get crossed lines on a phone call? Like hundreds of people talking at once?'

'Huh? Why?'

'Could you?'

'I remember it happening to your dad once years ago when he was trying to sort out the car insurance after that accident–'

'I need to go back. To Japan.'

Her mother folds her arms. 'We've been over this. We will, one day soon.'

Yūki switches to Japanese. 'I need to go to Osōma! To the house.'

'No way, it's impossible.'

'Some people are.'

'Only old people. Anyway, *why*?'

'Because Grandpa wants me to go.'

'I don't understand.'

'I keep dreaming about him, beckoning me.'

Mum sighs. 'Of course you do. That's why you're seeing Angela . . . Whatever happened to our rational girl who–'

196

Yūki snaps. 'She died, Mum. She's gone. I'm not her and I'm not the little girl who climbed the totem pole, and I'm not the one who went to bits at school. I'm just the girl who got caught in the wave, and that's it. I'm a tsunami girl.' She flaps her arms in frustration. It's the first time she's managed to say the word 'tsunami', and it sounds loud and horrible when she says it. 'I'm dead. In the tsunami, the stupid tsunami . . .'

Mum clutches her by the shoulders. 'Don't say that! You are alive and you are so precious to me. So precious.'

'Maybe I'm just a ghost and I should have gone somewhere else. I need to *do* something. I want to go back to Japan.'

Her mother stares back at her, and then hugs her hard.

'You are not a ghost, Yūki,' Mum mutters into her hair. 'If you were a ghost I couldn't feel you now, could I?'

'I need to be there again. I'm not really doing anything here.'

Mum sighs long and hard, then sits down on a chair, gazing out of the window for a moment. She looks small suddenly, deflated.

'Listen. Supposing you and me went to Tokyo at least. The anniversary of the disaster is coming up. We could go and see Kazuko and maybe go to some kind of memorial service or something. There's this down-to-earth priest near Kazu-chan's house, doing Active Listening and stuff . . .'

'I need to go to Osōma.'

'That's impossible. But Tokyo's doable. If you think it would be good for you. Not make things worse?'

'It can't feel worse than it does now.'

*

When Joel calls round next day she tells him about the crossed line and her plan in one rush. He gazes back at her, nodding, but kind of taken aback. When she's finished she waits for him to try and argue her out of it, but he simply says, 'Wow.'

'Wow what?'

'I've never heard you talk so much!'

'They say we can't go to Osōma. But some people are returning.'

'What about the radiation?'

'Some people are visiting their houses and they wouldn't let them do that if it was super dangerous. Would they?' She hesitates a moment. 'Do you want to see something?'

'What?'

'Something I drew. But you mustn't laugh. OK? Promise like a hundred times.'

'I promise a hundred times. Show me.'

She goes to the drawer, takes out the *Neo* magazine and the four attempted images of Half Wave, the fox – making sure to keep the mergirl drawing hidden – and hands them to Joel, anxiously watching as he looks at first one, then another, nodding in that non-committal way of his. Normally she likes the way he doesn't dive in to judge, but now it makes her impatient.

'Well?'

'They're good,' he says.

'You're just saying that.'

Joel looks her in the eyes. 'OK. I'll be honest. They're not terrible. But I like this one best.' He holds up the first hesitant, crumpled and uncrumpled, drawing.

Yūki looks at him. 'Right?!'

'You should do some more. You'll get better. The fox is great!'

'I need to get closer than Tokyo. What if I can't persuade Mum?'

Joel laughs – as free a laugh as he has ever given in her presence, as if she has said something ridiculously funny. 'I bet you could do anything if you set your mind to it! You decided not to go to school and look, nobody seems to be able to make you go back. What about all that samurai family spirit? You're a Hara, right?'

'Yes, I am,' she says.

She looks down at the smoothed out drawing of Half Wave.

'Do some more,' Joel says.

'I guess.'

Joel snorts. 'Um.'

'Um yourself.'

'How would you say you "love" someone in Japanese?'

She furrows her brow. 'Why?'

'Just a question.'

'Well, you don't. You kind of say "I like things about you". *Anata no koto ga suki desu.*'

'OK.' A silence hangs between them for a moment, and then he points at the first drawing. 'Well, there's things about this I really like. And I haven't seen you like this for ages.'

'Like what?'

'Alive.'

5

Ganbare, Yūki!

TOKYO IS A DARKER CITY this time.

As their taxi glides under the train tracks and stacked sky-scrapers of Shinjuku the neon is dimmer, some screens even black, as a cold rain falls. Areas that used to blaze with light are muted now. Mum has been quiet since they landed, fussing more than usual about passports and stuff like that.

Twice at immigration Yūki has had to say, 'Mum, I did all this myself last year.'

And Mum answered, 'I know, I know.'

'I'm not a little kid.'

But worse, she's having to fight bubbles of panic that keep rising up from her stomach, triggered by the Skyliner terminal, the rumbling subway and platform announcements, the winter cold that seeps in through the carriage doors.

She takes a breath now, watching the driver's white gloves on the wheel, and thinks again of the ghost girl in a taxi trying to go home in the rain . . .

Mum leans forward. 'Everything seems so gloomy.'

The taxi driver clears his throat. 'Energy saving. With all the nuclear reactors offline. It was hell last summer without proper air con and the rolling blackouts and everything.'

'Excuse me, but what do you think about the nuclear plants?'

'Keep them all switched off, I say. At least until we know what's happening with Fukushima. I'd not go within a hundred kilometres of the place.'

Yūki leans forward. 'But people are going home . . .'

'Had a journalist in here last week who told me some scary stuff. Nobody'll buy anything from there – not rice, not sake, not vegetables. I feel sorry for those yokels.'

Mum's voice lowers, still sticking to very polite language – but with a definite growl to it now. 'Excuse me, but you're looking at two of those "yokels". I grew up there. My father died in the tsunami.'

'I'm sorry. I apologise totally, I–'

'I was there,' Yūki adds quietly. 'I saw it all happen.'

There's an uneasy silence in the cab as they slide through the shadows under the train tracks near Shinjuku station. As they come out from under it the taxi's wipers smear what little neon there is across the windscreen in streaks of electric green and crimson. Yūki sees the driver glance at her, his eyes wide.

'You saw it? I really apologise again, young lady. But we're all worried about what might happen if they don't sort it out.'

'I heard students went and helped after the disaster–'

The driver sucks air through his teeth. 'It was good to see young people being idealistic and all. But I'd not want my daughter anywhere near that zone. She's just finished high school.'

'Thank you for your advice,' Mum says. 'We're not planning on heading north.'

They sloosh across the slick tarmac of Shibuya Crossing, mega screens dimmed or blank, past ranks of pedestrians waiting under their umbrellas.

'My sincere respects,' the driver says as he pulls up outside Kazuko's 'mansion' apartment block a few minutes later. 'And no charge for this ride.'

As Mum and the driver argue about the fare and the cold rain hits Yūki's face, little bubbles of unease rise up again, catching her throat like fizz in a newly poured Coke.

She does her breathing and thinks of Half Wave, of that dream image with his head lifted, and renewed hope in his eyes. The kind of hero who could save you. The kind of hero who would never give up – and her own head lifts, and her chest with it.

The wheels of her roller-case rumble on the wet tarmac as they make their way to the entrance and buzz the intercom.

Ganbare, Yūki, she whispers to herself. One more push.

But the new determined attempt to get Mum to take her north does no more than make Mum even more frazzled and annoyed, repeating what the driver said – and that leads somehow to a messy rehash of the last year and that morphs into a typical Hara sister argument. Half an hour later Yūki is slumped back listening to their rapid fire Japanese, frustrated.

'Come off it, sis,' Kazuko says, pushing the lightning from her eyes. 'I'm flat out on a new campaign, and I haven't got time to be trawling reams of paperwork. It's all a mess. From what I hear the house was trashed anyway.'

'But you're the one in Japan. You're the one who can make sure the house and the land are secure, chase compensation or something-'

'Yes, and *I* was the one trying to keep Father's spirits up and visit him like even just a couple of times a year, when you're so busy being Mrs Responsible with your middle class life in Cambridge. I'm the one trying to keep track of any royalties. That kind of stuff.'

'But come off it, Kazu-chan. I have a *full-time* job at the Psychology Department. And we've had our hands *full* with . . .'

Her voice trails off, and both sisters glance without thinking at Yūki.

'With me,' Yūki says flatly. 'I'll say it if you won't.'

'That's not what I was going to say, Yū-chan.'

Kazuko goes to pour her sister some more wine, but Mum holds her hand over her glass.

'Sis, we haven't seen each other for almost two years. And not since Dad died.'

'No need to become alcoholics though.' Mum sighs. 'Oh, whatever, go on then.'

Kazuko turns to Yūki. 'You didn't fly halfway round the world to watch me and your mum fight, right? I guess we all feel we haven't done enough. Just goes with something as weird and big as what happened.'

'Anyway, it's decided,' Mum says. 'We'll stay here and go to the temple. See that dishy Zen priest of yours, Kazuko, and honour Father there, and let's just try and make the most of this time together. Three Hara women united, right?'

Yūki gets to her feet, determined. 'But Grandpa *asked* me to come, and I promised I'd go back—'

'Sweetheart. It was just a dream, he's not there,' Mum says. 'He's not anywhere now.'

'People are still digging in the mud, looking for people, still finding people . . . We just gave up looking for him too easily. We abandoned him. I abandoned him – and I've got to go back, Mum. I have to.'

'Maybe she *should* go,' Kazuko murmurs. 'I mean, whatever helps. That palm reader by the shopping mall said—'

Mum sighs. 'Here you go with your mumbo-jumbo—'

'Shhh, Kaori. Can a little sister speak freely?'

'Why break the habit of a lifetime!'

Kazuko turns back to Yūki. 'It's good to see you so determined, Yū-chan. What does your therapist say?'

'She says I need to find some closure, so—'

Mum cuts in. 'Angela doesn't know the reality. And we have no idea – none of us – what's going on at the power plant. Or if the radiation levels they publish are just nonsense.'

Yūki shakes her head, pacing up and down in front of the sofa. 'You're not listening. If I don't go nothing's going to change.'

Mum sighs. 'Let's be sensible—'

'Noooo,' Yūki shouts. 'Let's not be sensible.'

Kazuko leans forward, lightning bolt swaying. 'Right! Let's not be sensible. Let's make something up together. We're good at that, this family. Think about what happened with our little brother—'

'Kazuko!' Mum fires her sister a warning look. 'Not now.'

Yūki's gaze flicks from one sister to the other, puzzled. 'Little brother?'

Mum looks away.

'There's no harm,' Kazuko says. 'She should know.'

'Know what?'

'Big brother really,' Kazuko says quietly. 'Two years before your mum here was born, Mother had another child. Their first one I mean. She and Dad had temporarily moved to Osōma from Tokyo, living in the family house with *our* grandmother. Tough as old boots that old bird, may she rest in peace wherever she is and play that *biwa* again . . .'

'It's not really the time for all this,' Mum says.

'What about the brother?' Yūki says impatiently. 'What happened to him?'

'Not much,' Kazuko says. 'He was stillborn. Mother took it really hard. Dad too I think. They'd had a bad time here, bit wild – so they packed up their apartment for good, and shipped up to Osōma and built the annexe and the studio. And slowly they picked up their lives, and our mother started her ceramics again and Dad was drawing and then your mum was born, and then – hey presto – your Aunt Kazuko was born too. Hooray.' She gives a little bow. 'But they couldn't get over that little boy. People didn't talk about that stuff then . . .' She glances at her sister. 'People still don't talk about it *enough*–'

'Kazuko!' Mum says, a real edge to her voice now.

'I want to hear the story,' Yūki says, perching on the edge of an armchair and looking both sisters in the face. 'I'm old enough to know.'

Mum waves a hand in defeat and Kazuko leans forward into the story. 'Well, they conjured up a ritual the two of them, your grandparents. Father made a *kokeshi* doll, you know the souvenir ones you see all over the place at hotsprings in Tōhoku - no arms or legs just the long bodies and little round heads. Once upon a time people used to make them for children, but there was a belief going around in the sixties that they were made for babies who died really young. So Jiro made a little boy *kokeshi* and Mum painted it up specially – she was so good with a brush - and then they buried it under the new studio. So that the little boy they lost would be with them, kind of guardian angel, you know?'

The story of the *kokeshi* is triggering some kind of memory now, but it won't quite come into focus. Yūki sits down, her mind churning. 'So he would have been my uncle? Why didn't you tell me about all this?'

'It didn't seem like a subject for when you were little,' Mum says. 'And what does it matter now?'

There's a silence in the apartment and the rain brushes against the big window, the lights of the city shifting in the drops sliding down the glass.

'And what happened then, Auntie?'

'And things were great for a decade or so, Dad drew and his work got bigger and bigger and Mother made her pots . . . and then – she died, and Jiro stopped drawing . . . and here we are and that's the recent history of the Hara family . . .'

Her voice trails off for a second, then the Kazuko-spark is back fiercely. 'But – but then you, Yūki – *you* – freaked us all out when you were old enough to talk properly and we all went to visit Father, because you suddenly started telling us you were playing with a little friend that only you could see, a *little boy*. Like a *zashiki warashi* – you know, a 'house ghost' – the kind that helps out in old houses or inns, and plays pranks, and stuff like that? We'd say, *Who left the light on in the* furo *bathroom?* and you'd say, *The little boy did it.*'

Yūki's spine twitches, and she sits up. 'Really?!' There's definitely something stirring in her memory – a sense of closeness, of a cosy secret held tight.

She looks at Mum, who is studying the bottom of her glass intently.

'It's true, Yūki. I'll admit, it really spooked me. You always talked about him when you were two or three, then he kind of faded, your imaginary friend—'

'But the best bit was this,' Kazuko cuts across her, 'when we asked you who the boy was, you said – that – he – lived – *under* – the – studio.' She counts out the beats of her punchline with her hand. 'Where Mum and Dad buried the little kokeshi doll.'

The silence descends again, lengthens, as the shivers go

running up and down Yūki's back. That does feel familiar – that sense of having a special friend – somebody you could rely on to be there always. She can feel the Osōma house and the bluff now, enveloping her, calling her.

'I guess you must have overheard something,' Mum says, very quietly. 'And you were lonely. We – I – did my best to get you a sibling, but . . .'

Kazuko pats her sister's knee and lets her hand rest there as she turns back to Yūki. 'Grandpa was delighted though, when you saw the *zashiki warashi*. He and Mum had got fed up with the rat race and materialism and stuff. He said there was wisdom in the old folklore. After they moved to Tōhoku he started to focus more and more on the old stories of ghosts and foxes and *yōkai* and things like that. It was his best work I think. Then Mum died and it all dried up.'

Yūki closes her eyes, trying to make the memory clearer, opening up that secret world again – and then she is with Grandpa and the sparks from the bonfire are zipping up off Little Mountain, and soon they will light the Susuki rockets and send them *shuuuuuu* into the sky, and the spirits are very close.

'I *need* to go,' Yūki whispers, eyes still scrunched shut. 'Can't you understand?'

Mum sighs. 'And can't you understand that a mother's most vital need is to keep her child safe, Yūki?'

'I'm not a child.'

'Sixteen is still a minor. Grandpa would agree.'

'No, he wouldn't! Remember how he used to swim at Obon,

and he was protesting about the nuclear plants years ago – and he was right!'

'And he could be wrong too. Go left when everybody went right just for the sake of it. A nail that sticks up can be good – but it can also be a pain in the backside sometimes!'

Suddenly the apartment feels very small and confined, and frustrated Yūki goes over to the window, her face reflected in the glass, hovering against the city beyond. Somewhere out in the night a siren rises and falls and rises again.

'I'm sorry,' Mum says gently. 'Sorry for saying that about Father.'

'It's important some nails stick up,' Kazuko says. 'But I have to agree with my sister for once, Yū-chan. You are too young to risk your health – not like us tough old chickens . . .'

Yūki gazes at the lights of Tokyo, breathing hard. Joel said, *I bet you could do anything if you set your mind to it.*

'Yūki, your aunt's asking you if you want another drink.'

There's no point arguing. She looks back from the window, her mind suddenly made up. The story of the lost uncle and the *zashiki warashi* is reverberating in her head and she knows what she is going to do. She looks at her half empty Coke on the table.

'Could we raise a glass to Grandpa?' she says. 'A proper one. I'd like to try some wine.'

Kazuko laughs. 'Just a tiny bit, sis? Three Hara women drinking together. Warriors! *Kanpai!*'

Night falls deeper around them and the rain clears.

Yūki makes a show of yawning and then excuses herself. She

powers up her phone, and taps out a text. It must be about three p.m. at home, school end.

Hi Joel. In Tokyo. Im going to take yr advice ☺

Almost instantly the reply comes back.

Wow. Great to hear from you. But what advice?! Did I give u advice?

About taking a risk. Thx for helping me. Don't reply now it costs me! Y ☺

She thinks about adding an 'x' but then just presses send, and flicks it back to airplane mode, carefully setting and checking an alarm, and making sure the volume is low.

She sits on her futon in Kazuko's cluttered home office, looking at the gig posters on the walls. One of them features three guitarists leaping high in the air, their long black hair flying around their heads.

There's a small mirror next to it and she looks at herself. Her hair, as ever, not quite straight and not quite curly, not quite brown, not quite black.

Slowly, deliberately she starts to twist her hair into one long plait.

It looks good, the hair darker, more definite – and it makes her look older somehow. Possibly more Japanese. When she's done she stands sideways and looks herself up and down and then takes the deepest breath she can find inside herself.

OK. I'm ready. *Ganbare, Yūki!*

PART THREE
Zone

1

A Song on a Cold Night

So, AT SIX A.M. ON the morning of March 10th 2012, Yūki is running as fast as she can for the overground station, the Tokyo air cold and clean and bright around her, her energy bounding back off the pavement.

At the corner of Kazuko's street a few crows are cawing from the lampposts, and she glances up as a solitary, masked cyclist swings past ringing his bell, just missing her.

Otherwise there's only the sound of her footsteps, her breath, the long plait bumping against her rucksack with each step, as she bounds round the corner by the Lawson store, past the little temple and then under the elevated expressway, early morning traffic thumping overhead.

A bearded, homeless man lifts his head from dragging the sack of cans he's collecting and shouts, 'Wow, so fast! Go, miss, go!'

She waves a hand over her shoulder and runs even harder for the overground.

It's a Saturday, and the station platform at Mejiro is nearly empty as she threads her forty-eight-hour pass (the only thing Mum entrusted to her yesterday) into the barrier. And then pats her pocket to feel the 30,000 yen that she's rifled from the envelope in Mum's handbag. About £180, enough to get there, and a bit more besides. And then I'll just have to pay her back, Yūki thinks, and apologise for like a thousand years.

She replays her escape: on soft tiptoe from Kazuko's office, past last night's takeout remains and her virtually untouched inch of wine, and then propping her note, written in super apologetic Japanese, on the kitchen table.

Mum, I'm really sorry but I have to go. I'll be fine and I'll be back day after tomorrow latest. I'll phone tonight. Promise. Really sorry again. Love you. Y

Then phone stowed in the bottom of her bag she dropped the six floors to the street, paused one moment with her hand still on the 'mansion' block front door, then let it clack shut, the sound still reverberating in the entrance hall as she rounded the corner by the cherry trees.

Now the Yamanote line's sing-song chimes are ringing out like normal at each station. The few passengers are absorbed in their phones or gazing at blank nothing through the windows like normal.

The main hall of Ueno station is busier as she weaves her way round weekend travellers getting an early start, jetlagged tourists stumbling off the Skyliner dragging their rumbling cases behind them like normal.

But nothing is normal. And the reason for that is nothing has been normal for months, for years. Trying to calm her heart, Yūki tries to fine-tune her plan as she strides into the ticket office. Running away is the easy bit, it's everything else that will be tricky. She knows that since the disaster the Jōban line only runs part of the way north, that the tsunami washed away the track south of Osōma and a train with it.

Taka's?

Don't think about it now.

At the counter the man pauses and gives her a long squint of a look when she asks for her ticket.

'No trains north of Hirono Machi. There's a bus transfer to Sendai. Are you sure that's where you're supposed to be going?'

'*Hai.*'

'Single or return?'

'Um, return?'

He scratches his head. 'You don't sound so sure?'

'I know where I'm going. Thank you.'

'Well. Take good care.'

'Thank you.' She stuffs the ticket and change into her jeans pocket.

Only after she has shuffled through the ticket barrier do doubts creep back in. Maybe the guy was just doing the *who-are-you?* thing. Or, maybe it really is dangerous – the radiation and stuff . . .

Shut up, she tells herself. Lift your head, do what you have to do.

The train rattles north through blustery showers. Every now and then she can feel her switched-off phone lurking like a lead weight at the bottom of her bag, and somehow, after a few stations have rattled past, it ends up back in her hand. She eyes its dead screen, her thumb hovering over the power button. But then she thrusts it away again, and turns her eyes determinedly to the window, waiting for the familiar first sight of the Pacific, hoping against hope that when she sees it the ocean won't send her straight into a shivering mess on the train carriage floor. Got to be a chance of that after what happened in Norfolk. A bit of the plait has come loose, and she focuses on making it better, tighter, more definite.

When the ocean does come – slices of silver-grey and white between the trees – her heart bumps a really big beat, and she braces, and then, miraculously, it calms down to something not much faster than normal. She takes a moment to rest as sun and cloud alternate and then, beyond Mito, sleet starts brushing the carriage windows, the weather closing in.

At each station Yūki feels cold air enter the carriage as passengers get on and off, and she ducks her head down, vigilant for a train guard looking for the sixteen-year-old *gaijin* runaway.

Police even? Will they be looking for her already? God, it's possible – Mum will be in a state.

She finds a flu mask in her bag and pulls it over her mouth and nose. With the plait and her features hidden behind the mask maybe that's enough of a disguise.

Iwaki arrives: a bigger station, so she checks extra carefully

218

as they pull in. The doors hiss open opposite her, but nobody gets on, just a guard standing there who glances at her from the platform, before his eyes sweep away again.

This is where Taka and his friend got on. As the cold and nothingness gust into the carriage, she looks at the empty seats across from her, and sees him smiling that lopsided smile, coming over, bragging about the kickboxing, touching the useless magic formula on the back of her hand.

She glances down at her wrist, the skin blank now. Behind her, down the carriage, someone laughs, and she finds herself wiping a tear or two from her eyes, pulling her hoodie up over the plait to try and get warmer. She sniffs hard, wishing she'd bought some food at the station, and rests her forehead on the gentle vibration of the carriage window, and watches the world blur as they pull out of Iwaki, trying not to think about anything, doing the breathing exercises to practise in case an attack comes, fighting little waves of jetlag, snuggling back into the crook of the seat.

She wakes with a start to find the train has stopped at a station she doesn't remember, and only catches the very end of an announcement: something a bit quick in Japanese about the bus that connects with services north of Sendai.

Everyone is getting to their feet, and an old man nudges her.

'Terminal stop, young lady. Hirono Machi is the end of the line.'

'Excuse me, but do you know how to get to Osōma Town?'

'Osōma? Near Odaka?'

'Yes. Sorry to bother you.'

The man shrugs. 'Taxi. If you can find one. And if they'll take you. The bus goes to Sendai, but it loops right round the evacuation zone. Route 6 is still shut – at least where it goes past the reactor. It's a total mess.' He peers at her as he knots his scarf tightly. 'So. Where are you from? Tokyo?'

'I'm from here,' Yūki says pulling her rucksack from the luggage shelf. 'I'm going home.'

The man's eyebrows arch up under the brim of his little hat. 'Oh! Really? Be very, very careful, won't you?'

She pulls the hoodie further over her head as she hustles after the other passengers, flicking her eyes left and right and trying to shelter in the midst of them. Knowing Mum she'll have alerted everyone from the police to child protection to the coastguard – and sure enough, there are two uniformed officers standing just beyond the doorway, scanning the passengers as they file out. Almost unreal, but it must be her they're looking for. Can't be defeated here, not this early on, and yet there's no other way out of the station, and maybe the disguise won't be enough. Yūki hesitates, dragging her steps . . .

Damn it.

There's a sudden screeching from beyond the officers, like the station tannoy is going wrong and squealing out feedback, and both policemen look to the right, one of them shouting something as he strides away towards the commotion. Yūki hurries to join the old man in the hat.

'Excuse me, but could you show me the way to the taxi rank?'

220

'It's not hard to find.' He peers at her again suspiciously. 'Shouldn't you be in school?'

'No,' she says brightly. 'I've been at a chess tournament.'

'Oh I see. I'm more a *Go* man myself.'

'I'm not very good, I'm learning.'

And chatting nonsense about the imagined tournament and how she won three and lost two she ducks past the remaining distracted officer and out into the bleak little concourse beyond. She glances towards the squealing and sees the second police-man closing on a young busker. A dark woolly hat is jammed on his head and he's crouched over his amp trying to get it to stop feeding back, waving his hand to acknowledge he's done something wrong. His voice is calm though as he calls out, '*Sumimasen*, sorry, I'll have it sorted in a moment.'

Yūki sniffs the air cautiously.

Really cold, and a wet sleet falling now. Otherwise OK. But then you couldn't smell or see or hear radiation, could you?

There's just one taxi left on the rank, an old guy plonked on its bonnet, smoking. When he hears her approaching he turns round and chucks the cigarette into the grimy slush at his feet. His face is blotchy, and the lines in it crease deeply as he looks her up and down, twice. Maybe not the friendliest face she's ever seen, but she has to get away from the police just in case.

She thinks of Mum's dire warnings about seedy men and cars. Then clamps her hand on her phone in her pocket and walks up to him. And anyway it's a licensed cab so it's probably OK.

'Um, excuse me?'

'Can I help you, miss?'

'I'm really sorry to bother you, but if it's not *too* much trouble could you possibly take me to Osōma? I'd be very grateful.'

'Osōma! Really?' The man frowns again. 'Have to go round the zone.'

'I'm going to visit – my grandfather.'

'I thought most of it was still in the "hard-to-return" zone.'

'He's – on the edge of it.'

The man grunts. 'I won't get a fare the other way, so I'll have to charge both directions.'

'Um, how much?'

'About 15,000 yen.'

'It's fine,' she says, trying to make her voice confident. Is that

223

a lot? Is he ripping her off? Can't be helped though, there's no choice . . . She smiles. 'That's totally fine.'

'Visiting your grandfather, you say?'

'Um, yes I haven't seen him since the tsunami.' The man still seems unsure, so she hurriedly adds. 'I was in it. I survived it.'

The driver nods, but kind of the way you would if you heard somebody had missed a flight.

'Lucky you. Jump in. So, what does your grandpa do?'

'He was a manga artist,' she says, without thinking.

'Oh! Retired, huh? Cushy. Buckle up, will you, the road's sketchy in places.'

The car smells a bit of cigarette smoke, but it's really good to be moving again – accelerating away from the station. She turns around and watches the spinning lights of the squad car fall away as the taxi's suspension sighs over bumps in the tarmac. But when she turns back again she sees the eyes of the driver seeking out hers in the rear-view mirror.

'Problem, miss?'

'No.'

'You cold?'

'A bit.'

He turns up the heater, and manages a half smile. 'It's a long way, so settle back.'

'I'm OK.'

'Your accent is a bit odd, if you don't mind me saying. Do you come from Kyushu?'

'I live in England.' Damn it, another mistake. What if the driver's heard some radio alert for a runaway? 'That is, I lived in England for a long time, but now I live in Tokyo.'

The driver nods. 'Fair enough.'

Yūki pulls the mobile from her rucksack again and eyes its blank screen. Can the police track your phone when it's off? Maybe you have to take the battery out or something?

The man clears his throat. 'I bet your grandad will be pleased to see you. A lot of the old folk in the *kasetsus* are lonely. Bad suicide rate. It's one thing to survive a disaster, but it's another thing *surviving* surviving, if you ask me.'

Yūki nods.

'What do your parents think about you coming? Whole reactor complex is a time bomb.'

'Is it really dangerous?'

'I'd rather be a starving taxi driver than one of those nuclear workers microwaving himself from the inside out. For a pittance.'

'And what about around the zone?'

'Who knows?' He puffs out his cheeks. 'Some of the evacuation area is very high, but a lot of it isn't too bad right on the coast, they say. Wind was going north-west when the explosions happened so . . . damn it, nobody knows anything really. Mind if I listen to the radio?'

She leans forward. 'You don't know a taxi driver called Jimi, do you, he works around Osōma and Tomioka? He's got curly hair.'

'What's the full name?'

'I don't know. Jimi's just a nickname, I guess.'

'Well, if he's still there I wouldn't think there's any work for him now. The contractors all go by minibus. Friend of yours?'

'I knew his son.'

'Ah. Got you. Sorry.' The driver clicks on the radio and a woman's voice fills the cab interior.

'. . . with the anniversary tomorrow residents still await news on compensation packages. In other news, the court case brought by bereaved parents of students of Okawa Elementary School in . . .'

'Terrible,' the driver grunts. 'All of them died, near Minami Sanriku. Would you rather I put music on, miss?'

'Yes, please.'

The driver flicks the station and a breathy Japanese voice singing heavily accented English fills the car.

'I'm crossing you in style someday, Oh, dream maker, you heart breaker . . .'

Yūki leans back, trying to loosen the tightness gripping her shoulders as the car bumps along and the slow jazzy piano and voice sail into the next verse, the driver beating slow time on the steering wheel with his index finger.

'Two drifters, off to see the world, there's such a lot of world to see . . .'

On the long straight of road ahead not a single other vehicle or soul in sight now.

For a slow half hour they head north, jolting over potholes, a few rays of sun still raking the mountains to their left as the afternoon fades, but to the east the sky looks heavy, buttressed by thicker,

226

massing clouds, and the ocean beneath, when she catches sight of it again, has taken on the bluey purple of a week-old bruise.

'Here we are,' the driver grunts.

'Osōma?'

'No. Evacuation zone.'

The road ahead is blocked by a high concertina metal gate pulled across the road. Red lights flash from its spikes and three men in helmets are standing in front of it, waving batons, directing the taxi towards a side road.

'We go round now,' the driver says, turning towards the sawtooth hills, the setting sun turning them to silhouette.

Yūki looks back through the gates, glimpsing weeds on the tarmac beyond, a line of bare cherry trees, a temple roof and a garage forecourt strewn with rubbish. There's a convoy of lorries just visible in the distance, their open backs covered with blue tarps.

'What are they doing?'

'Radioactive topsoil removal. You tell me where they're going to put it all, miss. Some poor farmer's back yard no doubt.'

A few hundred metres down their new road, a house that looks like it's been built recently stands amidst the dried remains of last summer's weeds, its windows dark rectangles.

Yūki leans forward. 'Did the wave reach here?'

'No. But the family probably moved to the other side of the country.'

For twenty minutes they head inland, the traffic non-existent apart from the occasional lorry or Self Defence Force vehicle.

227

Yūki's eyes flick from the taxi meter which is mounting alarmingly, to her phone which is somehow back in her hand again, to the darkening sky and the road. The driver is looking at her again: a long searching look in the shake of the mirror, that makes her shift on her seat.

'Is everything OK, Mr Driver?'

'So, how old are you?'

'Eighteen. Why?'

'Really?'

'Nearly.'

He shakes his head. 'I got in trouble last year for helping a few kids who came up here without permission. You really meant to be here?'

'Yes,' she says, glad of a chance to be truthful. 'I really am meant to be here. With Grandpa.'

'That's nice. *Ii ne . . .*' The man sighs a long, weary sigh that fogs the windscreen. He wipes at the condensation with his sleeve, then glances back. 'I lost my niece in the tsunami. She was about your age. Lovely girl. Life ahead of her. Don't waste yours, miss.'

'I'm trying not to . . .'

Out towards the ocean a faint glow still lights the undersides of the clouds, but otherwise the night is taking the empty landscape bit by bit.

2

Wave of Desolation

AN HOUR LATER SHE IS standing on the main street that leads from Osōma's train station, watching the taxi disappear into the gloom pooling under the hills.

Weeds have forced up through the bricked area in front of the station building, and the car park and bus stop are deserted. No lights in the waiting room, and when she looks back down the street, it's as if night has arrived in a great rush. Just a dim glow from a building halfway down on the left, and maybe another a little beyond that near where the sushi restaurant is, or was.

Quiet as the grave, Kazuko had said, but not this quiet. Normally there'd be a few cars, kids cycling home from after-school clubs, people going in and out of the little supermarket on the corner . . . But the Lawson *konbini* is dark, and the roads beyond are black, and the wooded hills beyond that even blacker, and it all feels so shockingly empty.

She shivers.

It was hard enough to persuade the driver to leave her here –
he had wanted to 'deliver her in person' to Grandpa, but Yūki had
spun some story about Jiro not being due back from Minamisōma
until later. Eventually the driver shrugged, took her money and
wished her to be well and safe.

Now her fake confidence has gone with his departing tail
lights.

The chill feels more intense than normal for March in Tōhoku,
and you can see what must be dried mud from the wave along
the pavement to the right.

The mud. For a moment her feet feel like they're stuck to the
ground. To the right a few houses have been badly damaged so
the tsunami must have come this far. Slews of rubbish have collected in the gutter and here and there are gaps where houses
once stood, like looking at a friend who's just lost a couple of
front teeth. All her energy and movement seems to have gone
with the taxi.

What now?

Get moving again, dummy. Ten minutes more. See what happens.

She wills herself into motion, her footsteps the only sounds as
she edges her way into the darkness and silence.

That one pool of yellow light is getting closer, beckoning, and
she hurries towards it instinctively. Yes, it's the little *ryokan* inn:
Kujaku Ya - the Peacock. The debris has been cleared away from
this stretch, and there are dozens of planted flowers, pinks and
pale blues valiantly shivering in plastic food tubs placed on the
concrete, flickering life in the darkness.

Maybe they're even taking guests? Just about enough money in the envelope still . . .

Wisps of steam are curling into the cold air from the vents above the kitchen window, a smell of cooking carried on them. Out of the corner of her eye she senses rather than sees movement – like a shadow has just passed and blocked what light there is and she looks that way to see the red vending machines where once upon a time she used to buy Cokes and Plum Fanta. It's blinking through its light sequence, as if someone's just put coins in and pressed a selection, but there's nobody to be seen. Suddenly something bangs to the bin at the bottom of the machine – shockingly loud in the silence – and she jumps.

'Hello?'

Nobody there, just the emptiness, and the little run of brave flowers, and dried sludge from the wave pushed to the side of the street.

Her index finger reaches for the inn's door release, but at that moment the thing goes rattling open, and through the wisps of cooking steam she sees a slim figure stooping to put on shoes in the *genkan*. The silhouette straightens to become a lanky young man, his head topped off with a cloud of curly hair . . .

And Taka materialises from the steam.

She blinks. It *is* him, surely!

A red towel is wrapped round his neck, and he's staring at her now with a strange look on his face. Kind of blank – like the expression if you were on a Skype call and the picture froze. Then that lopsided grin spreads back across his face.

'Shit! No waaaaay. It *is* you. I thought it was – I saw you coming from the station. What the *hell* are you doing here?'

The words are rough, but the tone is something more like wonder. Or even relief.

'You're OK,' she gasps.

'Of course I am. I'm always OK.'

'Oh my God, I'm so glad. *Yokatta*! I thought you were dead. I was sure you were dead!'

'Don't think so.' The smile fades. 'Not yet anyway . . . But what the hell are you doing here?'

'I – I ran away.'

'From England?!'

'Tokyo.'

'Ooooooh.' He shakes his head. 'That's bad. Listen, I'm like really sorry about your grandpa.'

'Why didn't you answer my text? Or when I called you?'

'Huh? Didn't get a text or anything–'

'Or were you just winding me up with that call?'

'What?'

'You called me. Last month, it was your number, and there was all these voices talking at once and–'

He holds up a hand, the smile gone. 'Slow down, slow down! I lost my phone, in the disaster.' He waves in the direction of the port. 'But I was so glad when I heard you made it. A guy told me he'd seen you and that grumpy Takeda woman the day after. I was glad. Super glad.'

A man's voice is shouting gruffly from somewhere deep in the *ryokan*. 'Taka-chan? Oi, where are you?'

Taka glances over his shoulder, waving Yūki away from the threshold. 'Quick. Make yourself scarce.'

'But I need somewhere to *stay*.'

'Well, *obviously*. I mean just hide round the flipping corner,' he whispers. 'My old boss from the sushi shop is helping out here. He's OK, but he might just turn you in. There was a policeman here an hour or so ago. Looking for a runaway sixteen-year-old? I guess it was you, right? I saw you get out of the taxi and I thought I'd nip out and save you a bunch of trouble. Wait by the vending machine. Try not to freak out, OK?'

He turns to the door, then hesitates and looks back. 'Hey, Yūki?'

'Yes?'

'You're not a ghost or anything are you?'

The tone in his voice makes the shivers chase through her again. 'I don't think so.'

'OK. Just checking.'

She waits uneasily by the vending machine, watching the steam from the inn shape wraiths on the air, feeling the night thickening around her, and flapping her arms for a bit to get the circulation going again. Now and then in her peripheral vision it is as if something shifts, but when she looks that way there's nothing. She shoves her hands deep in her pockets. It's so good to see Taka, but already a couple of times she's seen a shadow on his face, something that surely wasn't there last year. He looks older, maybe thinner. And the possibility of staying in the Peacock seems to be receding.

A few minutes later Taka is back. He's wearing a big parka and pulling a cart with a red plastic tank of something sloshing inside. The smile is back. '*Okaeri, Yūki!* Welcome home. So just how much trouble are you in?'

'A bit, I guess.'

'Are you hungry?'

'Very. Thirsty too.' She points at the machine, still blinking away beneath the tightly-balled cherry blossom. 'Something dropped – but there was nobody around.'

'It's gone bonkers. Just suddenly chucks out a drink at random since the electricity came back on the street.'

'Can I take it?'

'You must be crazy. No idea how much radiation the drinks in there got in the first weeks . . . But, ta-daa!!' He pulls a can of hot coffee from his parka pocket. 'It's black with sugar. Want some?'

'I don't really like coffee . . . Where are you living?'

'Home of course. Been back two weeks. Come on, I'll show you.'

Yūki hesitates.

'Come on. I won't bite!'

'Taka? I mean, how did you . . . ? What happened when . . . ?'

'When the wave came?' Taka shrugs. 'Long story. Come on. Unless you're worried I'm like some kind of weird pervert or something. I mean I am *weird*, but you don't have to worry about anything else.'

'No, no. You were joking about me being a ghost, right?'

He looks at her – his face suddenly dark again, then shakes his

234

head. 'Yeah, just a joke. To be honest, I've been kind of expecting you. Dad said you'd be back again.'

She must look surprised, because Taka laughs. He pulls the ring on the can. 'So I was kind of keeping my eyes open.'

'Expecting me?'

'Uh huh.' He takes a swig of the coffee. 'Sure you don't want some? You look like you're frozen.'

'OK, yes please.'

He hands the can to her and she swigs, but too fast and the hot bitterness scalds her throat.

'Easy. Have a bit more to warm you up. Can you carry it while I pull the kerosene? Let's get home.'

If life in Tokyo seemed dimmed, Osōma is simply a dead version of its old self as side by side they walk the streets on the edge of town. A few flakes of wet snow come again, a sudden gust of wind banging a loose board in a house to their right. It booms in the darkness, and Yūki's head jerks round.

'Right?' Taka says. 'It makes you jumpy as hell at night. There's only about eight of us come back since this part of town reopened at the start of the month. Most of what you hear isn't people . . .'

Yūki glances back at him, the sleet swirling into his face as he bumps the cart with the red can along behind him. Definitely thinner.

'What are you looking at? Have I got sauce round my mouth?'

'No. It's just I was kind of sure you were dead.'

'But here I am! Ever heard of Schrödinger's Cat?'

235

'Whose cat?'

'It's a kind of thought experiment in quantum physics. There's a cat in a box and a switch that's triggered by the random wobbling of this sub-atomic particle. Or something. And if it goes one way the cat gets poisoned and dies and if it goes the other way the cat lives. Until you look in the box to see which way the particle went the cat is both alive and dead. To the observer, right?'

'Doesn't the cat know, though?'

'I guess.' Taka scratches the back of his neck. 'Maybe I'm not explaining it properly. But it's like I was the cat, right? Until you looked in the box and came here. Now I'm definitely alive. Before, for you, I was kind of both.'

'Are you making fun again?'

'No way. That's me being super serious.' Taka shakes his head. 'So you ran away? Wow. I thought you were just one of those well-behaved little girls.'

'I'm not little now.'

'You know what I mean.'

'Mum and Dad just see me as this kid still, but I'm sixteen.'

Taka sniffs. 'I'm eighteen in a few months. But I don't feel it. I feel about fifty some days. And just like a little kid the next. Rollercoaster.' He mimes the climb and dive of a carriage with one hand in the night air.

'Taka-san, when did you come back?'

'To Osōma? Almost as soon as they lifted the evacuation order here a few weeks ago. The sushi guy came to look after his place – he's staying with Mrs Komori at the Peacock. She was the first back – on her own, really brave – and her husband is coming at the weekends to help clear up . . .'

'And you and your dad.'

'Yep.'

Taka's silent for a long moment as the cart rumbles behind him, the liquid sploshing around in the can. 'I was lucky. The wave reached our house and it messed the ground floor, but upstairs is fine. Then I went away for a bit. And then I came back. I was dead and now I'm alive again.' He glances at her. 'I'm kidding, again!'

'So, where did you go?'

'Doesn't matter.'

She glances at him. He looks less sure of himself now, like someone recovering from an accident or something. 'Are you really OK? And why did you come back?'

'So many questions! How about I ask you some?'

'Sorry. Like what?'

Taka stops and looks at her. 'Well, your parents are going to be like majorly pissed off with you, right? Do they know you're here?'

'I had to come. I was going mad.'

'What about school?'

'I'm not going.'

'So you're like a *hikikomori* or something?'

'No. I just prefer being at home.'

He laughs. 'Me too. So, what's your plan?'

The cold is biting deeper, and the wind keeps banging things

237

in the darkness. Suddenly she feels the need to be inside, to be warm and safe. 'It was like, I dunno, I – feel like I abandoned Grandpa. And . . .'

'And what?'

'And I keep dreaming about him, like all the time.' She hesitates. 'And I dreamt about you.'

'Oh?' Taka raises his eyes, a smile back on his lips. 'Really?'

'Nothing weird. Well, it was weird . . .'

'And what happened?'

'You were lying on the beach, wearing this yellow puffa jacket. Like – like the dead guy I saw that night.'

Taka opens his mouth to make a perfect round O. 'Was I dead?'

'Kind of, but kind of not.'

'That's reassuring, I think,' Taka says changing hands on the cart's handle.

'It's funny. Sometimes the dreams seem more real than being awake, you know? And tomorrow's the anniversary. So, that's why I'm here.'

Taka nods, sighs a deep sigh. 'And tomorrow's the anniversary.'

They walk on in silence, past dead traffic lights and piles of rubbish, the sleety snow brushing her cheek.

'Will your dad mind me staying?'

Taka kicks at a stone sending it spinning into the night. 'No. He's away – got a job to take somebody all the way . . . to the north of Sapporo.' He tilts his head to one side. 'But he'll be pleased you're here. You should call your mum . . . Dad said she punched my uncle once. Scary!'

238

The mention of Mum makes her feet feel heavy – the reminder of how much crap is waiting for her when she turns the phone on. 'Later. Just want a little bit of time here first.'

'To do what?'

'I want to go to the house, if I can.'

Taka pulls a face. 'That's difficult.'

'I really need to go—'

'I said difficult. But not impossible. I've been in there, Yūki. It's . . . really strange.'

This time his tone makes it clear he's not joking, and she comes to a stop. But Taka just puts his head down and trudges on towards the port area. In seconds the darkness and snow have wrapped around him, and he blurs in her vision.

'Wait!' She hurries to catch up. 'Strange?'

'Shit scary more like. Let's talk about it when we're inside. I freaked myself out a bit. There's more ghosts than people here right now.'

Her scalp tightens. 'Not really though?'

'Well, just look at what happened here.'

They've come out of the town proper and up onto the little road that climbs above Osōma Port. A faint light seems to be emanating from the clouds, or from the sea itself, and in that vague glow Yūki can just make out the devastation: pulverised remains of houses, workshops, boats, fish processing buildings below them. Hard to tell where one thing ends and another begins in the tangle of girders, panels, planks, bits of machinery, roof, wrecked cars and vans. A huge shipping container lies on its side amidst the wreckage, but the fishing boat has fallen from its perch in the port building. You can just make out where tracks have been cleared through the chaos.

'I've seen typhoons howl through here, but nothing like that day. The sound was just off the scale . . .' Taka whispers. 'Like a thousand garbage trucks emptying everything out all at once.'

Yūki gazes at the wreckage. Somehow worse than the morning after, the sheer scale and *deadness* of it all now way beyond what she pictured from her bedroom in Cambridge.

'I can't believe how much rubbish there is.'

She feels Taka stiffen slightly beside her. 'It's not "rubbish". Don't call it that, please. It's just people's lives in pieces.'

'Sorry. I didn't mean to—'

'I know.' Taka flashes her a smile then points up. 'Look!'

She follows his gaze to see a large half chunk of moon sailing free of the clouds. 'Waning gibbous.'

'What does that mean? Astrology?'

'Ha no! It just means it's getting smaller. The full moon the other night was just awesome, floating above all this . . .'

'What about the radiation?'

'It's OK here, most of the worst of it got blown inland, like east of Fukushima City – but there are hotspots so you have to be a bit careful. We got a gizmo. You all right? You look really pale.'

'I'm cold.'

'So let's get warm. Then we'll make a plan,' Taka says.

'Taka-san, I so wanted to talk to you. For months and months. It's like a sign, meeting you.'

He rolls his eyes. 'Karma? Destiny? Poor you, if I'm your flipping destiny! And you can drop the "san" you know.'

When she looks back at him there's no trace of the smile. In the gloom his face just looks as deadly serious as she's ever seen it.

3

Omurice at Jimi's

THE DOWNSTAIRS IS A MESS.

Saturated tatami mats are half ripped up and the smell of mould and damp hangs over everything. A sofa lies on its back and a big TV has fallen face down on a heap of magazines and books.

'You're really living here?' Yūki says, picking her way uncertainly across the threshold.

'Upstairs.' Taka points. 'And the kitchen's OK ish at the back, it's higher. Just got to be a bit careful with fuel. And fetch drinking water.'

'What about electricity?'

'Mrs Komori has it now and then. I charge my phone there. There was a big aftershock last week and they haven't got it hooked up here yet. Mobile signal comes and goes too. I keep everything I need upstairs - you get all kinds of things trying to get in.'

'Things?'

242

'Foxes. A wild boar the other day. I was washing at the sink and it scared the bejeepers out of me. There's a torch there by the door, flick it on, will you?'

She watches him heaving the red kerosene tank over the threshold in the dance of the torchlight. Is this really a good idea? There was that stuff Grandpa said about him being in trouble after all and she hardly knows him. Maybe it would be better to head back to the Kujaku and take a chance on Mrs Komori . . .

She reaches for the phone in her pocket, but when he turns back to her, his smile is so bright in the torch beam that her thumb slides off the button again.

'So, please make yourself at home.'

'I'm a bit hungry, but no problem if it's difficult.'

'There you go with that polite stuff again!' He starts up the stairs. 'I'll make you some *omurice* – there's still some rice in the cooker. It's about the only thing I'm any good at.'

'And when's your dad back?'

He shakes his head. 'Not entirely sure . . . Here, give me the torch, will you.' His hand brushes hers, a reassuringly warm point of contact, and then he lights up the stairs. 'See, the water only came up a few steps. The rest was fine.'

At the top they turn left into a big, tatami-matted room. A round stove is already throwing a circle of orange around it, and Yūki steps into the warmth with relief, ice cold fingers thawing. Taka flicks on a camping lamp, and then deftly lights an old fashioned oil lantern. 'It's all stuff from when me and Dad go camping in the mountains. Cosy right?'

A futon lies rolled to one side, a bunch of clothes neatly folded over a chair. Near the window on a writing desk is a two-ringed gas stove, a kettle and a dented rice cooker beside it.

'You absolutely sure it's OK if I stay?'

'Absolutely. Survivors' club kind of thing. Or you can bed down with the ghosts outside.'

She glances at the night filling the window at the far end of the room. 'Come on . . .'

'I told you. It's weird. I'll get some bedding.'

'Taka-san?'

'Yep?'

'Do you think the police will find me here? I mean, I don't care if they find me tomorrow evening – but I want to get to the house before they do.'

'Nobody knows I'm here apart from that old gangster and Komori-san and they're cool about it. I was supposed to stay in Osaka with my mum and her new bloke, but I hated it. I told them I was off to Tokyo to find a job. And then I came back here – to be with Dad. He always says his migraines go away when I'm around. He stuck by me when I was having a bad time last year . . .'

'Grandpa said you were in some trouble?'

Taka screws his mouth to one side. 'I'll tell you about it later, Yūki. But do me a favour and let your folks know what's going on. I'll get cooking . . .'

'Um, I really need the toilet.'

He points to a door. 'Just through there, first door, take the

244

torch. Listen, if it's just . . . a number one, don't flush. Sorry to be personal and all, just need to save water, OK?'

Back in the fold of the heater's warmth Yūki looks around properly. It's a traditional room, dark wood beams and paper-panelled *shōji* sliding doors. A stack of wavy books lie on a shelf near the futon – Japanese history, self-help books and one or two manga – and a chessboard is set out with a handful of pieces on the low table. Taka is cracking eggs, his movements precise.

'I'm getting all my food from Komori-san,' he mutters. 'Have a look at the view we've got while I make this for you . . .' He nods to one of the doors.

Reluctantly she moves out of the warmth, slides the door and finds herself in an enclosed balcony, with large square windows, their internal shutters gapped to frame the mess of the port area. Her gaze lingers on it again, remembering that first view of the devastation a year ago, and her slide down into hypothermia. Then drifts beyond it, up to the vastness of the ocean.

Her breath catches in her throat, fingers reaching for the cold glass.

A fleet of pale clouds are sailing above the black wall of the sea. The moon emerges again, setting lines of silver on the innumerable wave crests running to the horizon. The sense of space – of limitless power – nudges that thing lurking in its lair, and in her body she feels the extraordinary weight of the water again, the chaotic power of the wave, and she is back in the tsunami, tumbling and lost and giving up and everything is fading and . . .

'You must be really hungry,' Taka says from right beside her, startling her from the panic's grip. 'Come back, and let's get warm.'

Her heart is tapping away in her ears, but she follows Taka back into the main room, closing the ocean off with the sliding door, breathing in warmth, the first comforting sniff of the omelette, grabbing a breath.

'Everything fine, Yūki?'

'Yes, I'm fine.'

'Just let your folks know you're not freezing to death? I don't want to be done for kidnap or something. Not with my charge sheet!'

There's no putting it off, she knows that, and she takes another deep breath and reaches for her phone. The start-up seems to take for ever, and when she flicks from flight mode it takes even longer to find a weak, one bar signal. She waits, and then – heart sinking – watches the notifications popping up. Missed calls: 24, 25, 26, 27. Voicemail messages: 9. Texts: 24.

No way she can bear to listen to Mum or Dad's agonised voices, and she knows what they will be saying. And there are missed calls from Tokyo landlines and withheld numbers that might be police or something. Quickly she scans the texts, which basically repeat a few obvious lines over and over again:

Where are you? What are you doing? xx

Are you all right? Please call. We're not cross, but please let us know where you are.

Go to a kōban police box and let them look after you.

246

Kazuko chipping in: *You can tell Auntie anything, sweetheart. Anything! Just take care.*

And one from Joel answering her last one: *Risk? OK, cool. But pls be safe. Let me know how it goes. J* ☺

And one more from Mum: *Are you in Osōma? If so go to Mrs Komori at the Kujaku and call us. Just spoke to her. She promised to help. We love you. But please think what this is like for me. Mum x*

She feels a stinging stab of guilt now, and, afraid that the phone might suddenly ring in her hands, she hits reply to the last text and types super-fast: *I'm fine. Please don't worry. I will be back the day after tomorrow. Promise promise, I am safe and warm. Please let me do this. Thank you and sorry. I am OK. Yūki xx* and then hits send, holding up the phone to try and make the signal stronger.

As soon as she sees the 'sent' message she fumbles the phone off, and thrusts it into her rucksack, letting out a huge rush of breath.

'Well?' Taka calls from the stove, beating the eggs in a glass jug.

'I said I was fine.'

'You were lucky to get a signal. Did you tell them it's safe enough here?'

'*Is* it safe?'

'See for yourself.' He nods at a small yellow device on an armchair. 'Just push the button in the middle at the bottom.'

The Geiger counter is wrapped in plastic, about the size and

247

shape of a mobile. She presses the button marked 'on', and waits as the readout flickers a string of kanji before numbers appear. 0.48 µSv.

'What does it say?'

'0.48 something.'

'Micro Sieverts. That's fine. Not much more than background really. You'll get like a dental X-ray's worth every fortnight at that rate.'

'Isn't that a lot?'

'Not really.'

'How do you know so much about it?'

'You need to learn this stuff fast,' Taka laughs, pouring the eggs into a pan, setting the mixture sizzling, 'and I'm like really smart you know.'

She looks at the chessboard, relaxing just a bit at last. 'That day on the train – why did you say you were at a kickboxing tournament?'

'I was trying to impress you.'

'That's about the last thing that would impress me.'

'I realised that as soon as I said it. I'm not great at chat really. Or talking to girls. Dad says I read too much.'

'What kind of things?'

'Oh, all kinds of stuff. Weird manga. Quite a lot of science, you know stuff about cosmology, and even some philosophy and psychology believe it or not.' He grins. 'Chess books of course! Surprised?'

'Kind of–'

'Not what you expect from the son of a Tōhoku taxi driver? Thing is, taxi drivers are real thinkers, you know – they see a lot, hear a lot, have a lot of time to mull things over. He wanted me to go to university, but now I don't know.' He looks up. 'So? Any other messages? Like from the police?'

'One from a friend of mine. He helped me this year.'

Taka quickly nudges the sides of the omelette away from the edge of the blackened pan. 'Boy?'

'Just a friend.' She goes over to him. 'Taka-san, seriously, what did you mean about it being scary out there? You keep hinting at stuff, and then you stop.'

Taka focuses on the eggs. 'Well, it's probably just imagination, but . . .'

'But what?'

'OK.' He puffs out his cheeks. 'Well, I was in the zone – just inside, but quite near the sea. And it was getting dark. And I saw . . . a figure. A person.'

'A figure?'

'Yep, but he was like dressed all in white – and he was just standing there looking straight my way, and I called out to him, and he just kind of stared at me. And I suddenly felt really odd, and then he drifted, you know, across the ground. Instead of walking. Like he wasn't really there, or like he was projected, you know?' He shakes his head.

A shiver chases through her. 'A ghost?'

'*Funayūrei*. But it was probably just imagination, right? This place does things to your head.'

249

There's a long silence, just the sizzle from the pan.

'You're not pulling my leg?'

'Why would I do that? Shit, it's burning.' Quickly he spoons cooked rice with a wooden paddle into the omelette, folds it, and slides the fluffed up yellow half-moon onto a plate.

He plonks it on the low table near the heater, and beckons her to sit. 'Come on, eat while it's hot.'

Yūki's mind is still conjuring images of the floating white figure, a hint of the shiver still trembling in her back. 'What about you?'

'I had spaghetti Bolognese with Komori-san. She's an amazing cook.'

Yūki sits down and puts her hands together. '*Itadakimasu*.'

'If I had any ketchup I'd have written a nice message on it.'

'What would you have written?'

'I dunno. *Okaeri!* Or *yokatta* because I really am glad to see you. Is it salty enough? I've almost run out, but I put some soy and seaweed stock in it. Does the trick normally.'

She rolls the hot egg and rice around her mouth, sucking in air to cool it a bit. It tastes really, really good. '*Oishii*,' she says through the mouthful.

Taka smiles and takes another pull from his coffee can.

She takes another three forkfuls and then looks back at him. 'So, when you saw that figure you were in the zone, right?'

'Uh huh.'

'So what's it like in there?'

'It's kind of strangely peaceful somehow, but it's a horrible mess in places . . .'

250

'And what happened next? With this man you saw?'

Taka raises his eyebrows. 'He vanished, and then I *thought* I saw these other figures coming up out of the waves in the distance. It was late, and there was a bit of mist – and it scared the hell out of me. I just ran like crazy for home and chucked salt all over myself.' He takes another sip. 'But you know, there are loads of stories going around. A woman in Minamisōma told Mrs Komori that late one night the doorbell went – and when she answered there was nobody there, just a pool of water on the step – and her daughter's shoes, neatly placed together. Her daughter had died in the wave, right? Lots of people are trying to go home.'

'I read stuff like that online.' She takes another warm bite of the *omurice*. 'Taka-san, what happened to you?'

'Me?' He pushes a hand up into his hair. 'Doesn't really matter, does it?'

'It does . . . I want to know. I tried to phone you like a dozen times. And I asked Takeda-san if she knew. And then I got that weird call from your number, but it was like there were hundreds of people talking at once. Loads of people saying *moshi moshi* like they were all trying to be heard. I mean it could have been ghosts, like one of those stories about mobiles calling from dead people . . . ?'

'If they were ghosts they're not supposed to be able to say *moshi moshi* though, right?' Taka shrugs. 'It was probably just a technical fault, we get loads of things like that. Listen, you've got to drop the "san". Just Taka, right?'

'OK, sorry.'

251

'I'm glad you were thinking about me though. And dreaming about me! You sure we weren't getting it on?!'

She chokes on a mouthful of *omurice*. 'No!!'

Taka laughs. 'Sorry! Sorry . . .'

'How did you lose your phone, were you in the wave too?' Yūki says, trying to regain her composure.

'I think so.'

'You *think* so?'

His voice drops. 'I saw Shuto get swept away - you know the guy on the train with me that day?'

Yūki nods.

'As the wave went back out I managed to scramble out of our house and I saw him just get swept away in front of me.' He waves his hand out towards the sea. 'Shuto was only about like twenty metres away, but I couldn't do anything. He just looked - I dunno - surprised. I got down into the port as the water went back out, looking for him, and helped some people who were injured. It was awful - people face down in the mud, really banged up, you know. And I helped get somebody out of a car that was half buried and then that secondary wave came and I must have got hit by something and went under. And then I don't remember any more of that day. They brought me unconscious to the community centre on a stretcher. Bloody authorities didn't come for ages they were so worried about the radiation. And then the reactor went all Chernobyl on us and we got bused out to a school in Miyagi somewhere, and . . . I saw a couple of people die there in the gym.'

His voice has got thicker, quieter as he talks, so quiet now she can hardly hear him, and there are tears in his eyes, but he wipes them away and forces a smile. Tentatively Yūki edges around the table towards him, but he holds up a hand.

'I'm OK, I don't want to get into it now.'

'And you went to Osaka and then you came back?'

'I had to come back. Just like you.'

'Don't you care about your health?'

Taka is silent for a moment. 'It's stupid, I spent all my life wanting to get away from this place and then I couldn't wait to get back!'

'What about your dad?'

Taka puffs out his cheeks, looking away. 'Been here all his life, and his dad and his dad . . . You know, that kind of thing.'

Yūki edges back to her cushion. She listens to the silence beyond the room. 'Taka-san, you don't have to come with me tomorrow,' she says. 'If you don't, I'm going anyway. But it would be good if you did come. I'd like it.'

'Of course I'll come! I'm not letting you stumble around on your own! It's called the Difficult-to-return Zone for a reason, you know. We'll get there and remember your grandpa – and everyone else who died – and get back before it's dark.'

'Have you been as far as our house?'

'Not quite. The cliff road is washed out in places. And there are security patrols to dodge. And God knows what else we'll find – nobody's been doing much clearing up in the zone, Yūki. There could be bodies—'

But when Taka looks back a hint of his lopsided smile is there again.

253

'What?'

'Who'd have thought that stupid boy with the water gun and little Miss Manga would be going on a trip like this together! Tsunami Boy and Tsunami Girl!' He picks up the Geiger counter, glances at it, and peers away again towards the zone. 'I'll come with you on one condition.'

'What's that?'

'That you sign something saying it was all your idea. I don't want your parents blaming me when we get back. I've got to keep my nose clean.'

'I'm sixteen.'

'Yeah, you said. All grown up.' He looks at her. 'I didn't recognise you at first that day on the train. Hey, want to know what I thought?'

Yūki feels her cheeks growing warm. 'What?'

'I thought, *Wow, that's some cool foreign chick.* And then I realised–'

'And you thought, *Oh it's just that weird* hāfu *girl* or something.'

'I thought, wow, she's really something now. Hot. I like the plait by the way.'

There's no hiding that blush. The embarrassment, the omelette, Taka's joke about getting it on, the coffee's race all working together . . .

But then she feels odd, and reaches out to steady herself on the table as she hears a faint chattering from downstairs, glasses and crockery rattling, the door to the corridor joining in *kataka-takatakata*. She braces but the sound dies quickly away.

'You OK?'

'Was that an aftershock?'

'Just a little one. Get them all the time. Freaks me out when we don't get them! Let's get the stuff together for the morning and get some sleep.'

'Where?'

'Here of course. Only got one heater. I don't want you to freeze to death.'

Yūki gazes around the room. Beyond the tiredness there's a sensation of something like vertigo, something she can't quite place for a moment. Not anxiety, but a bit like it. Maybe, just maybe, it's excitement. Apart from a brief taste this morning running for the station it's something she hasn't felt for what feels like years. She looks back at Taka, shadows cutting angular shapes on his face.

'Taka-san? Did you think about *me*? I mean after the wave and stuff?'

He looks at her. 'Of course. I told you, I heard you survived so . . .'

'You could have let me know you were OK.'

'*I* didn't have a number or anything.' He points at his nose. 'Anyway I thought you weren't interested! I was hitting on you pretty hard on the train and you didn't seem to notice. Come on, let's get warm, and snug.'

'I knew you were hitting on me.' She eyes the futon.

He laughs. 'Cross my heart, I'll be a real gent. Dad brought me up that way.'

5

Into the Zone

IT TAKES A FULL MINUTE or so to remember where she is.

For once she has had no dreams: just a sleep that feels deeper than anything she's felt in a year or more. Or maybe there was a dream? Somebody singing – but she has no idea what the song was now, or who was singing it. Just an echo of an echo.

First light has turned the *shōji* panels pale grey. Taka lies curled on his side with his back to her, his upper arm flopped back in her direction, his hair a black mess on the pillow. She gets up, edging out into the cold and down the corridor to the toilet. The plastic slippers inside the door are like blocks of ice, and the toilet seat heating won't work of course, and she shivers as she sits there, thinking about the day ahead. A calendar on the back of the door shows a hot-spring pool in the snow and is flipped to March. But it's March last year. Her eyes move to Friday the 11th – nothing marked on the day, it just looks like it should have been a day like any other. No more, no less.

It all happened a year ago.

She tries to concentrate on the hot water and the steam in the photo and then goes back to the main room, looking at Taka sleeping. He looks younger somehow, not the cocky teenager on the train, not the gaunt-faced young man from last night. Almost like a little boy curled tight.

'Taka-san?'

'Mmmm.' He opens his eyes a fraction. '*Ohayō*. Morning. You said "san" again.'

'Sorry. We should get going. If we're going, right?'

'Yep. OK. Give me a minute.' He reaches his fingers towards her. 'Listen. I was awake in the night, thinking. I don't want to get you into any trouble.'

'I have to go, I told you.'

He sits up, rubbing his eyes. 'I know. But I mean what are you hoping to do?'

'I just need to be there at the time the wave came. Say a prayer, I don't know. I'm making it up as I go along.'

'We'll just have to be very careful.' Taka nods, stretching. 'I'll bring some incense – there must be some in the cupboard here somewhere. We used to go and do my grandparents' graves every year at Bon. Let's get there and back in daylight.'

'Why?'

'Because it's really hard to see anything in the dark, of course.'

'What do you think the worst is that could happen to us?'

'Very worst? Get a bit too much radiation and end up with some cancer or something in years to come. Get arrested . . .'

His features are a blur in the dawn light.

259

'You're OK, are you, Taka-san? You look thin.'

He waves the thought away. 'I'm fine. Needed to lose some weight.'

'Should we leave your dad a note or something?'

'He won't be back today. There's been a lot of snow further north.' He pushes a smile across his face and heads towards the toilet. 'Can you boil some water on the ring there?'

'Sure.'

'And let's get the heater going harder. And pack some supplies.'

Twenty minutes later, red bean cakes and a cup of tea warming her insides, Yūki steps out into the cold as Taka shuts the door firmly behind them.

'Aren't you going to lock it?'

'You're kidding me, right? In Osōma? Now? I mean unless some *tanuki* wants to steal my chess set . . .'

A single crow is flapping around the mass of wreckage below, and from somewhere far away there's the sound of machinery, but in the foggy air, it's hard to tell where it's coming from.

Taka slings a drawstring bag over his shoulder and switches on the Geiger counter. 'You ready?'

'Ready.'

'*Ikou.* Let's go.'

In silence they move away up the elevated road. Banks of dark clouds are packing over the sky and the air has the taste of snow about it. Yūki adjusts her half empty rucksack, anxiety and excitement both pushing her heart to beat that bit faster than it should be. But it feels so good to be moving again. For better or worse she's on her way, the last few kilometres to the house. To home.

'Last chance.' Taka looks back at her over his shoulder. 'You're really sure?'

'Totally, totally sure.'

'Sounds like you had some problems. In England.'

'I – I get these . . .' She can't remember the Japanese word for panic attacks. 'Sometimes I get very frightened – here in my chest – and I freak out a bit.'

'Ah, *panikku hossa*! OK, so what do I do if you get one?'

'Just remind me to breathe. Talk to me.'

'No problem! So let's talk now. Like we're just going for a stroll by the sea.'

'About what?'

'Normal stuff. Normal teenage stuff. Boyfriends, girlfriends, whatever.'

'To be honest, that's just as scary.'

He grins. 'Right?'

They're leaving the mess of the port behind, the road bending towards the community centre on higher ground. She pulls a woolly hat down harder over the plait.

'OK. So – so tell me what happened in Osaka, Taka-san?'

'Oh God. Argued with my mum's new boyfriend like crazy. He's a real loser. Had a brief fling with an older girl.'

She feels a twinge in her stomach and she reaches for another

261

topic. 'And what about that trouble here, before the wave. You didn't tell me last night.'

'It was another thing, with another girl . . .'

'Another girl?' she hears herself echo, wincing at the tone in her voice.

'Don't make it sound like that! They were both very short *things*!' Taka takes a deep breath. 'What about you, you must have been doing something in your room all this time?'

'Work for tutors that school arranged. Things my therapist gets me to do.' She hesitates. 'I tried to do some drawing.'

'Tried? You must be like amazing now?'

'No. I pretty much gave up for ages so I'm really bad.'

'Says who?'

'Says me.'

'What kind of things were you trying to draw?'

'A fox. And a kind of super hero.'

'We could do with one of those! I bet it was way better than you think. A hundred thousand yen!' He turns and smiles, then points ahead. 'Before we get to the community centre and the shrine there's a bend in the road. And just round that is the new checkpoint. So we have to detour. You ready?'

She remembers pausing below the shrine in the car with Grandpa that night: the paper charms shifting in the breeze, the foxes with their sharp eyes, the way Jiro stared into the dark space beyond the *torii. We'll come back tomorrow*, he had said. *I promise*. But he never got the chance.

'I'd like to see the shrine.'

'It's too risky. Sorry, Yūki. *Gomen ne*. We'll have to go round.' He glances at the Geiger counter clicking away in his hand, and shows her the readout: 0.85. 'No problem here, but if it gets way up – I mean four or five or above we'll turn back. Deal?'

She nods, and lifts the rucksack on her shoulders. 'I just want to get there. Even if we can't be there long.'

'OK, need to be quiet.'

It's a little brighter now, the sun just visible as a pale white disc behind the clouds. The road rises away towards where the trees start, but Taka beckons her to follow him as he takes a sharp right off the tarmac, through a narrow gate and along a faint path that leads across a field below the woods.

They're only about twenty paces across it when there's the growl of an engine from where the road disappears into the pines.

'Patrol. Run, Yūki!'

Taka takes off, hoodie flying back to set his hair loose, and she sprints after him, rucksack and plait banging on her back.

Over the sound of their pounding footsteps the engine is getting louder as they cross the open ground. In the middle of the field there's a telegraph pole choked by a tangle of bushes and Taka heads straight for it, throwing himself round and then down onto the ground. A heartbeat later, like a baseball player diving for home, Yūki slides into him with a thump. Her heart is bounding like crazy, but when she looks at Taka she sees he's smiling as he fights to get his breath.

'Already – exciting, huh? Can you see anything?'

Peering back through the bush she can just make out the road. There's movement between the last of the trees and then a police car slips slowly into view.

'It's stopping,' she whispers.

There's the sound of the handbrake, a car door opening, and then . . . silence. No footsteps, no voice calling out, just the faint rumble of the engine - and from somewhere behind them now another sound like muffled drumming. Yūki turns to see a few snowflakes falling and pockets of mist forming and moving on the grassy slope below. Things already feel a little strange here, and they're only minutes from Taka's house.

'What if he doesn't move? What if he's on guard?' she hisses.

'We'll just have to wait.'

'Is he looking for me?'

'Maybe.'

The wraiths of mist drift towards them, and she nudges a bit closer to Taka.

'Don't worry.'

'I'm not worrying. I–'

The ground beneath them is shaking now, and the drumming is suddenly very loud.

'It's a quake!' she hisses.

Taka shakes his head, and points back behind them. A black figure is looming out of the mist, getting larger very quickly, and seconds later a horse rears into sight, nostrils flared, thundering towards them. Its mane shakes as it runs, the steam condensing out of wide nostrils, and it hammers wildly past, sending up clods of earth. A few dozen paces beyond them the horse lets out an unearthly whinnying neigh, and then powers away.

'What's wrong with it?' Yūki hisses.

'Something spooked it maybe.' He shakes his head. 'I'm just glad we're doing this together.'

'Me too.'

From the road, there's a blurt of static from a walkie-talkie and the car door clunks shut – and then the police car revs once, twice and grinds away down the road towards the port.

Taka lets out a rush of breath, and glances at the radiation meter.

'Let's go. Race you to the wood!'

He gets there first by a long stride and comes to a stop under the pines. A huddle of wild camelia bushes screen them from the road, thick glossy leaves trembling in the wind and, ahead, a little path snakes away into the silent dark spaces of the trees.

A line of swans are passing overhead, heading inland, their wingbeats dragging their wild calls across the sky. Those migrating swans used to thrill her on winter visits – now they just feel sad and forlorn somehow.

'Are we in the zone yet?'

Taka shakes his head. 'This way. Need to be really quiet.'

He leads her into the wood, their trainers soft on the fallen pine needles and sandy soil. Every now and then a push of wind goes sighing through the canopy. The first time she's heard that sound since the endless night walk with Takeda-san. Seems like a lifetime ago, but somehow also as if it was just a few nights ago, the memories starting to flood back. She tries to cut them short.

'I think I came this way maybe,' she says, pulling alongside him. 'The night after.'

He gives her a quick reassuring smile. 'I guess you must've. Hush up a bit though, we're not far off the checkpoint.'

Sure enough, a few hundred metres further on, it's easy to pick out men's voices on the road, ahead and some way off to their left.

'That's it,' Taka whispers. 'They won't see us. There's some barbed wire ahead but it's kind of trampled down. Don't trip on it.' He glances at the dosimeter in his hand, then waves her on.

The voices of the men come closer and closer, and Yūki focuses on putting her feet down softly, her breath practically stopped in her throat. The bushes screen them, but it feels like any sound they make will be loud in the wood's silence. One step, then another, as the path leads them down into a boggier hollow to where the mist is pooling and thickening the cold air, then on in silence back up the other side. When one of the men coughs it sounds so close that even Taka half jumps. He grins, then signals away to the right, to where the track peters out in a mess of mud and dead leaves that squelch under their feet.

'Shhh, very quiet now.' He mouths the words more than says them.

A few paces further he points at strands of rusty barbed wire twisted in the undergrowth, pushing it down with his foot and waving Yūki over it, before leading them on down another slope.

266

Slowly the voices fade away, and after another hundred metres or so, he stops in the darkness, the light from the Geiger counter screen spilling up onto his face, sending shadows chasing across his features.

'What's it now?'

'One and a half. That bit of old fence marked the edge.' He spreads his arms. 'So. Welcome to the zone. Taka's Zone Tour starts here. No charge for our first guest.'

There doesn't feel like there's any real difference, no tingling, no change in the air temperature.

'Here, you take the dosimeter, Yūki,' Taka says. And maybe, as she takes the gadget from him, there *is* a subtle shift in the air around them. Like the silence is even deeper somehow, or the mist thicker.

She shivers. 'It's kind of exciting. Scary too.'

'Right?'

'Where now?'

'We'll keep off the road a while longer just in case. They sometimes send patrols down as far as where it got washed away. Otherwise just watch your step. And we just need to be careful for wild boar – they can be pretty stroppy. Keep an eye on the dosimeter.'

'Is this the way you went – when you saw the ghosts on the beach?'

'Yep.'

'I don't really understand why you took the risk.'

He waves vaguely towards the sea. 'Just curious.'

Those shadows on Taka's face had made him look so strange . . . She reaches out with a lightly curled fist and bumps his shoulder. 'Taka, you *are* real, aren't you?'

He reaches down and takes her cold hand and plants it against his warm cheek. He holds it there for a moment and she can feel the downy stubble that's sprouted there in the last year. He holds her hand a beat, looks into her eyes, then lets it fall.

'Real as you! Well done, by the way!'

'Well done, what?'

'You managed not to say Taka-san. Big step!'

She smiles. 'Tell me about what happened to you, Taka.'

'Nah. Something upbeat. I know. Tell me about this hero of yours.'

'It's not anything.'

He glances back over his shoulder as he starts to walk again. 'We're breaking the law together now and maybe frying our bits so you might as well drop the "I'm no good" crap. I'd *like* to know.'

The quiet is intense now, even the wind in the tree tops has stilled as they make their way down into another hollow. Their footsteps and breathing could be the only sounds in the whole of the zone.

Taka pushes his Japanese into super-polite mode. 'Please, Hara-san, I would be humbly grateful if you would possibly share this information with me.'

She smiles again, and takes the plunge. 'Well. I used to draw him all the time when I was small. He was a boy who lived at the bottom of the sea. He had to sing to the catfish – you know, who cause the earthquakes?'

'You mean Namazu?'

'A bit – but I had lots of them.'

'And?'

'And he fought baddies and rescued people, stuff like that. It was just childish type stuff really.'

'No, sounds great! What happened to him in the end?'

'I stopped drawing.'

'No, I mean what happened in the story?'

'It didn't really have an end or a beginning, you know, it was just like you do when you're little. He calmed haunted umbrellas and *kappa* and fought evil monsters. And sang songs.'

Taka laughs. 'Man, those *karakasa* umbrellas can be a pain!'

'If you're gonna make fun—'

'No, no. I'm not. I'd love to see some.'

'It all got washed away, I guess. But – but I've been trying to draw him again. A friend was nagging me to do it.'

'A friend? The boy who sent you the text?'

'Yep, Joel.'

Taka smiles. 'Boyfriend?'

'No. It's not like that.'

'Have you had a boyfriend?'

'Yes,' she lies, not wanting to sound like a little kid, then changes her mind. 'I mean, no. No I haven't. How about you?'

'That thing with the girl in Osaka. That was just – physical, if you know what I mean. And I went out with the girl from the sushi shop before that, but only for a few weeks. That's what the trouble was about . . .' He lets out a deep breath that condenses in the air above. 'Now she's dead . . . tsunami.'

'I'm sorry.'

'It was all over well before the quake. But it's so sad.'

They walk on in silence for a long minute.

'Taka, you said to be honest with each other, right? What was the trouble?'

He sighs. 'Well, she had been going out with this idiot from Fukushima City. He roughed her up a bit. So I kicked his ass – tried to – and he and his mates kicked my ass back. A lot worse. Broke two of my ribs! So I smashed his car windscreen and punctured all his tyres and spray-painted something really rude on the door and then he reported me to the police. And then we went out with each other for a bit.' He looks up. 'She was a good kisser, Kizuki. How can someone kiss that good and then be dead? Warm and so alive, then gone. Doesn't make sense.'

Despite the gloom she sees him blush, and he turns away, and walks on into the gloom. A single flake of snow comes spiralling down into the dark space under the trees, and she watches it fall for a moment, like something sinking slowly in dark water. Then hurries along the path.

'I'm sorry about your girlfriend,' Yūki says, as she catches up with him again.

'We weren't that much really. Change subject. Hey, did he have superpowers?'

'Who?'

270

'Your super guy.'

'Kind of. He controlled the sea. And he could run on the surface of the water. But mostly he saved people: sailors drowning or whales that had got beached.'

'And what was his name?'

'Han Nami. Half Wave – because he was little.'

'Or because he was like you, right? Half and half. Half Japanese, half English.'

Yūki stops again on the fallen pine needles.

'Well, no, I mean I'm quarter Japanese.'

'Yeah, but part this, part that, right? Part land, part sea, "where's home?" kind of thing?'

It seems ridiculous now, super obvious, but she's never thought of it before! He was always just Han Nami in her mind. Half Wave, because he was small.

'And everyone loved him, I bet? Super popular like you probably wanted to be?'

For a second she feels annoyed that Taka's spotted something so obvious, and is analysing her like he's some kind of expert.

'Well. It was just for fun, nothing serious.'

They're dropping further down into the depression in the woods. 'It sounds great, Yūki. Honestly. I'm not trying to be a smartass!'

'Grandpa was talking about him that day. Just before the quake.'

'And you're drawing him again?'

'I want to try and do a grown-up version. And – it's weird – when

271

I was in the wave, even when I thought I was drowning and every-thing, I had this really strong image of him. I haven't told anyone else that, it just seems so dumb.'

Taka is quiet for a while, scuffing the ground with his trainers. 'Well. Sounds like something you should keep working at . . .'

'That's what my therapist said. I've got to learn to draw properly first,' Yūki says. 'I'm just like all the other thousands of kids doing lame fan art and stuff—'

The dosimeter in Yūki's hand suddenly shudders, and she almost drops it as the alarm shrieks into the stillness. Wide-eyed she looks down to see the readout is flashing the kanji for danger： 危険

Taka grabs it. 'Shit! I forgot the sound was on.' He presses a button and kills the beeping dead. 'They might have heard it at the road.'

'Is it bad? The reading?' She'd been almost relaxing, but now her heart is bumping away again.

'Um, no it's OK. I've got the threshold set really low for you.' He looks around him. 'I guess lots of rain collects down here, so the radiation will be higher. I don't think I came exactly this way last time . . .'

'You *don't think*? We're not lost, are we?'

'Don't worry. One way is the sea, and the other way – about three kilometres or so – is the main road, you know Route 6. So we're somewhere between those. But we'd better move it a bit in case they heard us.'

There's a noise behind them then, and a soft crack of a twig or small branch, and then a sudden rustling off to their right. A few more snowflakes come spiralling down as they both spin around to look.

'Was that them?'

'No. Animal. Maybe a fox. Or a boar. We better get out of the hollow. We'll head up to the coast road. Let's move . . .'

6

Crushed Hearse

THEY RUN. TRAINERS SCRABBLING UP the steeper side of the hollow, through a thicker packet of trees, and on for another five minutes of effort before Taka checks the Geiger counter again, and then at last slows his pace. He glances back at Yūki, smiling reassuringly.

'OK, it's OK here.'

The sound of the wind has returned, making the sighing it always does in the pines or telegraph wires near the sea.

And beyond that, Yūki can hear something else now – a noise that is so much a part of the world here, of her childhood, that it takes her a long moment to realise what it is she's hearing: the slow break and drag of breakers as the Pacific moves relentlessly against the shore. Last night, and seen from the train, their voice was muffled by glass. Now there's nothing between her and the waves.

She stops, listening to the heavy thud as each roller shatters, and braces for the surge of panic – but again nothing seems to be coming, and she pushes herself forward to hurry after Taka.

Oblivious he's walking with a swing to his step now, humming a tune under his breath.

As she catches him her ears sharpen, and she realises it's a very familiar tune indeed.

'I know that tune. Grandpa used to whistle it all the time.'

'I heard it on the radio the other night. Stuck in my head now.'

'But what a coincidence. It must mean something. Do you know what it's called?'

'*Let's Not Forget*. Or something like that. I used to think it was just a lame old song, but loads of musicians and celebs did a version of it for the disaster relief so it's been on the radio a lot.'

'How does it go? I don't know the words really.'

Taka frowns. 'Something like: *"Let's not forget how the tears blurred my eyes,"* um, *"let's not forget happiness under starry skies."'*

'Can you remember any more?'

'*"Love and happiness lie beyond the stormy waves, love and happiness . . ."'* His voice falters, unsure. 'I can't sing, never could.' He looks at her. 'You OK?'

Yūki nods. 'I just thought the waves might give me an attack or something. But I'm OK. Let's hum it as we go?'

'Sure. We have to head towards the cliff now. There's a high fence that runs round the grounds of the old folks' home.' He picks up the thread of the song, and Yūki falls in beside him and hums with him and remembers the thousands of times she heard Grandpa whistle those familiar phrases, her feet finding the rhythm, fresh momentum swinging her legs, the plait tapping her

276

rucksack, the trees sighing, the waves coming closer and closer but it's OK.

It's going to be OK, I can do it, she thinks.

Probably.

A few hundred more metres of scrubby pine and fir trees – and they emerge back onto the coast road. To their left it curves away towards the distant checkpoint and Osōma, but to the right, after fifty paces or so, the tarmac simply vanishes. Beyond there's a fine mist or spray hanging in the emptiness, and beyond that she can see a chunk of roadway hanging down from the far side of a chasm, its twisted guard rail broken off and dangling towards the thunder of unseen waves.

And those waves really are crashing away now, detonating against the foot of the landslip like thunder. From out of the woods a high chain-link fence runs almost to the very edge and then turns ninety degrees to run parallel to the drop along the remaining sliver of roadway.

Yūki gasps. 'I was here with Mrs Takeda. I saw it. But I don't remember it being that narrow.'

'A lot more fell away in one of the big aftershocks. You sure you're up to this?'

'Can't we just go inland?'

Taka shakes his head. 'Even if we climbed the fence there's a huge pile of debris not far off and when I got near it the Geiger went crazy. It's always safer the closer we are to the coast.'

*

277

An echo of the song is still looping in her head, the first two lines repeating, and then rising up for the third.

'We can't stop now,' she whispers to herself. Despite the lift of the song, the pounding of the surf has made her legs feel like water, and her mouth has gone dry.

The waves boom and crash, and a fine salt spray drifts across her face. She edges forwards and the churning water below comes into view.

Oh my God.

She's aware Taka is talking to her, but for a moment all she can do is stand there, eyes on the pounding waves. She feels his hand on her arm.

'Are you OK, Yūki? Do you need to breathe? I can do it with you. Yūki?'

'I – I'm OK. Just give me a minute?' Her eyes cross the chasm and then climb the raw cliff to the twisted guard rail, to the safety of the road beyond. But it's slippery, and her gaze just slides back down to the breakers below, churning crushed-up cliff and roadway and fallen trees about twenty metres below her.

Everything swims in her vision and she is in the wave again, fighting, fighting . . . the shock and cold and the going-under and down. Breath held, the blackness and violence and roaring, the sensation of swallowing water, her lungs on fire. Not OK, not OK, not OK . . .

'Hey, Yūki! Take a damn breath, will you?' Taka's voice is right in her ear. 'Come on, in . . . out . . . iiiiin . . . out. Nice deep breath.'

She nods, and holds his gaze, and reassured by his dark

eyes, she does her best to mirror his deliberately exaggerated breathing. A ragged gasp comes, then another slightly smoother.

'That's it, Yūki. Take another. We can go back. No problem if you want to go back.'

'No. I'll be OK.'

'Just take a minute. Then I'll go first.'

Slowly her breathing deepens, and it stops feeling like her chest is locked, and she nods again and waves him ahead. But still her legs feel like they will crumple beneath her and she knows she is shaking a bit. 'I'm fine. Thanks.'

'You don't look it.'

'I'm fine. Let's go.'

Taka gives her a concerned smile, and then guides them both to the lip of the void – and then lets go of her gently and edges out along the remaining tarmac over the roaring water: a metre, two, three.

'See, it's OK!' he calls, looking back. 'Come on – grip the fence just in case, like this.' He freezes for a second, then beckons her frantically. 'That police car's coming back.'

She glances round to see the blue lights strobing through the last pines behind them, and then, before she knows what she is doing she is running, out onto the exposed metre or so of weedy tarmac against the chain-link fence. Taka's moving faster now, keeping his fingers locked into the fence, shuffling along like a distressed caged animal.

To her left at the edge of her vision the space is a void that wants to suck her back into the ocean. Her fingers claw for the fence, a few metres behind Taka, locking into the mesh of the cold wire, and she glances back again just in time to see the headlights of the car coming round the bend.

Damn it, can't be stopped now. Not this close!

She lets go of the fence, and barges past Taka to his left, trainers teetering on the very edge of the drop, running full tilt along the ribbon of road, the ocean and sky filling one side and the dark woods and fence the other, the strength flooding back to her legs and she is surefooted, almost effortless, almost like she's flying . . .

She hurdles the twisted guard rail at the far side and dives into a clump of bamboo, hoping against hope that they haven't been seen, heart hammering. A fraction later Taka lands in a heap next to her, breathing hard, his eyes wide.

'Idiot!' he gasps. 'I said hold onto the freaking fence!'

'I just didn't want them to get us.'

'Better if we're arrested than dead, right?'

Yūki points back, through the shifting bamboo. The police car has pulled up about fifty metres before the gap, its windscreen wipers intermittently sweeping the sleety snow that is falling again.

'He didn't see us,' Yūki pants. 'I don't think he saw us. We're OK.'

'See that white line?' Taka hisses, pointing.

The sketchy white paint runs at the very edge of the remaining tarmac, practically drawn on nothing now. From here you can see just how horribly undercut the cliff road is.

'You ran along *that*. God knows how it held your weight. Maybe your family *are* totally crazy after all. Shit, Hara-san. Don't do that to me!' He rolls on his back, gazing up at the clouded sky. 'What's Mr Policeman doing now?'

The police car grinds gears and then starts to back away, headlights shaking as it reverses into a three-point turn. 'He's going.'

'We'll have to go back another way,' Taka says, sitting back up, getting his breath. 'That's just not safe. We can go up to Route 6.'

'You called me an idiot. Then you called me Hara-san! Make up your mind.'

'Sorry,' Taka says. 'But you scared the hell out of me.'

'I told you I was OK.'

'You didn't look it. Was that a panic attack then?'

'I'm fine.' And she feels it, she really does feel fine. Out of breath, heart still tapping fast, but her legs feel better again. She sweeps the plait out of the way, and looks him in the eye again, about to tell him that. But to her amazement she sees tears gathering in his eyes. 'Are *you* all right?'

He wipes them away with a quick flash of his hand. 'Try and listen to me, OK? I want you to be safe.'

'Are you crying?'

'No, no.' He sniffs hard, then gets to his feet, and offers her his hand and pulls her up. 'I'm happy if you must know. Happy to be here with you. I cry when I'm happy.'

Yūki takes a long look into his face, then smiles and turns for one more long look at the waves. 'Let's go then.'

She tugs her eyes free of the water, and together they march on down the road, through last summer's browned weeds coming up through the cracks in the tarmac, and behind them, beating slow time against the foot of the broken cliffs, the ocean booms and bangs and then fades away to background noise and no more.

The road jinks through corners she has known all her life – but wildness and neglect have started to transform things, to reclaim it bit by bit. Weeds encroaching, eddies of pulped paper and plastic on the roadside that you'd never normally see. A black motorbike lies on its side gripped by tangled, dried blackberry tendrils. A house on the right, that Yūki used to hurry past because it was supposed to be haunted, lies half collapsed, the car on the drive covered with grime and bird droppings, and the whole place feels like it's been abandoned for years, not just twelve months. Beyond that a huge red pine lies across the road like a barrier, roots and soil exposed to the salt air coming from the sea, and another beyond that. They clamber over both in silence as sleet turns to snow and then back to sleet again, and the road snakes back towards the cliffs, trees thinning to show the wide sweep of the low-lying landscape before them.

Yūki stares at in silence. Destruction as far as you can see: houses shunted off foundations and rammed into each other, broken corners of other buildings like snapped Lego, huge piles of wreckage, overturned cars and boats. Virtually no trees left standing. A few crows flap across the scene, other-wise everything is still. The only structures left standing are the elementary school with its concrete bell tower and modern-looking main building.

Taka points at it. 'I remember you in school – I must have been in sixth grade and you were in fourth?'

'It was only a term and a half, while Dad was doing some field-work in Sendai or something. I don't think I remember you there though, Taka.'

'I guess I just blended in.'

'And I must have stuck out.'

'Just a bit! I heard most of the current kids weren't there when the wave came. The ones that were got picked up in a lorry in the nick of time. The wave must have been huge out here . . .'

'I saw it hit the school,' Yūki says quietly. 'It was as high as the roof.'

Taka taps her shoulder and points to a small path that leads away down the wooded hillside to their left. 'You can get to the beach that way. I was down there when I saw those figures . . .'

'The *yūrei*?'

'Shh. Don't say it out loud, Yūki. But it feels much better being here with you. Having someone to talk to and everything.'

They walk on as the road heads back through the trees.

'Did I really stick out at the school, Taka?'

'Just a bit. You were – like wrapped up in your own little world. Super intense.'

'Mum thought it would be good for me but it was even harder than back home really. Trying to fit in.'

'It must have been. I mean, I never feel I fit, and I'm born and bred here. Being left handed didn't help maybe. I just didn't feel like the others. That's why I used to get so worked up, I guess.'

'Did you really smash that guy's car up?'

'Uh huh. I just lost it.' He picks up a long piece of broken bamboo and swishes it through the air. The snow has stopped and there's even a hint of the sun pushing back through the veil of the clouds. 'Forget all that rubbish – what kind of a ritual do you want to do when we get to the house?'

'In my dreams Grandpa's always beckoning me . . . like I need to do something important for him.'

'OK. So we need to see the shape of it all. Let's try and be logical like a chess problem, right? If he's in your thoughts then it means you can't let him go, or he can't go, depending on whether we think ghosts are real or not. Either way, something isn't finished, right? Any idea what that could be?'

'On the bluff he said he had to fetch something, or do something. Maybe it's to do with that.'

Taka comes to a stop, swishing his bamboo fast up and down, and then suddenly lets out a weird kind of growl from deep in his stomach.

'What is it?'

He starts walking again, head down. 'Do me a favour, Yūki? Tell me what happened to you that day? I need to know.'

'What's up?'

'Tell me in detail what happened to you.'

So – hesitantly at first, then gathering speed until the words are tumbling out – Yūki tells him the fullest version she's ever told anybody. About how hard the house shook, of being on the bluff with Grandpa, about him looking sad, then suddenly energised again and going down to the house. The wave coming. The stupid whistle. A little bit about what it felt like in the water and the sense of giving up and how peaceful it felt for a moment on the edge of drowning. And then being on the raft with the little fox.

There's a long silence when she's finished, just the sound of their footfall for a minute or so as Taka wafts his bamboo sword at the weeds. 'Wow, you went through far more than I did.'

'I kind of worried I might have died, you know, Taka. It's stupid. I really thought that for a bit.'

He nods. 'I kind of felt that – when we were in the refuge centre in Miyagi. It was freezing cold and I couldn't help the old people around me and . . .' He keeps his head faced resolutely forwards. 'You said your granddad went back down to the house?'

'Yes.'

'Do you know why?'

'To fetch something, he said. It's so stupid – what could have been so important? *Modoranai*, right? You never go back. I don't know, but I keep feeling it's all my fault. I mean I should have stopped him. I just feel so bad . . .'

'You can't dwell on guilt,' he says, his voice croaky. 'Even on crap TV chat shows they know that much.'

'But I could have stopped him, right? So it's my fault.'

Taka stops again abruptly. 'OK, listen. I – there's something I haven't told you.'

'What? What is it?'

'The thing is. I – I haven't been totally honest about something.' He lets out another low groan. 'The thing is, it's *my* fault he died.'

'What?!' Her voice is really loud in the stillness around them. A crow takes off from nearby, cawing loudly. 'How could it *possibly* be your fault?'

'I'm soooo sorry. God. If he hadn't gone down to the house to call me he'd have made it then.'

'To call you? What do you mean?'

'Your grandpa called me. When the quake came I was on the way back from the station. I missed the 2.38 after Dad dropped me there. I'd left my stupid phone like an idiot and Dad gave me a lift, but I missed the train anyway. So the quake hit and I lay down on the road near home until it was over. Then I ran home to check the house was OK, and see if anybody needed help in the port. I was about to go down there when the phone rang – the landline. It was your grandpa on the phone, Yūki. The reason he went down to the house was to call and warn us that he'd had a dream about – about me drowning. It freaked me out to be honest, but I thanked him and then I went upstairs to look out of the window rather than heading out on the port road. And that's why I survived. Because of your grandpa. And he died. Ohhhhhhhhh God.'

Yūki's eyes are open wide behind her glasses. 'It was *you* he dreamed about? He told me about the dream, but . . .' She blows out a deep breath, trying to make sense of it all. 'What time did you get the call?'

Taka sniffs. 'Um, about two minutes before the wave came. He

286

saved my life.' He chucks his bamboo into the undergrowth. 'I'm sorry. I wish he'd lived and I died. I really do.'

'Don't be stupid . . .'

In all the versions of Grandpa's last minutes she has never imagined he was phoning Taka. But it fits: the way he seemed preoccupied on the bluff, the way he suddenly decided to go down. Just after he'd tried his mobile again. It's the kind of thing he would do. And suddenly it feels like everything has moved just a bit more – all the stuckness and repetitive memories in her head shaken by what Taka has told her. Kind of unsettling, but kind of good at the same time.

'Are you mad at me?' Taka whispers, his head bowed now.

'No! Of course not. But why on earth didn't you tell me earlier? Why didn't you get in touch with me or something?'

'I didn't know how to say it. And I had my own problems going on too. No excuse I know but . . .'

'What – what did he say?'

Taka closes his eyes. 'He said, *You're going to think I'm mad, but I dreamt last night you got drowned, so please get to high ground.* Something like that.'

'How did he sound?'

'He sounded fine. I said, *What about you?* and he said he was going to grab something and go back up to you on the bluff, just to be on the safe side. And then he hung up.'

It's like Grandpa has suddenly come back to life a little bit, whispered fresh words in her ear.

'Are you cross with me, Yūki?'

'He said he was going to grab something? Did he say what?'

'No. Does it matter?'

'Maybe. I think maybe it's important about why he went down to the house.'

'More important than warning me you mean!'

'No. That's not what I meant. You sure he didn't say what?'

'Honestly I'd tell you if it could make me feel less bad.'

'I wish you'd told me sooner . . . but I don't think you should feel guilty, is what I'm trying to say.'

Taka forces a smile. 'Then you shouldn't either, right?'

'He told me he'd had a warning dream. But he didn't say it was you.'

'Let's walk again. Keep talking if you want.'

Pale sunlight is smudged on the road, and she looks at Taka in front of her, his slim shoulders pulled up towards his ears.

'Taka?'

'Uh-huh?'

'For what it's worth, I'm just so glad you didn't die.'

He screws his face to one side. 'Hardly makes up for losing someone great like your granddad, does it?'

'No, but I'm still glad.'

'So am I. I think.'

He nods, fills his lungs with air and holds it. Then points down the road, into the trees to the right, and lets the breath go in a huge rush. 'OK. Do you mind if we do something really quickly? A favour I promised someone in the shelter. Then at least I don't have to feel bad about that too.'

'What is it?'

'We're near the retirement home. I promised I'd take a message to someone's wife there.'

'But there's nobody there now surely. And I want to get to the house.'

'There was an old guy and he was on the way out. It was freezing in the shelter and we were all on these thin mats and some of the old folks were dying right there, it was horrible . . .'

'Why? Radiation and stuff?'

'Just cold and shock, I think. He'd left his wife's ashes here and he wanted to apologise to her for abandoning her. It won't take a moment, but I promised I'd do it if I got the chance.'

'OK, if we're quick. I want to be there for 2.46 p.m.'

'I know, I know. Ten minutes.'

Around the next bend a driveway leads off between two large stone pillars, the sign for 'Osōma Sun Retirement Community' hanging at an angle from the gateway. The air feels stiller here, sheltered from the sea, and in the distance to the south, there's the sound of machinery – it must be the nuclear plant or some kind of clean-up going on beyond that in Tomioka. But it sounds worlds away as they pad up the silent driveway between shaggy bushes and bramble tendrils snaking out onto the tarmac. Taka glances back over his shoulder. Every now and then she feels invisible spider webbing on her face and she brushes it away.

'You came here before, Taka?'

'Yeah, but I got a bit spooked . . . didn't really carry out my promise. If you make a promise you gotta keep it, right?'

289

'Why?'

'Because it's the right thing to do.'

'No, why did you get spooked, Taka?'

'It just felt weird.'

'Did people die here?'

'I guess.'

The road takes another long swoop to the right and a sprawling complex of modern buildings comes into sight. Two cars are parked on a weedy parking lot – a little white one and a low, ornate Japanese hearse. A big tree has fallen right across the bonnet of the hearse, smashing the windscreen, leaving the carved dragons and gold clouds on the back bubbling up from the dead copper foliage. On the side of the small white car somebody has spray-painted a single word in English in shaky black letters; TERROR.

Yūki stares at it. 'Who did that?'

Taka doesn't answer: his eyes are roving the car park, the buildings beyond, as he marches to where the drive widens and sweeps under a canopy at the front of the building. An ambulance is parked at an angle there, but it doesn't look like it's moved for ages. The main doors to the home are wide open, and rammed across them the ambulance's heavy wheeled stretcher blocks the threshold. There's another small car park just beyond and Taka takes a quick peak at it before coming back to join Yūki at the entrance, following her gaze into the darkened interior. It feels like looking into deep, still water. Not a whisper of air or breeze, just a stillness so absolute it almost feels solid.

Taka shuffles his feet, one hand on the back of his neck. 'OK, just let me do this.' He claps his hands together softly, twice. In the silence the sound echoes away down the corridor in front of them. 'Mrs Uemura, I have a message for you from your husband, Susumu,' Taka whispers. 'He says, Kayo, please forgive me for leaving you. You can't come to me but I will come to find you. Thank you for your love and care.'

He bows and holds it for a long beat before straightening again and glancing at Yūki. 'Do you think that was OK?'

'Yeah, really nice. Can you hear something?'

Somewhere deep within the building there's the whisper of a sound – something like running water, punctuated by a faint *tap tap tap* that might be snow melting or a burst pipe.

She peers into the gloom again. On the polished floor a wheelchair lies on its side about ten metres in, and a few shoes and slippers are scattered around it. Beyond that a big stack of white towels or blankets have spilled from an overturned hopper. You can smell musty damp, bleach, winter lurking deeper here.

Tap tap tap.

Or maybe it's distant footsteps? And that sound of rustling or rushing is getting a bit louder, like a bunch of sparrows whirring.

'That's what I heard last time,' he whispers. 'I got this far and I thought I saw something down that corridor, just a glow.'

Yūki peers deeper, heart rate picking up. 'Really? Must've been fireflies or something, right?'

'In February?'

Taka flashes his phone torch into the darkness, and further down the corridor the beam falls on a big bouquet of flowers: white and orange chrysanthemums fizzing in a twirl of plastic, deliberately placed there obviously, and not long ago.

'Somebody else, marking the anniversary I guess,' Taka says quietly, looking back over his shoulder. The sound seems to fade again. Yūki is just about to tug Taka's sleeve and pull them both away, when a loud bang resonates deep in the building, like a door being slammed.

'No way!' Taka grabs Yūki's hand. His slim fingers are really cold, colder than hers now.

'Let's go,' she says.

'Can you see something?' Taka whispers. 'Look at the end of the corridor? Right at the end.'

Shivers ripple down her back. And – yes – is there something now? A very faint blur of light, about the size of a football, floating in the doorway at the far end? Towards them? Away? It seems to be moving but not moving, maybe getting denser, clearer. There's a whooshing sound in the darkness ahead, something coming closer, *rushing* towards them at what sounds like colossal speed. Instinctively Yūki ducks, and a second later whatever it is - not quite wind, but not quite solid either - rushes past their heads, setting Taka's hair blowing. She just about manages to stifle a scream, and before she knows it they are both running full pelt back down the drive.

Taka's eyes are wild. 'You see!'

'Birds? Wind?' But even as she pants out the words she knows

292

she doesn't quite believe it. It felt like something escaping – some huge pent up rush of energy, or emotion, or *something*.

Their sprint takes them past the 'Terror' car and the flattened hearse, round the first corner and she risks a glance back at the last moment but sees nothing but the parked ambulance. Her pace falters.

'Slow down,' she gasps. 'There's nothing.'

But Taka keeps a steady jog and he doesn't stop until he's made it through the columned gateway and back onto the cliff road.

When Yūki catches up, about to make a joke about him being more scared than her, he just slumps down on the road, head bowed. Cautiously she place a hand on his shoulder.

'It was probably just the wind, Taka. There must be doors smashed and windows open and it was just gusting through . . .'

'Come off it. That was weird.' Taka shakes his head. 'It just felt so sad . . . Did you see that round thing? Maybe it was a *nukenubi*, one of those floating head things. Or maybe all this,' he sweeps his arm at the landscape, 'is just getting to me.'

'So, let's just pray for it to be at peace. Whatever it was.'

She turns back towards the gateway and places her palms lightly together, and – taking his cue from her – Taka does the same and then together they bow in the direction of the retirement home as the wind shushes through the trees overhead.

Taka straightens. 'At least I gave the message. Do you think she heard me?'

'Let's imagine she did.'

293

Somewhere to the south there's a distant siren. It rises, holds a steady note and then falls away into the silence of the zone.

'Is that the plant?' Yūki says. 'What does it mean?'

'Probably just lunchtime,' Taka murmurs, but as he says it he glances at the Geiger counter again. 'You still got to eat, even when you're battling radiation. Brave guys.'

'Is the reading OK?'

'OK enough.' He rummages in his drawstring bag and pulls out a salt shaker. 'Just to be on the safe side. You know, like when you get home from a funeral.'

He tips a little salt into his palm, then takes a pinch and throws it over her shoulder, then his. 'I'll keep some for later.'

'Do you think we really need to do that?'

Taka nods, and turns away into the cold wind.

7

Welcome Home

AT THE BOTTOM OF THE hill a car lies on its side, sewn into the verge with last summer's weeds. And beyond that the tsunami devastation begins for real. Smashed piles of timber and huge chunks of board and masonry are heaped against fallen pines, small vans and cars rolled on their backs like beetles, their wheels useless in the air, slicks of dried mud and chunks of blue and grey and red plastic tangled with broken rooves tilted at crazy angles. Trawlers lie capsized in this silent sea of wood and metal and concrete and glass.

Nearer the ocean most of the trees have gone, and those that are standing are a dead-looking pale orange. Only the school buildings and an isolated concrete industrial unit near the sea stand intact amidst the carnage. The wind is sighing across the tops of the reeds where water still lurks in drainage channels, and the wet snow starts to fall again.

Yūki looks away to the bluff, the Hara house still hidden from sight.

Taka follows her gaze. 'Can you see something?'

'No. I was just thinking, how on earth did I make it through all of that?'

'I heard about two middle schoolers, and they were jogging home from school together. And they parted and took different roads and one lived and one died,' Taka murmurs. 'You were lucky, I guess, like me.'

'It didn't feel lucky at the time.'

'What I mean is there's always a bit of luck involved, right? And then sometimes you make good decisions too . . .'

Here and there across the wide landscape in front of them are thin poles, vibrating in the breeze, white flags whipping from each.

'They'll be where the SDF recovered bodies,' he says.

For almost a year she has imagined, fought for, longed for this moment – of somehow getting back to the house and trying to find Grandpa. But now with the house just a kilometre away across this alien landscape the reality of thinking about bodies is overwhelming.

'What – what do you think he would look like? If we found him now?'

'After a year of wind and rain and stuff, it's down to DNA, Komori-san said. Or dental records. Sorry. Try not to think about it.' He puts a hand on her shoulder. 'Listen, the odds of finding him have got to be like a million to one. They say some bodies went huge distances . . .'

'I know. Let's just get to the house now.'

Taka peers ahead. 'I reckon we should take the road that bends closer to the school. It's been cleared a bit, and everything's piled up between here and your place . . . I'll switch the alarm on again on the dosimeter.'

They drop down onto the flat ground, past heaps of wreckage, a dead house cut clean in two, its halves leaning away from each other. The counter is clicking away in Taka's hand as the buildings of Osōma Elementary loom in the snowy air, and he pauses to fiddle with it.

'I'll set the threshold a bit higher. Otherwise it'll be going off all the time.'

When they reach it, the school's outdoor swimming pool is filled to the brim with mud and debris.

'I hated the swimming lessons,' Yūki murmurs. 'I always felt so useless compared to everybody else.'

'Might have helped save your life though maybe?'

'I suppose.'

She glances once more at the diving boards poised still over the pool, and then quickens her steps past the big concrete frog sculptures along the side of the hall, one thing about the school which she did always love. Now they stare out from between whispering overgrown reeds.

Taka points up high above them to a dark greeny-black line smudged just under the roofline.

'Must be the high water mark,' he says. 'It's so lucky that lorry driver stopped.'

'Yeah, I think I remember seeing it.'

'That guy must have saved about fifty kids and their teachers. I think they're still trying to trace him.'

They walk on round the corner, the wind whistling in the broken windows above them, and on between the stilled violence of the wreckage. Being so close to the devastation silences them, the atmosphere more and more oppressive as they wade deeper away from the comparative normal of the cliff road.

'Tell me more about that hero of yours,' Taka says, trying to put a lift into his voice. 'So he wanted to live here and help people even though he came from the sea? Rescue people in distress?'

'It wasn't really very thought out.'

'But that was like you, right? Coming from somewhere else. But wanting to be here–'

She feels a flicker of irritation again. 'I've got a therapist, already?'

'Sorry. I was just thinking aloud that's all.'

He keeps walking, but Yūki's feet come to a sudden halt, and she looks back at the abandoned school and the remains of the coastal community, imagining the power of the water scouring the land, then turns round to look at how far it is to the higher ground. A kilometre or more. Even if the kids had run as fast as a ten-year-old can run they'd have never made it. She looks out in the direction of the sea, hidden by the junk and the dead trees, and a picture flashes in her head of Half Wave running on the skin of the waves, blue hair bright, heading for the school. A hero you could rely on. He'd know what to do . . .

'I thought you were in a hurry!' Taka calls.

She glances at her watch.

12.50. The weather is closing in: wisps of sea mist mingling with the cold snowy air and broken buildings, her breath clouding as she runs to catch up. In front of her Taka is veiled by the thickening air for a moment.

'Taka!'

He waits until she catches him. 'I thought I heard a dog. Did you hear it, Yūki?'

'No. I was just thinking about something.' That image of Half Wave is in her head, an idea hovering somewhere on the edge of thought.

'This is worse out here than in the woods if you ask me,' Taka says. 'Let's do what you need to do. It wasn't far from here I saw the you-know-whats.'

'If you don't want to come any further–'

'I want to come,' Taka says firmly. 'I just don't want to hang out with freaking *funayūrei*.'

'Angela said ghost stories after disasters are just your mind trying to work it all out.'

'Well, no offence, but I guess Angela – whoever she is – never hung around a tsunami zone after dark. Or saw their friend drowned in mud. Or . . .' He waves his hands at the carnage. 'Well, I guess you had it worse than me so I'll shut up. Can't you hear it? Something barking.'

Yūki cocks her head. 'Maybe?'

'If it's a dog, loads were abandoned . . . some starved but I guess there might be some living wild out here. Might be fierce.' He steps off the road and picks up a broken-off chunk of post. 'Or could be a fox. Were you really on a raft with one?'

'I thought he was a dog at first, but it was only when I'd got hold of him I realised he was a fox. I think he liked me.'

Taka's face lifts, the lopsided grin back. 'Your family and foxes!'

Even though it's still day the air has become gloomy again. Although she must have walked this road a hundred times, it's hard to keep bearings with the bluff drifting in and out of view through the mounds of broken stuff. Everything has changed. Houses that stood there all her childhood are now no more than concrete plinths, or shunted and rammed into the side of another one across the road. Trees have been shredded or totally ripped away. When they get to the little cemetery its rectangles of black marble lie in a tumbled mess like a child's abandoned building blocks. Close to the road a chunk of pale stone lies on a black plinth: a Buddha head about the size of a melon, his neck jaggedly broken, but the soft hint of a smile still lifting his features.

She lifts the head up in her hands. It must still be a good eight or nine hundred metres to the house, but this looks incredibly like the head off the little Buddha that sat beside the Godzilla in Grandpa's garden. Couldn't be, could it?

'Come on, Yūki. It's really bad luck to take stuff from cemeteries.'

She sets the head down upright, turning it to gaze towards the sea. And as she does so there comes the faint sound of an animal's claws sprinting on the tarmac.

But when she turns around, there's nothing to be seen. Shivers go through every vertebra, lengthening her spine.

'You heard it too, right? Ghost dog probably . . .'

'Taka, do you have any idea what happened to Mrs Takeda's dog?'

'Good old Pochi? Yeah, I heard one of those students who came up from Tokyo to help after the disaster found him. Apparently this guy was like some kind of a punk or something – but it's one story with a happy ending. Takeda-san gave him a hug if you can believe it!'

The road rises slightly towards the bluff now, into thick skeins of broken wood and metal, but her feet pick up the pace, her pulse quickening *doki doki* until it's all she can do not to run as she clambers over the worst bits, trying not to look too hard at the shoes and bits of clothing jammed in the mess. Pulled from houses, or off people who drowned, or . . . No, don't think about it. Keep moving, keep breathing.

A few sickly looking trees this far inland are still standing, and she recognises the gangly red pine where three roads used to meet, and they turn left, and round a conical mound of broken up stuff, and emerging from the mist in front of her she sees it at last: still proud against the bluff stands the Hara family house.

The land around is swept clear of the familiar bushes and trees. Windows darkened, stuff spilling from the doorways, the whole house looks like a storm-damaged ship floating on the brown and grey clutter of debris. The road towards it has been partly cleared and she starts to jog, then run full tilt for where the

301

gate used to be, weaving through the mess, jumping over a crate, heart pounding now as she crosses the last few dozen strides.

And reaches home.

She pauses on the threshold, one hand resting on the big ornamental rock like she used to reach for the edge of the swimming pool. Made it!

She grabs a deep breath, taking in the damage before her.

There's no sign of the gate. And everything beyond it from the garden is totally gone too – mannequins, ornamental trees, the postbox, Grandpa's collection all washed away to be replaced by mounds of fishing gear and broken bits of who-knows-what piled against the raised *engawa* around the house. The only things that remain: Godzilla lying face down in dried mud, and the big stone lanterns shattered where they fell. Beyond, the big ground floor windows of the sitting room are smashed open, the front door ripped on its hinges. You can see torn *shōji* through the broken front of the old building – and black holes and gashes in the white paper panels.

The silence is intense.

Just the sigh of wind and snow in the *hinoki* and pines and firs above, the fluttering of a blind in one of the upstairs windows, her heartbeat light and quick.

She waits, allowing her heart to come down a beat or two, and closes her eyes.

'Grandpa. *Tadaima*. I'm home,' she whispers.

The bear bell under the eaves rings softly once, twice, and she opens her eyes again. There's movement on the hillside above and she looks up just in time to see a scatter of crows take to the wind there.

Nothing else. But it felt a bit like she was being watched for a moment – that prickly feeling you get when somebody has their eyes locked on you.

Just imagination.

Never say 'just' before you say 'imagination', Yū-chan.

Taka is jogging up from behind, breathing hard.

'Wow,' he calls. 'It stood up to the wave pretty well. But what a mess. And that big mound of stuff back there made the counter click like crazy. Doesn't seem so bad here, but we shouldn't hang around too long, Yūki.'

'I want to have a good look round.'

'For what?'

'I mean it would be really terrible if he was just lying close by. I did look for Grandpa that day, but maybe I missed him?'

'OK. But – like I say, I'm not sure there would be much left. Sorry.'

'A skeleton? Or would there be . . .'

He pulls a face. 'I don't know. I saw one of those Buddhist mummies once on a school trip. Near Yamagata. All dried skin and stuff and it gave me nightmares for weeks and weeks. I made the mistake of telling Shuto and he took the piss out of me.'

'Thanks a lot.'

'I doubt your grandpa would be here anyway, but let's look. Just in case.'

She shoves away the thought of skeletons and mummified bodies – and imagines as hard as she can the sound of Grandpa's rough voice whispering in her ear.

Okaeri, Yū-chan. Welcome home.

Yūki looks at the trainer in her hand. It's covered in mud, but the silver panels are bright light underneath when she smears the filth away. Unmistakably Grandpa's. She remembers him miming his running action, beaming at her, so alive.

She glances up at the bluff. He was only joking about coming to get these, but it's as if Grandpa has taken a big step closer to her again. After all these months of dreams and nightmares and imagining here is something solid and real. Not much, but something. A mucky right-footed trainer, maybe the last thing he bought.

Taka has clambered out to stand next to her. 'I saw those that day at the station. I thought, wow, she's got a cool granddad . . . Where did you find them?'

'There was one in the *genkan* and this one was right here. I don't know how I missed them when we went in.'

She puts it with the left, as if he's just stepped out of them and left them neatly by the door.

'Yūki, just to reassure you. I had a quick look round again – in case he was still here. His body I mean. I don't think he's any-where close by.' He puts a hand on her arm. 'So you don't have to worry about that at least.'

'Thanks. That's kind.'

Taka puffs out his cheeks, looking around at the chaos. 'Can't shake the freaking guilt. God, it's a mess in there . . . worse than our place. What do you want to do?'

'Let's make a kind of shrine. Find anything useful.' She looks back at the house. 'But I already got this . . .' She holds up the photo from the broken frame on the landing: Jiro and Anna staring into a flash bulb, young smiles frozen, glasses raised for ever in some smoky club in 1970s Tokyo. 'Can you get out the incense?'

'Did your grandpa like *shōchū*?'

'Maybe. It's like whiskey, right? He liked that.'

'Close enough. Then I've got an offering from me.' Taka smiles and reaches inside his drawstring bag and pulls out a tall can. '*Kanpai*. Cheers Hara-san.'

Yūki hears the hiss of the ring pull as she goes back up the steps and onto the walkway, then steps over the broken glass into the living room. Grandpa's art books lie pulped to a soggy mess on the floor, the *Garo* magazines and *gekiga* soaked with them and covered in mud and mould. She pulls one free from the mound that doesn't seem too water damaged, and wipes the cover with her sleeve to reveal a beautiful Ainu warrior princess, her mouth tattooed like a fierce smile. It's signed 'Hara Jiro, 1970'. Perfect.

She pushes on through the dining and living rooms again, scouring the sludge for anything else useful or meaningful. But there's very little visible above the muck, not a trace of any of Grandma's pots, or the Tezuka Award which she knows - despite Grandpa's feigned indifference - that he was super, super proud of, and can't have been too far from hand. And she thinks of the black biscuit tin and searches for it quickly in the dining room, but gives up after five minutes. Not a hope. Probably buried far out at sea by now, and besides, her watch hands are creeping towards 2.46 p.m.

Back on the walkway Taka is wedging a bundle of incense into a broken flower pot filled with soil.

'Is this OK?'

She nods, then crouches down, spreading out the curled photograph and weighing the edges down with the silver trainers, setting the sodden comic book carefully beside it.

'Wow, perfect,' Taka says, touching the cover. 'She's something, really cool! Not sure I'd mess with her!'

Yūki gazes at the girl's warrior smile, imagines Grandpa bending at his drawing desk to ink her to life. So certain and sure in the lines they bring a smile to her own face more than forty years after he drew them.

'You did bring matches, didn't you?'

'Of course!' Taka says, fishing a chunky red lighter from his pocket. 'Um, do you want to say something? Or shall I just light it?'

'What's the time?'

'Pretty much bang on. 2.46 p.m.'

'Then light it, and we'll think about what happened. Remember Grandpa and everyone who died.'

'I never know what you're supposed to do when you pray, to be honest.'

'I think you just do what feels right for you. Ready?'

Taka crouches down, cupping his hand to protect the flame. The black bundle flares and then starts to chug out cedar smoke, and together they stand side by side, facing the photograph, and Yūki bows. Her eyes fall again to the trainers, the young man smiling at the flashbulb and the young woman leaning into his side.

Beside them the Ainu warrior girl stares up at her, proud – an outsider, a nail that sticks up just like the man who created her.

She takes a breath and closes her eyes and remembers the house shaking and dancing around them for those long, long minutes and how solid and real Grandpa was throughout the ordeal. How warm and strong his hand was . . .

After that, what was he thinking, when he went down to the house? What was he thinking when he died?

The wind gusts a bit and then dies. She smells the incense and then lets the breath go.

'Grandpa,' she says quietly. 'Please rest now.'

'And please accept my apologies,' Taka mutters, setting the can down next to the photo. 'May you and everyone . . . be well . . . wherever you are. We're sorry we haven't found you yet.'

Yūki stares at the photo, then away to the top of the bluff.

Imagine being a crow and you can be a crow.

Imagine being in love and you can be in love. Imagine being a superhero and you can jump right across the sky!

She lets her mind climb up into the snow above the house.

Her watch has ticked past 2.55 p.m. They'd have been heading up onto the bluff now this time last year, Grandpa still walking, talking . . . Maybe we should have done something up on the hill, she thinks. Some kind of ritual there?

Maybe it doesn't matter, the main thing is I'm here.

But in truth she feels a little flat now. Like something more should have happened, or they should have done something more definite. Too much to expect him to suddenly materialise like in some anime story.

'Taka?'

'Uh huh?'

'Did Grandpa say anything else on the phone? You were probably the last person he talked to, right?'

'I suppose I was.' He screws up his face, thinking hard. 'I asked if you were OK.'

'What did he say?' Yūki whispers.

'He said something like, you'd be fine. Because you were stronger than you thought you were.'

The incense curls around them, shaping in the chilly air, and her heart lifts in her chest.

'That's nice. Anything else?'

'Like I said, that he was going to get something and go and join you.'

'He really didn't say what that thing was?'

'I'd have told you, wouldn't I? You OK?'

Yūki looks around, the fog is pushing in from the sea, shrouding the landscape. The bluff drifting in and out of view.

'How's the radiation reading?'

'3.8.'

'I kind of felt like he might be here, you know?' She looks again at the trainers. 'Maybe we should wait for the time the wave came, I mean – after all that's when . . .'

'OK, but I just don't want to be here when the light goes.'

Yūki nods. 'You really think you saw the *funayūrei*?'

'You saw what I saw at the old folks' home.' Taka scratches his head. 'What would your grandfather do? If he was here?'

'He'd be creative, or do the opposite of what most people would do—'

'Ahh, an *amanojaku*, right?'

She looks confused.

'It means when you do something one way because everybody else does the opposite. *Amanojaku* are demons really.'

'He wasn't a demon.'

'It's just an expression, I meant it as a compliment! So, what would he do?'

Yūki points to the bluff. 'We used to make a bonfire up there, at Obon, to send the spirits home.'

'So let's make one,' Taka smiles. 'It might attract attention though.'

Of course, it's the perfect thing to do! 'I don't care. Let's make one here, as big as we can.'

Taka holds up the lighter in his left hand and sparks it twice, grinning.

312

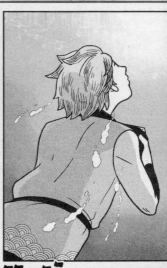

チリリリリ Chirr... チリリリリ Chirr...

The work has made her warmer, and Yūki takes off her hoodie to gaze at the flames. Taka is lobbing another chunk of board into the fire, and the blaze leaps higher, sparks dancing on the hot rising air. He turns to look at her, eyes bright as they catch hers.

'More, Yūki?'

'More! Lots more.'

As the minutes have lengthened the crackle of the fire has replaced talk, her arms and legs more and more energised as they work. She drags a shattered piece of bookcase to the flames and levers it on and then watches the flames bite at it.

The Geiger counter lies forgotten on the deck, and beside it an old photo album that emerged from under a smashed chest of drawers in the garden. Most of the photos are gone, but some are still in their plastic pockets, smudged by condensation and mould, glimpses of Grandpa and Grandma on holiday, maybe thirty years ago or more, walking hand in hand with their two small daughters. A Christmas here and Mum and Dad and Jiro and Anna all lined up on this very spot, the image faded now. The house when the trees were smaller.

The higher the flames the more her heart lifts. Smoke billows shrouds over them making their eyes sting and then clears again. At the edge of the crackling she thinks she can hear something now and then – a sound like the wind rustling through summer leaves, or water running. And every now and then there's that sense that they are being watched, that makes her glance up at the bluff or out into the blurred sea light.

She remembers Jiro's non-committal grunt when they waited

for the spirits. Don't scare away anything that might be there, Yū-chan, just wait, just wait.

The wind falters, and the flame and smoke are lifting straight up now. Something in the bonfire gives way, and the crash sends another tumbling mess of sparks up into the air.

'Enough?' Taka says. 'I'm knackered. And we should think about going soon.'

'Can we sit and watch it for a bit? From the house.'

Taka flicks his gaze out towards the sea. 'OK. Just a bit.'

'I've waited so long, I can't go just yet.'

'Sure. We need to eat something anyway. And I've got another can of that *shōchū* highball. Dad had some stashed away . . .' He fishes the supplies from his bag and sets down the can.

'Do you drink a lot?'

'Nah. Just special occasions. This is a special occasion, right?'

'Very.'

She looks at Taka's slimmed face, his dark eyes reaching for hers.

'How are you doing, Yūki?'

Her cheeks are warm from the flames. 'I am very well thanks to your honourable presence, Taka-san.'

'Hey c'mon, I thought I told you to drop the polite stuff.'

She punches him lightly on the shoulder. 'I was just kidding.'

He smiles. 'Well, you got me.'

They go to sit on the edge of the walkway in front of the old house, beneath the gashed *shōji* and broken windows, but still within reach of the fire's warmth, and eat *onigiri* rice balls and biscuits in silence.

316

Taka takes a pull from the can and offers it to her. 'Peach flavour. Do you mind sharing?'

She eyes the can's mouth, wipes it with her sleeve and takes a sip – and then splutters as the fiery mix hits her throat.

'It tastes strong!'

Taka reaches gently for the can. 'Don't have too much though, if you're not used to it.'

'Taka?'

'Mmm?'

'What do *you* think happens when we die?'

He looks up, considering, closes his eyes for a moment. 'I was thinking a lot about this. Reading and thinking when I was down south.' He looks back at her. 'OK, this is like another thought experiment right? Where's *konoyo*? This world?'

'Well, here. Right here.' Yūki points at the ground in front of her.

'And if you think of typical heaven? God and clouds and stuff.'

She points her index finger up.

'And hell?'

She jabs her thumb straight down.

'Easy, right. So, the question is: where is *anoyo*? That *other* world? Where the spirits return after Bon.'

'Um, well . . .'

'You don't know where to point, right? It's here, all around us, sort of. But it's not *konoyo*. It's alongside us somehow.'

'You haven't answered my question.'

'Because I haven't got a damn clue.'

317

The fire ticks steadily away, and Yūki stares back into it for a long while, then glances over her shoulder into the darkened interior of the house.

'It'll take ages to repair it all. I'm going to do it if nobody else will. One day.'

'I'd help you,' Taka says quietly. He hands the can back to her and she takes another sip. She can feel the *shōchū* warming her stomach now, and takes another mouthful of the cold, fiery liquid and feels Taka edge closer to her, the side of his body just nudging against her.

'Is this OK, Yūki?'

'Yes. *Daijōbu*.'

'I'm not trying anything on,' Taka says. 'I just need to feel close.'

'It's nice.'

'I've been pretty lonely. I mean, everyone my age is gone – or dead.'

Something bangs loudly in the fire, and they both jump, and look at each other and smile – then settle back. And she leans a bit more firmly into him.

'It felt like you were going to say something when we were lighting the incense, and then you changed your mind.'

'Doesn't matter. Let's be quiet.'

'Are you sure?'

'This feels good. Right now.'

She feels the glow of the fire on her face and hands, Taka close beside her, and gazes into the fire, watching as it brings the front

318

of the house to life, and the minutes pass and lengthen. The wave would have come by now, she thinks. Maybe this was when I was in it. Or when Grandpa died . . .

Taka's breathing has become heavier, and she feels his weight leaning into her.

Maybe he's asleep.

It'll be about 7 a.m. back home. Joel has come to mean a lot over the last few months: his friendship has helped to get her here. But she's never felt as close - been as close - to a boy as now. She thinks about the 'physical' stuff with the girl in Osaka, the good kisser at the sushi shop, feels a twinge again of envy in her stomach. Maybe I need to give him a sign? It seemed a moment ago that he was going to say something or even that they might kiss when he looked at her or something, but then it passed.

'Taka?'

'Mmmm?'

'Are you asleep?'

'Yes.'

'I dunno, could you - kind of - hug me?'

He leans back against the old building, and eases her so she's half leaning back on his chest before putting an arm around her.

'Like this?'

'Yes. Thank you.'

The snow falls a bit heavier, the downward motion hypnotic, flakes melting as they hit the ground. Now and then little gusts of

wind come and set the snowflakes dancing, but otherwise everything is calm. Taka adjusts his position.

'So, tell me what it was like here at Obon, Yūki?'

'It was – magical.'

'Magical? We just went to our family grave and cleaned it,
y'know, regular stuff.'

'It was warm and we all sat round the big table in the old house
and Aunt Kazuko would tell stories about gigs going stupidly
wrong, and Mum and Dad and her would drink a bit and laugh for
once instead of being super uptight like normal. And then we'd
build the fire up on the hill, Grandpa and me.'

'Sounds amazing.'

'Well, sometimes there were big rows too. Dad felt he didn't
fit and his Japanese was sooo bad. And Mum and Aunt Kazuko
could have arguments . . . It wasn't perfect.'

'Families, right? Hey, pass the drink back, will you?' Taka takes
the can.

'Sorry. You have the rest. Would you really help me repair this
place?'

'We might have to wait a bit. But yeah.'

'Can you hear something? Shhh.'

'It's just the fire.'

'No. Something else . . .'

To be honest she's not totally comfortable in this position, and
either jetlag or exhaustion or maybe the drink is muddling her
head a bit – but she doesn't want to move and break the contact
either. Should she do more? Just enjoy this moment. Think of

Grandpa. Think of the fire and Taka. Think of Anna and Mum and Kazuko growing up here, playing out here . . .

She closes her eyes, hears the fire crackling, smells the lingering waft of incense and smoke. The wind is soughing through the pines overhead. Some other sound with it? Kind of close and far away at the same time . . .

She can hear Taka breathing, and together they drift down into dreams they won't remember as the snowflakes fall gently and the light fades and the Geiger clicks away on the steps behind them and the wind gently flips the pages of the blurred photo album.

Out on the old marshland the reeds are whispering.

A car settles lower in the wreckage with a groan, sending rust flakes into the salty black void beneath.

Concrete frogs gathering snow on their eyelids, gazing at the sea.

Beyond that the ocean keeps up its relentless beat, each wave building, breaking, rolling back from the ruined sea wall, the waves getting louder, louder . . .

A white owl screeches down from the bluff, hunting radioactive voles in the night.

And a small fox picks its way into the circle of the bonfire.

It sniffs at Taka's bag, then creeps towards the sleeping figures, whiskers just millimetres from Yūki's hand. Gently, it licks her fingers, then – as she stirs – darts towards the back of the house, gone in a flash of orange.

321

Suddenly Yūki is awake, struggling up through the fog of sleep, the thick taste of the peach spirit in her mouth.

Darkness has filled the eastern horizon. Not quite night yet, but the day is almost completely gone. Taka is breathing deeply behind her now, his chest rising and falling.

And that sound is back – a persistent thrumming that's so familiar, but that she just can't place.

She listens harder.

Maybe it's coming from above? Yes, like it's coming down from the bluff.

Carefully she lifts Taka's arm from her chest, and eases unsteadily to her feet. The sound growing in her ears, she makes her way around the walkway and down the two stone steps at the back of the house. The back garden lies before her, cluttered with debris and dried grey sludge, with the studio's empty carcass to her left.

A fleeting glimpse of a something or someone moving at speed up the old path on the bluff? She blinks. Maybe nothing more than the sense of movement, but it sparks her into motion and she runs though the mess and then scrambles up the land-slide from the quake, the mud shot through now with weeds. Quickly she clambers to where the bird feeders used to be, the hillside here scoured by the wave, then higher and higher, panting as the path steepens through tangled blue netting and buckets and bits of plaster board turning green. The wind sigh is gone, just her heartbeat now, the rustling of undergrowth and her ragged breathing, and then from out of those rhythms comes

Grandpa's song about the tears looping in her head again. It feels like something special is about to happen and she pants the tune uncertainly under her breath as she scrambles towards the summit of Little Mountain.

Below the rock slab she pauses. 'He-llo? Anyone here?' Maybe it was just a security patrol. Or somebody else marking the anniversary? Or the police?

She takes two more deep breaths, and surges for the top, arms and legs like pistons, that sound audible again, filling her ears.

When her eyes fall on the old lookout post her knees buckle beneath her.

Stuck neatly in the ground where she and Grandpa always kept their vigil, almost at the exact spot where they parted a year ago, is the old plastic windmill toy. Its blades spinning like crazy, the sound filling the hilltop, her ears, her head – drowning everything out, even the loop of the song.

8

Anoyo/Konoyo

SHE GAZES AT THE SPINNING toy.

The wind is picking up, blowing it harder as she approaches, her spine buzzing, all trace of sleep and confusion pushed away in a rush of adrenaline. There's a sudden rustling in the under-growth to her left and her eyes flick away to see leaves moving as if something or someone has just pushed through them.

'Hello?' she calls uncertainly. 'Anyone here? Hello?'

She turns to look out across the desolate landscape to the sea. Nothing but a blur of twilight and mist and snow, and the windmill pulls her attention back, its colours merging as it spins.

Yūki edges closer. The air feels kind of different the closer she gets to it – warmer, sweeter, like somehow the bonfire's glow is reaching up and around her, pulling her in . . .

Summer days up here, humid warm air, the sweat on her skin, the cicadas calling *miiin min miiiiiiin min* as evening drew on, the moss soft and green underneath her as she looked out at the immense Pacific rolling a thousand shades of blue all the way to the horizon, clouds towering over, and thunderstorms brewing, and the distant sound of the Osōma *matsuri* festival. The drainage channels running to the sea where naughty *kappas* lurked waiting to pull you in and give you a fright, and evening coming and the pages of a manga flapping in the warm breeze. The sound of her pencil scribbling furiously, trying to finish a story before the sun went down. Voices from the house below, laughter maybe and then Grandpa calling her name as he came stumping up the bluff, a bag of Susuki rockets and bangers in his hand, his voice calling through the pine trees that still held the warmth of the day beneath them. And scribbling the last few bits of colour down and getting ready proudly to show Jiro her work. The last of the sun still on the ocean beyond, corrugated blue and grey and silver . . .

OK, Yū-chan. Now it's time to work our ma-ji-kku!

That sense of companionship and belonging, of being close – not just to Grandpa but to the magic of this place.

Where the windmill's stick pokes into the ground the earth looks like it has been freshly turned.

She takes two more steps towards it, and as she reaches out it slows, and the very faded pink and orange blades, with their tiny flowers on the end of each tip, take shape from the blur. Gently she pulls it from the ground.

The breeze catches the sails again, and she feels it vibrate as it spins. It looks and feels just like the one from the front garden but how on *earth* could it have got up here? Maybe someone found it and just stuck it in the ground? An SDF member or another grieving relative. Maybe better just to put it back.

She jabs the post into the soft ground, and feels the tip strike something hard. Puzzled, she does it again and hears a distinct metallic clunk, and the next second she is digging like a wild fox with her hands, pulling away the loose earth and stones and dead pine needles to reveal a flash of bright yellow.

She gasps – then paws more earth away, fingers scrabbling until the whole of Grandpa's old black biscuit tin is revealed. Dented, but intact – its lid stuck down with clear tape, the round sunburst still radiating bright yellow.

She sits back on her heels. 'Oh my God.'

It's the one that was sitting on the table, this day a year ago, before the quake, before the wave, before the radiation. She leans in again and pulls it free, pushing the plait out of her face with a muddy hand, heart going like crazy, then rips the brittle tape loose, and prizes the tight lid off.

Shivers run like cold water all over her skin: the sketchbooks are crouched there as she has expected to see, all of them – russet orange, green and indigo coloured covers and her childish handwriting shouting up at her. But she *hasn't* expected to see the thing that's resting on top of them: a slim, faded, utterly beautiful *kokeshi* doll. He's obviously a boy, his features drawn really subtly, and with blue hair – blue hair! – flicked over the rounded head. And lower down scrolling waves are brushed in a darker blue across his body.

'Oh my God!' she whispers again.

She turns it in her shaky fingers, watching the waves roll and knows at once it is the doll that Grandpa and Grandma put under the studio, after they moved here, after they lost their little boy.

But it's more than that.

The face - the feel - of the doll is super familiar, as if she's known it all her life, as if she's coming face to face with someone she hasn't seen for a very long time indeed.

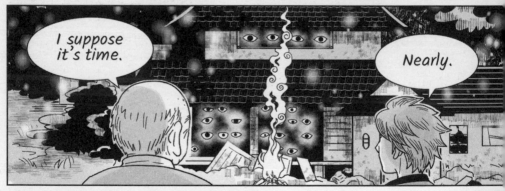

I suppose it's time.

Nearly.

I have one more favour to ask. Then a place I need to go.

I will do my best, Hara-san.

The wind is riffling the pages of the concertina sketchbook, flipping images of Half Wave, the *kappa* monster grabbing a bright green cucumber, the curling blue seas and saw-tooth mountains.

'I don't understand,' Taka says. 'You buried this up here on the day of the wave?'

Yūki shakes her head. 'No – I – I just found it here. Somebody *put* it here. I dunno. It doesn't make any sense.'

'Maybe your grandpa buried it up here before it all happened? Jeez, you're shivering like mad, Yūki.'

She shakes her head. 'The windmill was down *there*.' She points back to the garden. 'The sketchbooks were on the table . . . maybe he survived and climbed up here and buried it and then . . . but he can't have done. The house was wrecked. Maybe somebody else . . . ?'

She looks up at Taka to see his eyes are red, as if he's been crying. 'Are *you* OK?'

'I was calling you for ages, Yūki. I thought you left me here on my own. I had this weird dream that all these eyeballs were staring out of the house and when I woke up you were gone. I looked everywhere. In the end I guessed you might have gone up here.'

'I'm sorry. I didn't mean to worry you.' She waves her hand at the tin. 'But I just don't understand it, Taka.'

She can still feel the shivers, but that sense of being enfolded in the warmer, humid air is lingering. Her gaze sweeps the bluff again, then the surrounding darkening landscape – and her

330

head swims for a moment. She squints through the snow that has smudged her glasses and puts the book down to wipe them quickly on her hoodie.

Taka puts a hand on her shoulder, giving it a squeeze.

'I'm weirded out, Yūki. Does it feel odd to you? Up here? It's like everything is buzzing, or static or something.'

'Does it feel warmer to you here? I don't know . . .'

'I thought I heard cicadas when I was coming up the hill, but you couldn't in March. Unless the radiation has confused them . . .' Taka looks out to sea and pulls a face. 'Maybe we should get going?'

'Are you scared?'

'Yeah.' He tries a lopsided smile, but it doesn't quite sit right on his face. 'Listen, there's something I wanted to tell you, but . . .'

But Yūki's eyes are back on the blue sketchbook, turning a page to reveal another mountainous breaker and Half Wave leaping triumphantly from its back. 'It's not even water damaged,' she murmurs, then she picks up the faded, blue *kokeshi* doll again. 'Taka, this is what he went to get.'

'That old doll?'

'I used to play with him. Not the doll, but the boy.'

'OK, you're not making much sense, and you're kind of freaking me out, Yūki. I haven't checked the dosimeter in ages . . .'

'Just give me a second more.'

Another rush of tingling races across her skin, and her head swims again. But something wonderful is taking shape inside it: a story that's forming out of the destruction around them, from the bonfire sparks and piles of wrecked lives and sighing reeds and pines on the hill and snow clouds and a windmill toy and broken land. A new story about Grandpa – and a boy with bright blue hair.

A boy who could save you . . .

'Did you hear what I said?' Taka says, gently. 'I'm sorry. Your superhero looks amazing, but we can look at it all back at my house, right?'

She looks around again. The last sparks are floating up from the fire below, fireflies spiralling into the murky air . . .

Yūki closes her eyes, and breathes in the weird mix of smells, of summer and winter and bonfire and earth as the wind makes the pines dance. Too much to expect to actually see Jiro, of course, that *is* just for imagination.

She feels Taka shake her shoulder again. 'It's already dark, Yūki. How did it get dark so fast? We've got to get–'

His voice stops dead, and she distinctly feels his body go tense beside her.

'Taka? What is it?'

'I can hear a car. Out on the marshes.'

'There can't be.'

She opens her eyes and stands up, following his gaze into the snow swirl and falling night. There does seem to be something moving out there now – on the edge of being visible, like a piece of the darkness is moving – and there's the faintest of shaky lights dancing in front of it. If it is there, it's going quite fast, blinking in and out of existence as it weaves through the piles of tsunami debris. Her head goes all swimmy again, and she crouches down, one hand resting on the earth. Any trace of the bubble of warmth is gone, and the ground is cold and hard.

'It's Dad!' Taka gasps. 'Come on, we've got to catch him.'

'It can't be, can it? How would he get around the roadblocks?'

But already Taka is hurrying away, back to the rock slab and the path down to the house. 'Come on! He's come to get us!'

'But how would he know where to find us? Wait!'

Yūki stares out into the gloom, but sees nothing now. When she looks back Taka is already out of sight and she grabs the tin, the doll and the windmill and stumbles after him, the snow sticking to her glasses, slipping on the wet grass and pine needles, skittering down the rock, trying not to drop her treasures, but desperate to catch up. 'Wait!! Wait!'

She finds him waiting impatiently for her halfway down the black hillside. 'Here, let me take some of that. But come on, for God's sake. We've got to run.' He's peering out between the branches and pointing now as – about a hundred metres away – a silhouette of the car is just visible for a second or two, gliding through the night, accelerating away again to the south into the labyrinth of wreckage-choked roads. 'He's looking for us, Yūki.'

She hands him the windmill, wipes her glasses again on her sleeve, and looks back out towards the ocean – and freezes. Further out, beyond the shaky headlight, there are white shapes moving in the darkness – thin, pale figures moving slowly towards them.

'Taka, can you see them?' she whispers, transfixed.

But already Taka is gone, dropping down the hillside as fast as he can go. She takes one more look – doesn't see the spectral shapes, then thinks she sees them again – and hurries after him, the tin clutched tight in one hand, the other grabbing branches and saplings to steady herself, down and down, across the landslip, across the long whisper of the grass past the wrecked studio, leaping up onto the *engawa*. Rounding the corner to the front of the house she finds Taka staring at the dosimeter.

'Taka, I think I saw—'

'Just grab your bag – stick all that in it and let's go. Come on!!'

335

He peers out into the night. 'He just went past – that way! I can hear the engine.'

'Did you call him to come?'

'What?! No.'

'Then what's he doing out here?'

'Looking for me. I think I can still see the tail lights . . .'

He grabs Yūki's hand and practically pulls her from the raised walkway, down the steps, through the wreckage and past the smouldering bonfire and into the night.

'Taka,' she gasps, 'I think I saw *funayūrei*. They're coming.'

Taka glances back at her, eyes wild and kind of scary. 'I told you.'

And then together they run – the laden rucksack banging on her back – away from the Hara house and deeper into the night, chasing the two tiny dots of red flickering through the wreckage as the sea wind nips at their faces.

Dad! WAIT!

e's stopping.

Taka! I can give you a ride.

Dad, what are you doing out here?!

Need to get you out of here.

Everything's fine.

How did you know we were here?

Got a message to pick you up.

People think the road is blocked but I know back ways.

Are you OK, Taka?

I'm fine.

How are you?

Sorry about the state of the car.

Taka, what's going on?

No need to be afraid.

I'll drop you here. For now. Take care.

I hope you're OK, Dad.

I miss you.

I'm fine, son.

I love you.

9

Realm of the Galaxies

Yūκι AND Taka stand silently looking at the pale taxi rammed nose first into the reeds shivering in the river's bed. One door is wrenched open, and water and mud are choking the wheel arches. Somewhere away to their left something splashes in the darkness and a moment later a bird of some kind shrieks in alarm. Yūki jumps, looks away towards the sound, then back to Taka, but his eyes have stayed locked onto the sight before them.

'It's Dad.'

'I don't understand, Taka . . . it's been here ages. You can see that.'

But already he is scrambling down the bank to the crumpled remains of the car, its bonnet jammed into the far bank of the channel, the windscreen smashed and frosted in the dance of torchlight. Faded red lettering on the roof light spelling out JIMI'S TAXI OSŌMA.

Wide-eyed now, Yūki stares down at the car, bound by reeds and tangled weeds to the muddy river bed, then she too is sliding down the bank to find Taka already half inside the broken body of the car, his torch flicking around in the gloom.

'Taka, what's going on?!'

He looks back up at her, eyes bright. 'It's his car, Yūki. Help me look in the ditch!'

'I don't understand.'

'He died. In the tsunami, Yūki, don't you understand? We've got to try and find him now we've found the car. I never got this far, but he's here somewhere . . .'

His voice is kind of wild now, even more so than back on the hill, and full realisation dawns on Yūki in a rush.

Her shoulders drop. All along it has felt a bit like Taka has still been holding on to something, on the verge of saying something - and now it makes sense. She squelches into the mud and water and joins him, peering into the musty cab.

'Taka, I'm so sorry.'

'I'm going to look around. Help me.'

There's a good thirty centimetres of mud in the footwells. In the faint light she sees the string of prayer beads tangled around the rear-view mirror and unhooks them carefully. She gazes at them and then goes to find Taka, and places the beads in his shaking fingers.

'I can't find him, Yūki.'

'What about the *funayūrei*?'

'I've got to find his body. I don't care.'

'OK, I'll help. But you said - you know - there might not be much to find. And the radiation is high so . . .'

343

'Just a few minutes. Please.'

Together they scour the banks of the river, mud and water soaking their legs, clogging up their shoes, the torch flickering across flapping sheets of plastic and broken pieces of cars and houses.

About twenty paces from the wrecked taxi the sight of a crumpled black puffa coat in the reeds makes them both catch their breath – but it is just an empty shell.

'Was that his, Taka?'

'Not sure. Could be . . .'

But of Jimi nothing else is to be found.

Eventually, after ten more minutes, Yūki puts a hand gently on Taka's shoulder.

'You saw it, right? You saw the car moving back there, Yūki? I'm sure I did.'

She thinks back over the muddle of the last half an hour or so: the panicky descent from the bluff, the glimpse of those pale shapes out there on the marshes, the flickering light. Had that been real – or just tiredness and the emotion overloading them? They *felt* real though, Yūki thinks. And maybe she *did* see the car – just for a second – a headlight flickering far out amidst the sea of wreckage, and it had all felt super intense as they fled the house, the radiation alarm still shrilling as they ran for what might have been red tail lights dancing away into the distance. Taka had looked back past her shoulder and his eyes opened even wider as he beckoned her frantically, and with the radiation alarm shrieking, the *shōchū* and adrenaline all pulsing round her body,

344

she had given in to fear and ran and ran and ran. Sometimes she had thought she heard the engine, sometimes not, but Taka wouldn't stop, and they jogged on, then scrambled, then ran again, deeper into the zone on a road that started south towards the nuclear plant before jinking inland towards Route 6. Twice they came to a dead end where a bridge was washed away, and had to backtrack. Dead cars loomed out of the darkness rolled on their sides, and a white fishing boat reared up on a great wave of black wreckage, and, for a third time, they found themselves heading towards the void of the ocean. Taka had hesitated, and Yūki peered back towards the Pacific waves. No sign now of those figures, even if they were out there somewhere – and they had jogged on another hundred metres, the road bending back inland and up a slight rise in the land, a wider drainage channel coming towards the road, as a stitch snagged tighter at Yūki's lower left ribs, and suddenly Taka was running hard again, beckoning over his shoulder.

'There's a car in the ditch. It's Dad's!'

Her hand is still resting on Taka's shoulder. 'I think I saw it. I think I saw the tail lights . . . I dunno. At least we found it now, right?'

'I saw it driving for sure. You must have seen it, Yūki. But I couldn't see Dad at the wheel though, just the taxi. Oh God . . .' His voice thickens, falters, and his shoulders slump and start to shake – quietly at first, then harder.

Yūki waits a long moment. 'Is that why you wanted to come into the zone, Taka? To look for him?'

345

Taka sniffs hard, wiping his nose with the back of his hand. 'I'm sorry. I just can't quite - believe it. It's too real, the car here and everything.'

'Take your time. Try and breathe a bit,' Yūki says, rubbing his hand with both of hers. It feels like ice.

'I looked and - looked,' Taka says, the words broken up, 'looked - on the edges of the zone, tried everywhere - everything. I just couldn't bear the thought he - was still out there. But I never came this far. Got too spooked, and the - radiation was high.' He takes a huge breath in, then pulls the Geiger counter from his pocket and glances at it. 'Shit. It's still high. We'll have to go.'

'Then let's say a prayer. And go. We can come back again . . .'

Together they stand in silence on the far bank and gaze down at the taxi, and put their hands together and bow.

Taka sniffs hard again, and then whispers, 'Sorry, Dad.'

'You did your best,' Yūki says. 'You couldn't do any more. Nobody could.'

Taka shakes his head, takes one more look at the cab in the shifting reeds, and then turns inland.

'Do you want to talk about it, Taka?'

'Just give me a minute. Please? And I need to make sure we go the right way.'

The road snakes through the broken remains of homes on the far side of the river, then climbs very slightly to higher ground. Slowly the piles of wreckage fall behind them and the houses now are intact, but all darkened and empty and still. The sludge

346

in Yūki's trainers reminds her of the long night walk with Takeda-san, but somehow there's not a hint of panic in the memory. And even the fear of the *funayūrei* is fading as they climb slowly away from the flatter land and the tsunami zone. She glances back and sees nothing but night and the faint glow of the ocean beyond.

'How are you doing, Taka? Do you want to tell me more about it?'

'I'm OK. A bit cold. Really cold.'

'Me too.' She pauses and looks back into the darkness. 'But why didn't you tell me about your dad sooner? I still don't understand. Sorry, but I could have helped you more.'

Taka is shivering hard, still fighting to control the tears, and Yūki reaches out to take his hand with both of hers again.

'I dunno. I thought if I said he was away – to everybody – then maybe somehow he was just away. And he would come back, somehow. Or at least I could stay in the house.' He sniffs. 'It was so hard, with nothing found, so . . . I dunno, I just liked to imagine he was out there driving his taxi somewhere. Maybe giving lifts to people who need help. Stupid.'

'It's not stupid. But we shouldn't have secrets. Not after what we've been through. We're friends, right?'

'Yeah, of course.' He forces a smile, and checks the counter again. 'We need to keep moving. I'm OK.'

The road cuts through a deserted industrial area, buildings damaged by the earthquake or neglect, doors gaping open to pitch black interiors, and they hurry on. Beyond that there's an abandoned conveyer-belt sushi shop, its signpost fallen

347

diagonally across the road. They scramble under the rusting metal, and then they are on the deserted tarmac of the larger Route 6.

A traffic sign points right towards Namie, Odaka and Osōma, and they walk on past a deserted garage, a convenience store, a noodle vending machine with all its lights out. Not a vehicle in sight and no sound at all now but their footsteps and their breathing as they walk down the middle of the tarmac. A can tumbles past in the cold wind heading towards the emptiness behind them, the nuclear plant beyond that.

'What if someone sees us?' Yūki asks.

'Road's still shut. And if the police or something does come along we'll get home a bit quicker. Doesn't matter now, does it?'

'Was all that true about you going to stay with your mum and her new guy?'

'Yeah, I spent a lot of the last year there.' He sniffs again. 'But I came back a few times to get as close as I could get. Moved back as soon as they opened the zone a bit. I lied to them about going to Tokyo. It's so weird here now – I've known this bit of road all my life, but now it's like being in a film or something.'

Round a slight bend they see a big square building set back from Route 6, the word *PACHINKO* silhouetted on the roof in darkened neon letters against the smudgy moonlit clouds. The *pachinko* hall itself is a hulking dark shape beneath, pieces of pale blue cladding fallen to the tarmac beneath.

Taka hesitates, and then starts to walk towards it.

'Taka? What are you doing?'

'Just wait a minute?' he calls over his shoulder. From some-where deep inside the deserted building a sheet of metal is clanking slowly in the breeze.

'What are you doing? I thought we had to go,' Yūki puffs as she runs to catch him.

Taka has stopped halfway across the weed-strewn parking lot, and is gazing at the *pachinko* parlour, flicking the prayer beads through his fingers. 'The thing is . . . the thing is Dad was on the way to the old folks' home, Yūki, then Tomioka. He was right in the open when the wave came . . . If I hadn't forgotten my phone that day he wouldn't have had to take me back to the station and maybe—'

'Don't! Don't, Taka. You can't think that. The wave would probably have got him anyway. And maybe you'd have drowned on the train. *And maybe and maybe* is a waste of time . . .'

Taka's shoulders slump, his slim face broken, pale.

Yūki rubs his arm. 'Come on, let's get going. We need to get warm.'

But Taka's eyes are still on the *pachinko* parlour. 'I dunno – it's like you said, it feels we haven't done enough for Dad, to remember him or whatever. I just wanted to find him . . . Why him? Why not *me*? I miss him so much, Yūki.'

'He seemed really nice, always. He must have been a good dad.'

'Yeah, he was.'

'I always wondered why he was called Jimi?'

'You know, like Jimi Hendrix, the guitarist. Dad's wild hair kind

349

of looked the same so he got that nickname in the seventies, when he was growing up. Everyone called him that, like for ever.' He puffs out his cheeks.

Yūki glances back in the direction of the Hara family house. 'Listen. I had half an idea, up on the bluff. Can I ask you a weird question?'

'OK.'

'If you could have one more moment with your dad, what would it be?'

Taka glances at her. 'Does it matter?'

'Of course it matters. What would you do? Where would you like him to be, right now?'

'I dunno, just take a ride with him. Or go to that conveyer-belt sushi place and chat a bit. Or come and play some *pachinko* with him. Here. I'd have been allowed in this year . . .'

'Then let's imagine he's here, Taka, playing *pachinko*. Just like normal. Content. Imagine it's all bright and full of life and your dad's there.'

The piece of metal clanks again deep inside the darkened building.

Taka shifts beside her. 'And then?'

'And then he kind of will be there, right? That's what I think anyway. We can leave him there for now.'

Taka's silent for a moment.

'I mean – I don't mean to tell you what to do, Taka–'

'No,' Taka says. 'No, it's good. Let's do it.'

'Really imagine he's here, Taka. And then he will be.'

350

And together they stand gazing at the dark shape of the building, and Yūki closes her eyes and makes the lights blaze in her head.

Route 6 is still silent and empty as they walk on past an abandoned 7-11 store, a casino, a strip of black windowed restaurants with names like 'Surf Paradise' and 'Pleasant View', already being lost to bamboo and undergrowth. When she looks up the clouds have cleared and the moon is low and a huge array of stars are tilting over their heads above them.

'They're so bright,' Yūki says, trying to lift Taka's spirits. 'The stars are really bright. Look!'

'Yeah, it's because there's so little light pollution right now. Must be what it looked like a hundred years ago.'

'I can't see the Heavenly River though. I could always see it from Little Mountain . . .'

'Wrong time of year. We're looking out *away* from the middle of our galaxy now.' He takes a breath, pulling himself together a bit, pointing up. 'It's called the Realm of the Galaxies that part of the sky. There's a comet too, but my telescope got washed away so . . .'

'So you *are* like really smart.'

Taka snorts, but a smile lifts his face a bit more. 'I did say.'

'Your dad would be proud of you.'

'Pack it in or you'll have me crying again, Yūki. I've done enough for today.'

They walk on in silence again, gazing at the emptiness around them. A sudden rustling makes them jump, and when Yūki flicks the torch that way a raccoon blinks at them and scurries away into the night with something in its mouth.

Outside a small *konbini* store on a corner, a heap of news-papers is still bundled up and mushed by rain and wind. When Yūki stoops to look at them the date says 11th March 2011.

'How's the radiation now?'

'Getting better – if we turn right here we'll come to the Port Community Centre. They've cleared the topsoil along here.'

'Are we out of the zone?'

'Not quite. Very close.' Taka glances at his watch. 'God, it's three-thirty a.m.'

The darkness is thicker here under the trees, but, after another hour, in the distance Yūki sees the stars are fading in the Eastern sky ahead of them.

Taka looks round. 'You OK?'

'Yep.'

'What are you thinking about?'

'Taka, was it you?'

'Was it me what?'

'Did you put the box and the windmill up there, on the hill? When you were out here before?'

She glances up at his slim face just as he looks away into the trees. 'Course not.'

'Honestly?'

He looks back at her, features blurred under the pines. 'How would I know where to find that stuff and where to bury it?'

352

'Maybe when Grandpa called you – he said something about it all?'

'I literally have no idea. What's with the windmill?'

'Grandpa always had one just like it in the front garden.'

'People put them out for children who died, you know. Ever been to Osorezan in the north? It's full of them whirring away in this totally bleak landscape, remembering all the kids who died.' He shudders.

Yūki stops abruptly. 'I always thought they'd just put it there for me when I was little or something. But It was for somebody else.'

'What do you mean?'

'It's a long story, I'll tell you it properly later.'

It all adds up: the *kokeshi* and her childhood *zashiki warashi* friend and the dead little brother and the windmill. You can thread it all together. Half Wave too.

'Mind if I hold your hand, Yūki?'

She raises her eyebrows. 'Why? Are you scared?'

'No, dummy. Because there are things about you I like, of course.'

'That would be good.'

When his hand finds hers it feels warmer, and they walk on, each lost in thought as the ocean draws nearer and the light grows through the trees. She squeezes Taka's hand.

'We did it, Taka.'

'It was good to find Dad's taxi, but . . .'

'Do you feel better?'

'Kind of. Not really. I dunno, with chess you get these really neat solutions and you just think, ahhh, right and it all falls into place. This just feels like a mess really.'

'A mess?'

'Maybe a little bit better.' His eyes search hers out. 'How about you?'

'I thought Grandpa would be more THERE you know. It was like he was calling and calling me for months and months.'

'Did you see those things out there, Yūki? Tell me you did or I'm going mad.'

'I did.'

'And what about Dad's taxi? It was out there, driving along, wasn't it?'

'I saw it,' she says, and gives his hand another firm squeeze. 'Just for a moment.'

Fifteen minutes later they come to a little junction Yūki recognises. To the right the old coast road runs away towards the washed-out section and the Hara house now far beyond, and to the left is Osōma Port and town. The surging of the waves comes again now, the dawn lifting the horizon, and a second later the ocean is there. Her gaze drifts out across the gathering light on the sea, and then they turn for Osōma.

'We should cut around the checkpoint,' Taka says. 'Back into the woods.'

Ahead of them now is the dark shape of the little Inari shrine, the *torii* glowing dimly, one guardian fox still on its side, one staring sharply at them, the waves sighing to their right.

'Just let's see the shrine,' Yūki murmurs. 'Doesn't matter if we're caught now. We were there the night before, and he said he needed to come back. We'll pay our respects.'

'I don't have the energy to argue with a Hara,' Taka says, smiling through his tiredness. 'If that's what you want, then whatever.'

As they draw near you can see a handful of bouquets of fresh flowers have been placed on the top step. Some photos just visible, nestled in the crinkly cellophane wrapping, and bottles of water and sake, and four or five bright *mikan* fruit shining like bright orange suns amongst them.

The pulse of the sea is louder, merging with the tapping of her heartbeat.

When she bends to look at the photos, the faces of the lost and dead stare back through the plastic: two young children – a boy and a girl, a middle-aged man sitting on a motorbike beaming at the camera from ear to ear, two elderly men and a white-haired woman each in their own separate image, dignified, silent.

Taka joins his hands in prayer position and closes his eyes, and she does the same, bending low.

She thinks about Grandpa pausing here that last evening and that strange look on his face – and imagines him somewhere out there in all the ocean. Or high above looking down. Or walking up slowly from behind them.

Never say 'just' before you say the word 'imagination'.

She lifts her head. The light is brighter now on the sea, the colour returning to it, soft blues and turquoise and light rippling to the sky, vermilion *torii* framing it, blurred a bit by the wind in her eyes . . .

Looking around she sees:

. . . the standing fox looking at her sternly

. . . Taka's black cloud of hair blowing in the wind, his lips moving silently in some prayer or private thought

. . . the pines swaying, swaying, the road leading away towards the cliff fall and home.

And Grandpa standing right there in the middle of the tarmac as bold and clear as day.

He taps the tarmac with his stick, silver trainers bright – and then smiles, and points at the high corner of the opening to the shrine building. And she knows what she is going to do.

Rushing forward she slips the rucksack from her back, taking out the plastic windmill toy.

'What are you doing?' Taka calls, hurrying to join her.

'I'm sending the little boy home.'

'What?'

'He belongs here. With Grandpa. With the sea.'

She takes the faded blue *kokeshi* doll from her pocket and gazes at him for a long moment. The waves painted on his body are just visible in the returning light, his features calm: a slight lift to the mouth and eyes as if on the verge of a smile.

'Grandpa and Grandma put him under the studio,' she says. 'And then I played with him when I was tiny. A *zashiki warashi*, you know?'

'For real?'

'We'll leave him here.'

'Don't you want to take him?'

'No. He needs to stay here. Hold him.'

Yūki climbs to the top step, and clambers onto one of the foundation stones that supports one of the main pillars for the roof.

'OK, now pass him up to me.'

She takes the doll gently, then on tiptoe places him high up on a beam, tucked so he is sheltered and safe from the wind and staring eyes. You can see a sliver of the ocean from where he stands.

She makes sure he is safe, that he can see the waves, then slowly her fingers release him and she scrambles down, tears building behind her eyes.

'Now what?' Taka says.

'Now we'll – leave something to cheer him up, of course.'

She takes the windmill and props it amongst the other offerings and the wind catches the sails at once and it starts to spin – the familiar *chirrrrrring* merging with the waves – and her tears are flowing at last, overflowing.

Taka lets her cry for a moment, then puts his arm around her.

'*Daijōbu?*'

'*Daijōbu.*'

'I know what happened,' she whispers. 'I know how the tin got buried up on the hillside.'

The whirring of the windmill fills her ears and eyes, and she lets the tears fall for a while longer. And then she lifts her gaze up into the morning sky.

They both jump at the whoop of the police car siren, and blue light flickers across the darkened shrine. Through her drying tears the headlights are blurred and Yūki can't see the officer driving it. He passes them and stops just beyond the shrine. The rear door clunks open, and they hear him call out, 'Jump in, you two. I've been looking for you all night. I'm taking you to the police box in Osōma.'

Taka reaches for Yūki's hand as they walk to the car. 'Just a minute.'

'What?'

He reaches into his shoulder bag and pulls out the salt shaker and shakes a small white mound into his left palm. 'Chuck some over your shoulder, and then I'll tell them it was all my idea.'

Yūki takes a pinch of the salt and throws it over Taka's right shoulder. 'We're in this together.'

He grins, and throws the rest over her shoulder, and then strides to the car.

'Hello, officer,' Taka says brightly as he gets in. 'Lovely morning!'

'As long as you're safe,' the officer grunts.

Yūki takes a last look at the shrine, the spinning windmill – and then climbs in after Taka. The electricity of that last moment at the shrine is still coursing through her.

The driver coughs. 'Tell me, you *are* Hara Yūki right? Hara Jiro's granddaughter?'

Yūki looks at the rear-view mirror, but the angle is wrong and she can't quite see his face.

'Um, yes.'

359

'I'm pleased to meet you at last. Your grandfather told me a lot about you.'

Bit odd the way he said that.

'I'm sorry to have caused you trouble,' Yūki says. 'It was all my idea. Taka-san just helped keep me safe.'

The officer shakes his head. 'There's a lot more than radiation out there.' He laughs. 'I presume the character for "Yū" in your name isn't the one for phantom?'

'No. It's the one for courage.'

'Of course. Fasten your belts, please.'

The police car rumbles towards the port area and Taka leans closer to her.

'Hey, Yūki-san. You are glad you came then?'

'Very.'

'What are you going to do now?'

'I'm going to start drawing again. For real.'

She turns to look at him - and he raises his eyebrows in that cheeky 'well, here we are' kind of way she first saw on the train. There's a kind of dizzy sensation in her head - not tiredness or jet lag, just the feeling like when you're about to take a risk but you know it's good. Like the moment when she hopped the rope to climb the totem pole and life felt bigger.

Much bigger.

She leans towards him.

Well. I'll drop you here.

Another officer will take your statements.

Will we be arrested?

It was good to meet you. I have to meet someone now.

Epilogue

It's THREE YEARS LATER, JUNE 2015, a bright day of lifted cloud and sudden unexpected warmth.

Yūki is heading down into the middle of Leeds from the Art College with a package under her arm. She can smell the ink from the freshly printed pages wafting up from the padded envelope, still feel the excitement as she pulled the finished booklet together and stapled it in the workroom. It's taken her three years, and it's far from perfect, she knows that, but THE INCREDIBLE ADVENTURES OF HALF WAVE is done. Her first year illustration project.

For three years she hasn't been to Japan, but Osōma and Grandpa and Taka have hardly been out of her mind for a moment. All through the determined return to school, the switch of A level choices to include art, her foundation year, she has been drawing and drawing and drawing. And Joel has encouraged her all along, and they're still friends, and briefly were more than that, and then friends again, because Taka is with her all the time. And if Joel's disappointed he hides it well, as slowly they gather a few more friends around them. And the panic attacks aren't totally gone, but they are getting fewer and further apart.

And half her mind is always in Osōma.

Hundreds of drawings of things she's told to draw, but even more of Half Wave and Grandpa and a new companion for Half Wave – snippets pinged to Taka over Facebook, long hours text chatting on Messenger and Skype weaving a story together.

She shows him her progress, and he shares the struggles of the community as it comes back to life around him: water shortages, people working through grief and trauma, radiation monitoring and thousands of bags of low grade waste piling up in the fields. The cold in the winter, the heat in the summer. Ghost stories, of course, and sad stories about people who have found it too hard and given up the fight . . .

And the day when Grandpa's body is finally found and identified some twenty months after the disaster.

But good things too: the wild return of the samurai horse festival in Minamisōma and Odaka, people gradually moving back as the evacuation zone shrinks a little.

Yesterday he told her about a mass tree planting out on the coast, pushing thousands of saplings into the soft soil to replace the ones lost in the waves. And a concert where a visiting jazz musician from Italy brought them all to their feet in the dining room of the Kujaku and everybody danced.

'Maybe you should put that in your comic?' he messaged.

'It's too late!' Yūki typed. 'It's done!' And fired a string of smiley emoticons and ghosts to follow. And then a heart.

And now here it is in her hands.

In the post office she checks the Japanese and English versions of Taka's name and the address again, then turns the package over on the counter and carefully, perfectly, draws Half Wave riding a softly curled breaker.

Underneath, in Japanese, she adds:

I'll see you at Obon. Can't wait. Yūki X

終THE END

Glossary

bentō: a compartmentalised Japanese boxed lunch, either made at home or bought in a shop, railway station etc. Typically contains rice, fish, pickled and cooked vegetables, sushi, soy sauce, seaweed.

biwa: a four or five stringed Japanese lute, the biwa is teardrop shaped and played with a large plectrum. Often used to accompany the singing of classic stories.

engawa: traditionally refers to the wooden flooring around the edge of tatami matting, but now more usually to the raised walkway, either external or internal, around a house. It will be outside the *shōji* (paper screens), but still generally sheltered under eaves, and in modern buildings sometimes behind glass. The one at Jiro's house is exposed to the elements . . .

funayūrei: literally meaning 'boat spirits', funayūrei are a type of vengeful spirit or *onryō*, usually of drowned seafarers, generally appearing at sea, but also on land in some stories. Taka uses the term loosely to include any ghost or wandering spirit of a drowned person.

ganbaru, ganbarimasu: plain and polite forms of verb meaning 'to do one's best'. Like all Japanese verbs different levels of politeness and intent can be made by changing its form. *Ganbarō* is the plain volitional: 'let's do our best'. *Ganbare* is a very direct command – only for encouraging oneself or cheering your team. *Ganbappe* is the Tōhoku dialect version.

gasshō: hands joined in Buddhist prayer position, fingers up, expressing reverence, gratitude, request and respect.

genkan: inside a front door, a Japanese porch area, usually lower than the rest of the living space, where shoes must be taken off and left. The lower floor level helps contain any dirt coming from outside, and marks the important transition from *soto* (outside) to *uchi* (inside). Brief visits, including delivery transactions, will often take place in the *genkan*.

hedoro: sludge, slime or ooze, in this case on the sea floor.

ittekimasu: typical Japanese expression when departing from home or office for a short while. (Rather than *sayōnara*, which implies a longer parting.) Literally means 'I am going and will come back'.

kami: a word for the gods or spirits of Japanese Shinto belief. A kami can be anything from a waterfall, a force of nature, an ancient tree, to a dead warrior or Emperor, a clan ancestor, a mythical animal or deity. With both positive and negative aspects they must be both respected and placated.

karakasa: an abandoned umbrella that develops a life of its own, a karakasa is a *yōkai* (ghost/monster) that can easily give the unwary a bite.

kokeshi: traditionally made in the North East Tōhoku region, the rounded kokeshi doll has been both a traditional hotspring resort souvenir, and a gift to new-born children. Recently, they have been the inspiration for Nintendo's Mii avatars.

konbini: from the English loan word 'convenience' meaning any small supermarket or convenience store.

kotatsu: a low-level Japanese table with a sunken recess underneath for your legs. Often in cold parts of Japan a quilt and heater keeps the lower body snug and warm. Super cosy!

mokumokuren: an uncared-for house, particularly an abandoned one, may develop *mokumokuren*. The broken shōji panels will suddenly blink into life, each lit by a disembodied eye and usually with undesirable consequences for anyone who sees them.

moshi moshi: traditional Japanese phone greeting, from the verb *mōsu* 'to speak or declare'. Various folklore attached, including the belief that ghosts can't say 'moshi moshi', and hence a way of proving on a phone call that you are not a yōkai.

Obon: Buddhist ritual and festival, generally taking part in mid-August, when deceased spirits are welcomed back to family shrines. Graves are cleaned and washed, and ritual dances take place throughout Japan. At the end of Obon the spirits are shown the way back to the other world with *okuribi* – 'sending fires'. As ever, Grandpa Jiro has made his own creative version of the festival.

Osorezan: a mountain in the far North East of Honshu – generally translated as 'Mount Dread' - set in a bleak and barren landscape of white rocks and ash, bubbling noxious pools and hotsprings. It has traditionally been seen as an entrance to the underworld. Blind mediums and Buddhist priests wait to guide those enquiring about departed loved ones.

pachinko: a kind of vertical mini pinball crossed with a slot machine. Pachinko parlours are typically full of light and sound. A technicality allows tokens to be exchanged for prizes outside the parlour and is thus a form of gambling. As Jiro says though, gambling can be a mug's game . . .

ryokan: a Japanese inn – ranging from humble and cheap, to luxurious and mega expensive, usually with tatami rooms and

371

futons, Japanese cuisine, and often with a communal or hotspring bath. Eat, relax and soak away the cares of the world according to budget.

Shindo scale: as opposed to the Richter scale – which measures absolute power of an earthquake - the Japanese Shindo scale gives a measure of what a quake actually feels like in a particular place. Starting at 1 and ranging up to 7, with increments marked 'upper 5, lower 6' etc. The 2011 Great eastern Japan Earthquake measured 9.1 on the Richter scale, and a maximum 7 on the Shindo scale at Kurihara in Miyagi prefecture. In Fukushima it was upper 6, which the Japan Meteorological Agency describes as 'impossible to stand up, cannot move without crawling.'

tadaima: traditional greeting on returning home after a short absence. Literally, 'just now (I'm back)'.

tatami: standardized flooring mats, made of rice straw cores and covered with soft woven rush. Never wear shoes - or even slippers – on tatami. Traditionally rooms are measured by the number of tatami it takes to cover the floor.

Tezuka Award: named after manga pioneer Osamu Tezuka, and awarded by the manga publisher Shueisha since 1971.

zashiki warashi: the spirit of a young child – usually aged about 5 or 6 – said to playfully inhabit the parlour or storage rooms of old Japanese houses. They can help with chores, but also play pranks including stopping people from sleeping. Despite their mischievous streak it is regarded as good fortune to have one in your house. Stories abound from Aomori, Miyagi and other Tōhoku prefectures – and there are reports in living memory of them playing with real children.

Acknowledgements

I DON'T THINK I HAVE ever felt such a debt of gratitude in the writing of a book . . .

First and foremost my thanks to the people of Odaka, Fukushima who welcomed us so warmly, shared their painful experiences so openly, and supported my research so positively.

In particular: thanks to Karin Taira of *Real Fukushima* who was our first point of contact and who guided us on an early tour of the radiation evacuation zone so expertly and thoughtfully; to Tomoko and Takenori Kobayashi of the Futabaya Ryokan, whose spirit and determination in everything from radiation mapping to the renewal of Odaka is so truly inspiring; to Shuzo Sasaki and his inspiring father Seimei-san for very helpful conversations; to Yuko Hirohata for showing us her tsunami survival route and her powerful spirit; and to Kazuto Sugita for friendship, photographic support and excellent curry.

Further afield, my thanks to Bob and Tomoko Murphy – then of Fukushima City - who shared their experiences of 3.11, radiation fears and aftershocks in such detail, and for all their friendship, and translation services over the years. *Gassho* to Rev Taio Kaneta of Cafe de Monku for enlightening exchange via email about everything from ghosts to improvised therapy. (And thanks to Dr Chris Harding for putting us in touch.) My heartfelt thanks also to Kazuko and Nozomi Matsui. Kazuko-san's brother Yoshio was a much loved quasi grandfather to our boys, and is very much missed. (And probably seeded this story.)

Huge and heartfelt thanks to my great friend Nanase Shirota. Nanase has been my most important Japanese teacher – and sensitivity reader – and her doctoral work on the art of listening in Japan has been very useful and thought-provoking. Thanks, *Sensei*, for so many interesting conversations, and for good times too, from Omoide Yokocho in Tokyo to here in the UK. And many thanks Dr Brigitte Steger (of my old university faculty) for putting us together!

I am very grateful – and hugely relieved! – that Bella Pearson welcomed Tsunami Girl to Guppy Books. Thanks, Bella, for curating this project with such care, skill and attention during times of unforeseen crisis. And thanks to all the rest of the team at Guppy, and to Ness Wood for the lovely cover design. I am also deeply grateful to Tamsin Rosewell, bookseller extraordinaire and so much more, for being a kind of guardian angel to this project. And, my thanks of course as ever, to my special agent Kirsty McLachlan.

Chie-san, 本当にありがとうございました – thank you for realizing the manga part of this book so beautifully, and for standing in for Yūki! It has been a thrill watching the manga come to life, and a joy to work with you. And thank you to mutual friend and comic artist Emma Vieceli for introducing us.

My thanks also to Martha Stevns for her generous loan of her beautiful house in Mosset, France where the first draft of this book was written, to Nanase's parents Michiko and Takafumi (and

Futa!) for superb accommodation on the second research trip, and to Flo Bull, Giuseppe Bassi, Alessandro Trapani, Will Dalziel, Holly Pullinger, Sylvia Gallagher, Rachel Blue and also to the many part-Japanese, part-British UK students I've met on school visits for conversations that have helped shape this book.

Almost finally, thanks to my wonderful sons: Joe, for stimulating conversations on Shinto and kami and remembrance; and Will, for deep manga dives, and for drawing the first Half Wave character concept. Your university studies are both proving very helpful to your dad! (And you have both inspired parts of this story.) Thanks, too, to my mum – Maureen – for steadfast encouragement and love.

And finally – and vitally – deep, deep thanks to my wife, Isabel. I can think of no better companion for exploring radioactive disaster zones. Or for life in general.

Julian Sedgwick

THANK YOU VERY MUCH TO Julian, Bella and the team for this great opportunity. Julian, you have trusted in me for my artistic interpretation of your story. That was a great encouragement. Everybody in the team was so patient and considerate. I deeply appreciate that . . . !

Also, I am thankful to my housemate who is always easygoing even when I am stressed out by chasing the deadline.

Finally, even though we live far away from each other, I am always thankful to my parents, family and cat in Japan. They are my gasoline to get going everyday.

Chie Kutsuwada

Julian Sedgwick is the author of six books for children, and co-author of the graphic novel *Dark Satanic Mills* and Carnegie-shortlisted novel *Voyages in the Underworld of Orpheus Black*.

On the way to realising his childhood ambition to be a writer, Julian read Chinese and Philosophy at Cambridge, before working as a bookseller, researcher and script developer for film and TV, and Zen shiatsu therapist.

The first book in his *Mysterium* trilogy – *The Black Dragon* – was published by Hodder Children's Books in 2013 and won the Rotherham Children's Book Award. Following completion of the *Mysterium*, he returned to his fascination with East Asia and set his *Ghosts of Shanghai* trilogy in war-torn, ghost-ridden 1920s China.

Julian lives near Ely, Cambridgeshire, is married and has two grown-up sons. He still combines writing with his work as a therapist. In his spare time he draws as much as possible, juggles torches and knives - and waits for the weather to get cold enough to go fen skating.

www.juliansedgwick.co.uk
Twitter @julianaurelius
Insta @Julian_Sedgwick

Chie Kutsuwada is a UK-based Japanese manga creator and illustrator who is specialized in delicate and emotional drawing style and storylines. Chie creates stories as well as illustration, such as *King of a Miniature Garden* in *The Mammoth Book of Best New Manga II* and *Moonlight* in *The Mammoth Book of Best New Manga III*, which was shortlisted in the Manga Jiman competition organised by the Japanese Embassy. She has also worked on classics and collaborated writers, including *Shakespeare's As You Like It* and *Musashi Miyamoto's The Book of Five Rings*. Recently She contributed to the bi-monthly illustrated column *Mondo Manga* for Japanese magazine, *Mainichi Weekly*.

Chie also attends many manga-related events in and out of the UK and runs manga workshops at schools, libraries and museums including The British Museum, The British Library, Wellcome Collection and The Barbican. She has also worked on projects for Channel 4, CNN, and Wagamama.

chitangarden.wix.com/chiekutsuwada
facebook.com/chitangarden
Twitter @chitanchitan
Instagram @mcmc69